D1623832

Grey Griffins

GREY GRIFFINS

The Clockwork Chronicles | Book 1

THE BRIMSTONE KEY

DEREK BENZ & J. S. LEWIS

LITTLE, BROWN AND COMPANY
New York Boston

Copyright © 2010 by Grey Griffin Industries, LLC

www.greygriffins.com

All rights reserved. Except as permitted under the U.S. Copyright Act of 1976, no part of this publication may be reproduced, distributed, or transmitted in any form or by any means, or stored in a database or retrieval system, without the prior written permission of the publisher.

Little, Brown and Company

Hachette Book Group
237 Park Avenue, New York, NY 10017
Visit our website at www.lb-kids.com

Little, Brown and Company is a division of Hachette Book Group, Inc.
The Little, Brown name and logo are trademarks of Hachette Book Group, Inc.

First Edition: June 2010

The characters and events portrayed in this book are fictitious. Any similarity to real persons, living or dead, is coincidental and not intended by the author.

Library of Congress Cataloging-in-Publication Data

Benz, Derek.
  The Brimstone Key / Derek Benz & J. S. Lewis. — 1st ed.
    p. cm. — (The Clockwork chronicles ; bk. 1)
  "Grey Griffins."
  Summary: As the four friends known as the Grey Griffins begin school at Iron
Bridge Academy, where children with special powers like theirs are trained to fight
evil beings, rumors surface that a mad scientist known as the Clockwork King is
back, and the Griffins must defeat his robotic war machines before total devastation
is unleashed upon the world.
  ISBN 978-0-316-04522-3
  [1. Magic—Fiction. 2. Schools—Fiction. 3. Robots—Fiction. 4. Adventure and
adventurers—Fiction. 5. Good and evil—Fiction.] I. Lewis, J. S. (Jon S.) II. Title.
  PZ7.B44795Br 2010
  [Fic]—dc22

                                                                      2009038518

10 9 8 7 6 5 4 3 2 1

RRD-C

Printed in the United States of America

DEDICATION

Jon:
For Dwight K. Schrute, who understands that robots should be made with a six-foot extension cord just in case there is a robot uprising.

Derek:
To Ioulia & Noah: In deepest affection. As ever. Forever.

To Courtney Jeanne: The best Frank Hardy a Joe could ever have.

ENTS

THE GREY

THE LEADER: Max Sumner

After his grandfather's mysterious death, Max learned that his wealthy family was a part of the secret Templar society. He became the Guardian of the *Codex Spiritus*, an enchanted book that holds monsters, evil faeries, and other dangerous creatures captive within its magical pages. The *Codex* can change shapes, from a book, to a ring, to a gauntlet capable of channeling Max's family power: Skyfire!

THE INVENTOR: Harley Davidson Eisenstein

Built like a linebacker and incredibly smart, Harley is a technological prodigy who designs gadgets critical to any successful monster hunt. Unlike Max's wealthy family, Harley and his mother are barely getting by. But he's not bothered; he knows that happiness isn't measured by how much money you have in your bank account.

GRIFFINS

THE SLEUTH: Natalia Romanov

Fearless, fiery, and intensely smart, Natalia uses her keen
observational skills and her analytical mind to solve any mystery.
As a part of her sleuthing kit, Natalia carries a Phantasmoscope
that allows her to see into the faerie spectrum. Since a close friend
betrayed her, Natalia has had a hard time trusting other girls. She
feels more at home with the Griffins than with anyone else.

THE CHANGELING: Ernie Tweeny

Ernie became a changeling after a transfusion of faerie blood,
which gave him super speed, rapid healing, and enhanced
eyesight. But there's a catch: whenever Ernie uses his powers, he
becomes more faerie and less human. Despite that risk, he has
vowed to fight evil as his superhero alter ego, Agent Thunderbolt.

THE KNIGHTS TEMPLAR

The Knights Templar is an ancient society that has sworn to
protect mankind against unseen dangers like monster invasions
and zombie uprisings. In recent months, the Templar were nearly
exterminated by an army of werewolves called the Black Wolf
Society. They are slowly rebuilding their strength.

THE NIG

TERRIFIED, MAX SUMNER FORCED HIMSELF TO WALK down the long corridor. Water dripped from the ceiling, as an eerie light flickered through tattered sheets of plastic strung across the end of the hallway.

Max didn't notice the fallen bicycle until it was too late. He tripped, cutting his shin. But he couldn't turn back. Not now. The front wheel spun as he walked toward the light. When he finally reached the ragged sheeting, Max pushed it aside and stepped through. The temperature plummeted and breath rose from his mouth like a ghostly serpent.

Crunch...

Max looked down at a rotted yellow bag half-filled with decaying newspapers and swallowed hard. Then he heard the faint whistle of drills, and Max was certain that the stench in his nostrils was blood.

He passed a discarded sneaker, then a baseball cap with the name JOHNNY GEIST written on the lining of the bill.

"Help me..." a small voice begged.

Max raced through the doorway ahead only to find an empty room. It was some sort of laboratory with rusty instruments and tools that lined tarnished trays. Glass jars filled with mysterious liquids crowded dilapidated shelves, and a faint red stain ran along the concrete floor toward a drain. A steel table with leather straps for hands and feet stood in the center of the room. Then Max felt a cold hand on his shoulder.

Max pulled away and turned to look into the eyes of a young boy. He was dressed in a striped shirt and jeans, with a lone sneaker on his left foot.

"Did you call me?" Max managed to ask. "Are you Johnny?"

The boy said nothing but continued to stare, unblinking. That's when Max realized that instead of eyes, there were camera lenses in the boy's sockets. And worse, the veins in the boy's pale arms were pulsing with a silver-blue glow. No matter where Max's eyes fell, he found machinery in place of humanity. There wasn't much left of the boy, but the single tear running down his silicon cheek was real.

Max's stomach lurched and he tried to look away, but the same cold hand forced him to look back. This time the boy was gone. Ernie Tweeny, one of Max's best friends, was standing in his place.

"Help me…" Ernie moaned through blue lips. Max stumbled back and fell against a tray of rusty instruments, sending them clanging to the floor. As Ernie walked into the light, Max saw that part of his friend's skull had been cut away, revealing a mechanized brain of whirling gears ticking like a clock.

Max cried out as strong hands took hold of him from behind, lifting him into the air. He struggled against the invisible grip as his arms and legs were strapped to the table. A convex mirror hung over the table, and strangely, it wasn't his own face looking back at him. Somehow Ernie had taken his place. Max fought to break free from the straps as a man in a stained lab coat walked into view. He was tall, with neatly combed silver hair, and as he turned to face the table Max's blood froze. He would never forget those eyes. They were intelligent, cold, and as sharp as the scalpel he held in his gloved hand.

The man raised the gleaming instrument.

Max screamed. Then he woke up.

PART ONE

IRON BRIDGE
ACADEMY

THE UNMARKED
PACKAGE

Max Sumner pedaled his bike through the quiet streets of Avalon, Minnesota, trying to shake the nightmare from his head. He had been awake all night, too frightened to go back to sleep. The only thing keeping him from taking a nap was the last summer meeting of the Secret Order of the Grey Griffins. Max didn't want to be late.

With school starting on Monday, the four friends had decided to spend their last day of summer vacation reading comic books and watching movies in their secret headquarters—a tree fort that Max decided to call the Griffins' Aerie. Over the last year, Max, Harley Eisenstein, Natalia Romanov, and Ernie Tweeny had faced everything from leprechauns to six-armed ogres, and just about every monster in between. Their adventures had brought them closer than ever, but they were about to embark on their most intriguing quest yet — the Grey Griffins were transferring to a new school.

Iron Bridge Academy was a private military school run by the Knights Templar. The curriculum was designed to train students to combat unseen forces from the darkest of nightmares. The academy had been shut down for nearly a century, following an explosion that destroyed most of the buildings. Now the doors were opening again.

There were only two ways to be admitted into a Templar academy. The first was through birthright, which Max possessed. The Templar also chose individuals from the general populace who had extraordinary talent, intellect, and ingenuity, so Harley, Natalia, and Ernie were extended invitations as well.

By the time Max reached the Old Woods, Harley was already waiting for him.

"What are you doing?" Max asked as he set his bike down. Harley had a screwdriver in one hand. In the other, he held a palm-sized device with its electrical guts exposed.

"Just making a couple of adjustments," Harley replied as he replaced the casing and screwed it back together. "It's a tracking device."

Harley handed Max a metal chip and told him to put it in his pocket. Harley then twisted a dial on his invention, and the dark screen flickered to life. Two flashing green dots instantly appeared. "That's us."

"What about Natalia and Ernie?"

"I gave them ID chips this morning," Harley replied. "According to this little gizmo, they should be here right about . . . now."

Max turned to find the other two members of the Grey Griffins coasting down the gravel road on their bikes. Natalia's red hair was woven into braids that flew behind her. Ernie's vintage World War I Army helmet bounced on his head.

"I thought you were excited about transferring to Iron Bridge," Max heard Natalia say.

"I was, but King's Elementary is the last normal thing in our lives," Ernie explained. "Once we leave that behind, it'll be nothing but a bunch of rigid rules."

"Come on, Ernie, you know that's not true," Max said. "We're going to accomplish things that we never dreamed we could do."

"And what about all the other changelings at the academy?" Harley added. "You'll finally be able to put together your own team of superpowered humans. It'll be like a real-life comic book."

"I never fit in anywhere I go," Ernie complained. "Trust me, Iron Bridge isn't going to be any different—changelings or not."

Natalia sighed. "Look, Ernie. According to Brooke, we're kind of famous."

"Yeah, right."

"I'm serious. Everyone at Iron Bridge thinks we're heroes because we helped defeat the Black Wolf Society."

Ernie smiled.

"Don't get ahead of yourself," Max warned. "Brooke may be exaggerating."

Brooke Lundgren was the only honorary member of the Grey Griffins. The boys wanted to make her membership official, but Natalia wasn't quite ready to share the spotlight with another girl. Brooke knew that Natalia didn't mean anything by it. A close friend had betrayed Natalia, so it wasn't easy for her to trust other girls. Besides, Brooke had her own troubles. Her dad, Baron Cain Lundgren, had been given the directorship of Iron Bridge Academy. He had a reputation for being strict, and Brooke hoped that the other students wouldn't hold it against her.

"I knew it was too good to be true," Ernie sulked.

"What if I told you that my mom stocked the fridge with tons of junk food last night? Would that get your mind off school for a little while?" Max asked.

The Aerie was constructed of three separate buildings linked by suspension bridges and rope swings. It boasted air-conditioning, a cobblestone fireplace, a working kitchen, and hidden rooms with trick entrances. When the four friends reached the central building, Ernie scaled the ladder and pressed his thumb against a hidden sensor pad on the rafter. It had been installed as a safety precaution against prowling monsters. The lock on the door released with a *click,* and Ernie rushed straight to the refrigerator. In a matter of moments, his arms were overflowing with snacks.

"Hey, Harley, clear the table, will you?" Ernie asked as he tried to balance all the food.

"Clear it yourself," Harley replied, sitting down to read through a stack of comic books. That's when he saw the strange box wrapped in brown paper. It was unmarked, except for a faded Templar cross stamped on the top. "What's in the package?"

"Maybe it's our next assignment," Max said. "I overheard someone talking about an infestation of Vampire Pixies."

Natalia looked skeptical. "Since when do we get assignments in unmarked packages?"

Max shrugged as Ernie dumped the pile of food on top of the box.

"Ernest!" Natalia reprimanded. She began clearing away the snacks.

"What?" Ernie sat down and opened a bag of chips. "Did you expect me to hold that stuff forever? I have super speed, not super strength." With that, he shoved a handful of chips into his mouth and started smacking away.

Max broke the seal and pulled out a simple wooden box. Curious, he flipped the latch and opened the lid. Inside was a red velvet sack tied with a length of golden rope. He started to untie it, but Natalia grabbed his arm.

"Wait." She reached inside the box and pulled out a piece of paper. Written in looping script were the words WIND STEM TO FIND HIM.

"Wind the stem?" Harley read aloud. "What does that mean?"

Max opened the little sack and turned it upside down. "Let's find out."

An object fell into the palm of his hand. It was a brass beetle, no more than two inches long. A perfect symphony of etched brass and silver filigree, the mechanical creature sat unmoving.

"That's so supersonic!" Ernie said, and wiped his mouth with the back of his hand. As the self-proclaimed "world's first real superhero," Ernie had decided he needed a catchphrase. So instead of describing things as *awesome* or *amazing*, he called everything *supersonic*.

Overwhelmed by curiosity, Ernie grabbed the beetle. With his greasy fingers, he wound the stem several revolutions. Inside, a series of gears engaged, and the beetle started tick as if it were a pocket watch. When Ernie set the beetle on the table, small brass legs unfolded. Then the mechanism spread its wings and lifted into the air.

"Whoa!" Harley stepped back as it zipped by his head while circling the room. "What is that thing?"

"Quick! Close the windows!" Max called.

Unfortunately, the mechanical creature had already spotted an open window and flown into the forest.

Max jumped over a stack of comic books and ran toward the escape slide. "Don't let it get away, Ernie! We'll be right behind you."

INTO THE DEEP

"It went in here!" Ernie shouted as he followed the beetle into the mouth of a tunnel that led beneath the forest
floor. The mechanical creature hovered in place just out
of Ernie's reach. Then, as the other Griffins burst onto
the scene, the beetle took off once again, leading them
into the darkness.

They hurried through the slimy passageway but lost
the beetle as they came to an intersection. There was no
sign of where it had gone.

"Can you still see it?" Max panted, his lungs burning.

Harley glanced down at a blinking light on his

navigation device. "I was able to tune this to the vibration of the beetle's wings. It should be right through here…"

The ground started to shake as debris fell from the ceiling.

"Cave-in!" Ernie shouted.

Suddenly the floor fell away, and they dropped into the darkness.

Ernie slammed against something hard and started to slide. He clawed at the rock walls, but he couldn't stop his momentum. The others were screaming as he rocketed down the underground slide, shooting over rises and around bends. Air rushed against him, nearly peeling his cheeks from his face. But just when Ernie thought that he was going to lose consciousness, he shot out of the tunnel and landed in a puddle of motor oil.

"Ernie, is that you?" Natalia called out from the darkness.

Ernie couldn't see much, but he could feel slime oozing around his ears as he stood up. "Does anyone have a flashlight?"

"Here we go," Harley answered. He lit a few flares and tossed them on the ground, careful to keep the flame away from any oil.

They were unusual flares that couldn't be doused by wind or water. Harley had received a supply from a Special Forces unit of the Templar Knights called the Tactical Headquarters for Operations and Research. Most people just referred to the group as THOR.

THOR agents protected the world from dangers that most people were unable to see — rogue trolls, evil witches, armies of werewolves, and a host of other nightmares that would force the bravest civilian to run, hide, and pray for mercy.

The bright flames from the flares exposed a small room with cinderblock walls. It looked like a bomb shelter from the Cold War. The floor was bare, and the low ceiling consisted of little more than crumbling concrete.

"What is this place?" Natalia asked.

"It looks like my grandma's basement out at the farm," Max replied as he ran his fingers over the wall.

"Does anybody know what this motor oil is doing down here?" Ernie grumbled. He was trying to scrape the syrupy goop off his face.

"As long as you stay away from the flares, you'll be fine," Max said. "I'm more concerned about finding a way out of here. Are you wearing the compass that's supposed to lead you to safety?"

"It's called a Navitrometer," Ernie said. "And I already tried it, but I think it's broken. The needle keeps spinning in circles."

"I think we fell through a ventilation shaft," Natalia remarked as she studied the ceiling. "It's too steep to climb back out, and the only door I found is locked."

"Let's spread out and try to find the key," Max said.

As the Griffins looked around, they could see a large drainage grate in the center of the floor. The room appeared to be empty except for a pile of scrap metal in the far corner.

"This has got to be some sort of environmental violation," Natalia commented as the beetle circled her head.

Max pushed aside a few large pieces of twisted metal before pulling out something that looked like an iron football. When he held it close to one of the flares, he could see two round eyes of amber glass and a small mouth that was little more than a slit. Connecting rods dangled from its neck, and the head was dented and heavily tarnished.

Ernie gasped. "It's a robot!"

Harley handed Max a flare and then took the head and examined it. "I don't think so. There aren't any chips or electronic components."

Max raised the flare, and all at once dozens of lifeless eyes looked back at the Griffins from the scrap heap, some of them eerily human. It was as if a hundred mechanical figures had been torn limb from limb until there was nothing left but parts. Then Max spotted a pair of camera-like eyes that reminded him of the boy in his dream.

"What's wrong?" Natalia wondered as she watched his face turn pale.

"I've been having nightmares again," Max replied, his breathing shallow as the details flooded back. "I was in a laboratory, and someone was crying for help. His eyes had been cut out and replaced with cameras, just like that." Max pointed to the eyes staring back at him from the scrap pile.

"That's disgusting," Ernie said.

Max turned to his friend but figured it was better if Ernie didn't know he had been in the dream, too. Ernie tended to overreact to things like that.

"Look at this," Harley said.

The brass insect was crawling on the floor nearby. Like a watch, it seemed to be slowing down, but it was still moving purposefully toward a round metal door that was recessed into the wall. With all the interconnected gears, timer springs, and turned metal, it looked like a bank vault. There were seven stainless-steel turning wheels etched with mysterious symbols, all arranged in a vertical line.

"What is this?" asked Ernie. "A puzzle?"

Natalia examined the door with her Phantasmoscope, a multi-lens magnifying glass that allowed her to see through faerie magic. "Whatever it is, it's our best chance of getting out of this hole." She felt overwhelming sense of being smothered but fought against panic. Losing control wouldn't change anything.

"What if we radioed Logan?" Ernie asked. "He'd know how to get us out of here."

Max shook his head. "We're too far underground. The radio won't work."

Logan was not only the head of the Templar THOR division but also Max's personal bodyguard. Logan had grown up as an orphan on the streets of Glasgow, where he became a street fighter to earn enough money to survive. In time, the Templar found him and offered the Scotsman a place in their ranks. Under their guidance, he became one of the deadliest men in the world. More important, he loved Max like a son.

Natalia adjusted a series of interchangeable lenses that flipped over the top of her Phantasmoscope, and peered through the mysterious workings of the door. "I don't see any obvious traps or anything supernatural. The gears are attached to rollers that are connected to tracks where the door sits. I think it's just a big combination lock. All we need to do is find the right combination."

"Where do we start?" Max asked.

"I've got a hunch," she claimed before turning the middle wheel. Natalia stopped when a symbol with three wavy lines lined up with an arrow on the side of the door. The wheel resisted at first, but with a groan of rusty metal, it finally gave way. As it did, a sudden gust of air that smelled like dead fish wafted up from the drain.

The beetle started hopping wildly, striking its head against the wall beneath the lowest gear.

"I don't think our little friend liked your choice," Harley observed.

The beetle was growing more frantic as it clawed at the bottom of the door in mechanical desperation. Then the sound of rushing water echoed up through the drainage grate. It was followed by a small trickle, and soon water was pooled around Ernie's shoes. Before long the Griffins were sloshing through ankle-deep water.

Max turned to Natalia. "We've got a problem."

She rolled her eyes and sighed. "Why does this always happen to us?"

"Because somebody doesn't want us to find what's on the other side of that door," Harley called. "Hurry up and break the code, or we're going to have to swim."

"I need a clue…somewhere to start," Natalia complained. "There are more than thirty symbols on each wheel. Do you know the odds of cracking that code?"

"It doesn't matter," said Max, watching the water rise. "We have to do something!"

Across the room, Ernie pounded on the door and screamed for help while Harley redoubled his effort to find a hidden escape hatch.

Max could still see the brass beetle struggling below the surface, and it triggered an idea. "What if this thing knows something we don't?" he asked, reaching down to grab the mechanical insect. He handed it to Natalia.

"Look," she said, her hands trembling as she examined the beetle. "There are seven symbols on the wings, and seven wheels on the door. So the beetle has to be the key."

"Then let's match the symbols and see if the door will open," Max said.

"Whatever you do, you'd better do it quickly," Harley warned as the water approached his waist. "We have only a couple minutes before this place fills up to the ceiling."

Natalia spun the first wheel, then the second, aligning

the symbols to match the beetle's wings. The water continued to pour into the room as she quickly turned three more wheels, moving from top to bottom.

"Oh no!" she shouted, realizing her mistake as the water rose to her chest. "The last two wheels are underwater."

"Tell me the symbols, and I'll match them," Max said.

Natalia flipped the beetle over to get a better look, but it slipped from her hand and fell into the water. As she fought back tears, Max dove to grab one of the flares. As advertised, it was still burning when he resurfaced to catch his breath. Max could see Ernie standing on his tiptoes, trying not to swallow any of the water that was quickly approaching his nose.

Max took a deep breath and dove once more. His fingers scraped frantically against the floor as he gripped the flare in his other hand. Then he caught the glint of brass from the corner of his eye. Max stretched and took the beetle in his hand just as the oxygen in his lungs started to run out.

As he broke the surface of the water, Max could see that Harley had found one of the other flares. Ernie was flailing about as Harley struggled to help him tread water. It wasn't an easy task, even for someone as strong as Harley.

Natalia was close enough that Max could see the panic in her eyes. "We're going to make it," he told her. Natalia nodded, her teeth chattering as Max fumbled to find the last two symbols on the beetle's wings: an iron cross and an anchor.

He tossed the beetle aside before plunging back into the dark water. He found the wheels easily enough, but he had to drop the flare so that he could use both hands to spin them. Without the light to guide him, Max could barely make out the symbols. He was reasonably sure that he had lined up the iron cross. Aligning the anchor symbol, though, wouldn't be as easy.

The last wheel was locked by decades of rust, and it wouldn't budge. Max struggled, his lungs screaming for oxygen. As he started to black out, Max closed his eyes and succumbed to the darkness. Memories washed over him like a torrent: family gatherings around the Thanksgiving table...Iver smiling down at him like jolly old St. Nick...Logan protecting Max from an onslaught of werewolves...his mother kissing him on the cheek...his father's last words— *"If you turn your back on me, you turn your back on your destiny..."*

With a jolt, Max opened his eyes and tightened his grip on the wheel. He gave it one last twist, spending the last of his energy. This time the wheel moved. As Max struggled to stay conscious, he thought he could see the anchor symbol lined up. Suddenly there was a rumble, and the entire chamber shook. Then the water around him started to swirl until it became an uncontrollable vortex, pulling Max in its deadly current.

REACHING INTO THE PORTAL

The crashing water was violent. Max was smashed against the walls until he was nearly senseless. Then all at once, the water fell away, disappearing down the drain in the floor. The Griffins were thrown to the ground, where they lay like marooned fish gasping for breath. Max stumbled to his feet. "Is everyone all right?"

"Alive and kicking," Harley announced with a groan, helping Natalia and Ernie to their feet.

"Thanks to Natalia," Max added. "Nice work."

Natalia smiled as she wrung out her braids. Then she pointed at the door. A piece of it had slid away, revealing a small circular inset. They all watched as the beetle crept inside the opening, extending its legs into tiny holes. Then, with a whir of gears, the beetle began to spin, first one way, then another, like a combination lock. Finally, with a *click*, the door began to rumble, rolling away to unveil a dark room beyond.

"Whoa," exclaimed Harley, stepping through the doorway with his flare held high. "You need to see this."

The Griffins followed him into the circular control room. Against one wall was a wide console covered with buttons, switches, and levers. Blueprint diagrams hung in procession on the other walls. The floor was littered with concrete that had fallen from the ceiling, and there were several rotting chairs.

"I think it was some sort of testing laboratory," Harley remarked as he examined the blueprints more closely.

"Or a control room," added Ernie. "But for what?"

"A mechanical army," Harley said, looking at schematics. Each machine was bristling with weapons and shielded with armor. "Maybe that's what all those spare parts were back there."

"Vesper rockets?" Max exclaimed, reading through an inventory manifest. "And magneto rifles?" One machine looked like a cross between a minotaur and a tank. "Whoever designed this stuff had a crazy imagination."

"That person is also very dead," Natalia added. "This blueprint is dated May 1916. That was during World War I. It's for something called the Brimstone Key, but this drawing doesn't look anything like a key."

Max looked at the strange rendering of a cylindrical object with the words METEORIC IRON written next to it.

"I can't believe that technology like this existed back then," Harley remarked as he picked up another set of schematics. "This thing is a walking fortress. It even has retractable Gatling guns and rocket boosters. Can you imagine running into one of these?"

"It's called a Dreadnaught," Max read from the paper Harley was holding.

"Do you think that beetle was delivered to us by accident?" Natalia asked. "I mean, why would it lead *us* down here?"

"Check this out," Harley said. He placed the Dreadnaught blueprint back on the table and walked over to a floor-to-ceiling mirror. Attached around the frame were cylinders with compression hoses linked to an array of glass canisters. They were filled with a hazy blue liquid. Four motors, one in each corner, were arranged at angles, and they powered hundreds of interconnected gears.

"It's a portal," Max said.

Natalia frowned. "Are you sure?"

Max placed his hand on the surface of the mirror. It chilled his skin. "I'm positive."

Portals, known scientifically as interdimensional teleportation singularities, were enchanted doorways that could take a person anywhere in the blink of an eye. Some opened doorways to a particular place, while other portals could move a traveler through time. They were incredibly rare because they were simply impossible to find—that is, unless someone had a special talent. Max was just such a person.

"So how does it work?" Ernie wanted to know. He was getting anxious to leave.

Harley examined the motors and cylinders. "I think you have to turn it on first...you know, like a motor." He indicated a switch on the right side.

"Aren't portals powered by some kind of enchantment? Why would you have to turn it on?" Natalia wondered.

"There's only one way to find out," Harley answered. Then he took hold of a crank on the side of the frame and began to turn it. As he did, the blue liquid in the glass vials began to boil. After a minute of hard cranking, Harley flipped the starter switch. All at once the motors rumbled to life and soon they were driving the array of gears in a circular parade of motion. Harley stepped back. "That's incredible..."

Natalia studied the mirror. Its surface rolled like a wind-blown lake, and when Max touched it, a ripple went out from his finger in a series of rings. "Okay, you're right," she conceded. "It's a portal, but how do we know where it leads?"

"I think I can answer that," Max began, placing his hand on a series of dials on the left side of the frame. Taking in a breath, he turned one of the dials and all at once a brilliant shaft of sunlight poured through the mirror's surface, blinding the Griffins in momentary wonder. As their eyes adjusted, they could see that the portal led to the roof of a tall building in the midst of a sprawling city.

"That's Minneapolis!" Harley exclaimed.

"Which gives me an idea." Max began to turn the dials in different directions, sometimes together, sometimes one at a time, each time changing the scene on the other side of the mirror. "I think I have it!" he exclaimed a few moments later. "The first dial has some preprogrammed places that the mirror usually connects to, but the others let you control the destination." He turned the final dial two clicks, then stepped back with a smile.

The interior of their familiar tree-house headquarters appeared before them. It was just as they had left it a few hours earlier, with the box that held the beetle still sitting on the table.

"How did you do that?" Natalia asked.

Max thought about it for a moment. "I don't know," he admitted. "It's like I always knew how to use it, but I've never seen one of these before."

"That's weird," Ernie said. "But I don't care. All I know is that I want to get out of here."

He started to step toward the mirror, but Max held him back. "Wait a minute. What did the note say that came with the beetle? 'Wind stem to find him'? Who were we supposed to find?"

"Anyone who would hang out down here has to be insane," Ernie noted. "And that means I don't want to meet him."

"You should take a look at this, Max," Natalia said as she stood next to a glass display case.

22

"Are those Round Table cards?" Ernie asked, reaching out to grab them.

"Ernie, don't... it might be a trap!" Natalia warned.

Once again, it was too late.

In his excitement, Ernie had already pulled the deck out of the case. The other Griffins held their breath, waiting for the ceiling to fall or for the floor to open up and reveal a pit of vipers. Luckily, none of that happened.

"See, they're just cards," Ernie said, holding them out triumphantly.

Round Table was a popular trading-card game with Templar youth, but it was also used as a training tool so they could learn the strengths and weaknesses of enemies without the fear of injury.

Harley took the cards and started shuffling through them. "I haven't seen any of these before," he said. "Look, there's a Reaper, a Dreadnaught, and... wait, who the heck is this guy?" He handed the card to Max.

Across the top he read the words CLOCKWORK KING. There was a cadre of mechanical soldiers in the background, similar to the machines from the blueprints. The focal point, however, was a hard-edged man. His skin was etched with fine lines, his silver hair and mustache were trimmed to military efficiency, and his nose was as straight as his posture. He was dressed in attire from the last century, with a black dress jacket, a high collar lined with the emblems of his rank, and a red sash draped from his left shoulder.

The man's eyes struck Max like a hammer, and he staggered backward. "That's him."

"Who?" Harley asked.

"The guy from my dream."

"We need to show this to Logan," Natalia advised. "He'll know what to do."

"Wait a minute. Did you guys see that?" Ernie asked. "His eyes just blinked."

Max looked at the Clockwork King. He had the impression that the man on the card was examining him with great interest, and it was unnerving. Then, with a smile of horrifying malevolence, he winked. There was a flash and the card disintegrated into a shower of dust. The Griffins stared at the floor in stunned silence.

"Okay, that was C-R-double-E-P-Y," Ernie announced.

At that moment there was a deep rumble. A massive fissure raced along the ceiling, sending dust raining down on their heads. It was followed by a series of timed explosions. All at once, the world began to fall.

"The portal!" Max shouted, pushing his friends toward the mirror.

"What about the blueprints?" Natalia cried. "It's the only evidence we have..."

There was another explosion.

"No time!" Max ordered.

With a shove, Natalia followed Ernie and Harley through the portal mirror. Max took one last look at the mysterious control room and then dove after his friends.

A Message from the Grave?

A rift opened up in midair, and the Griffins tumbled back into the tree house like apples dumped out of a basket. They had just enough time to look through the hovering portal to see the ceiling of the control room collapse. There was a flicker, and then it was gone.

Max staggered to his feet, helping the others to do the same. Their faces were white, their breath labored.

"I feel like I was turned inside out," Ernie confessed, checking his body for missing parts. Max agreed. Only he would have described it as being disassembled and reconstructed without anesthesia.

"I wish I had brought a camera," Harley said with regret. "The schematics for those machines were amazing."

"At least we found these," Max said, fanning the Round Table cards across the coffee table in the center of the room.

As the Griffins recounted their adventure, a small dragon floated through the window to perch lazily on the refrigerator. There was a flash of light, and suddenly the dragon was gone, leaving behind the form of a furry spriggan. It was a catlike faerie with large eyes, a coat of spiky fur, and a leathery tail. Spriggans were shape-shifters, but this particular faerie was more. It was a Bounder Faerie. After Max had freed the spriggan from her prison, she had sworn to protect him for the rest of his life. The only problem was that she wasn't around much.

"You missed out on another adventure, Sprig!" Ernie exclaimed. "There was this cave with killer traps, and a pile of dead robots...oh and..."

Uninterested, the spriggan yawned before licking her paw absently.

"I just wish we knew how the scarab beetle got here," Natalia said as she examined the note that had come in the package. She held the parchment up to the light before pulling out her Phantasmoscope to check for traces of magic. "Nothing!" Natalia complained. "Not even a fingerprint or a loose hair. I can't solve a mystery if there aren't any clues."

"Maybe it was a ghost," Ernie suggested.

"Look, I know this is going to sound crazy, but what

26

if Iver sent the package?" Max asked, nervous of the reaction.

Nobody said a word. After all, Iver was supposed to be dead.

Olaf Iverson, whom everyone affectionately referred to as Iver, had been the proprietor of the Shoppe of Antiquuities. He also had been a surrogate grandfather to the Grey Griffins, not to mention a member of the Knights Templar. That was, until Max's father reportedly had killed him.

"But this isn't Iver's handwriting," Natalia pointed out, holding up the note.

Max shook his head. "Maybe someone else sent it for him. Think about it. If anyone wanted us to find a set of Round Table cards, it would have been Iver. It wouldn't be the first time he used them as a clue."

"What about the blueprints? Or that pile of metal body parts?" Natalia pointed out. "Iver never mentioned anything about robots before. Besides, if he really is alive, where has he been hiding?"

"I know it doesn't make sense." Max sighed. "But if there is a chance Iver is alive, don't you want to find out?"

"Don't be ridiculous!" Natalia exclaimed. "Of course I do, but there's no way. He would have contacted us by now."

"We need to talk to Logan," Ernie said as he walked out of the bathroom, his face finally cleaned of the oil.

Max sighed as he shuffled through the cards. "You're

probably right, but I don't want to tell him anything until we have more information. Natalia, do you still have that remote-viewing card for the Templar Library?"

"What do you think?"

"Good. We need you to do some research. Can you track down the cards that we found?"

"I've already made a list," she replied, patting her *Book of Clues*. "I'll do a search for the cards and for anyone called the Clockwork King. I'll even look for the Brimstone Key."

"What about me?" Ernie wondered.

Max set the cards back on the table. "I thought your grandparents were still in town."

"Yeah, but they're flying back to Phoenix in the morning, so I'm supposed to go home and play board games. I hate playing with them. My grandpa cheats."

"Then I guess that leaves me and Harley to check out Iver's shop."

"I can't tonight," Harley said. "Someone gave my mom tickets for the Twins game. We're supposed to leave in about an hour, and I don't want to miss it, because it's their last home stand before the playoffs. How about tomorrow night?"

Max didn't want to wait, but he wasn't about to go to the Shoppe of Antiquities alone. He hadn't been back there since Iver had disappeared. There were too many haunting memories, and he wasn't sure he could handle it alone. The only problem was that if they wanted to find out who had sent the beetle, Iver's shop was their best lead.

28

TRANSFERRING
IS NEVER EASY

Rain fell on the morning of the first day of school. Pungent smells from the forest swept over the road as Logan drove the Griffins in the Sumner limousine. Max still hadn't told Logan about the cards. Every time he tried, something had come up. Besides, Max was too nervous about the Griffins' first day at Iron Bridge to concentrate on much of anything else.

His grandmother sat in the passenger seat. A woman of elegance, Grace Caliburn was telling the Griffins about the time she met Max's grandfather. "I was fourteen, and he was a year older," she said quietly. "Those were simpler times—wonderful times—before the war. And Scotland was a magical place for an American like me."

"So you boarded at Stirling Academy?" asked Natalia. "I would hate to be away from my family for that long."

"It was more common in those days, but it was still difficult. I suppose some of the students will board at Iron Bridge, but I've heard talk that a good many families are moving to the area."

"You went to Stirling, too, didn't you, Logan?" asked Ernie.

"For a time," the Scotsman replied, bristling. Logan kept his life as private as a bank vault.

"And?"

"Stirling isn't for everyone. Let's just leave it at that."

"Which brings up a good point," interrupted Natalia. "If the Knights Templar is a secret organization—and no one knows it exists—then why build a school in plain view? The secret is bound to get out. I mean, the whole town is snooping around, trying to get inside that gate."

Logan nodded, keeping his eyes on the road. "I wouldn't worry about it. Baron Lundgren has taken care of the details. Besides, this isn't the school. It's nothing more than a facade."

"A what?" Ernie asked.

"It means that it's a trick," Natalia interjected.

"True enough," Logan agreed. "That building is actually a depot for an underground railway that will take you to Iron Bridge."

30

"You mean the academy isn't in Avalon?" Ernie pressed. The worried tone in his voice was mounting.

"It is and it isn't," Logan replied.

"What's that supposed to mean?" Ernie asked.

"In a manner of speaking, Iron Bridge is on the island in the middle of Lake Avalon."

"Wait a minute. We've been there, right?" Harley said. "The simulation chamber where we trained a few times is part of the school."

"Exactly."

"I don't get it," Ernie said, more confused than ever. "If Iron Bridge is on the island, why don't we just take a boat?"

"Too many questions," Logan said. "If I were you, I'd be more concerned about getting to class on time."

"The Templar have worked so hard to hide the academy, but what if one of the students blabs and the whole town finds out where it really is?" Natalia wanted to know.

"They won't."

"How can you be sure?" she pressed.

Logan's silent response signified that the conversation was over. Natalia sat back, arms crossed in dissatisfaction. Logan was an enigma Natalia had never succeeded in understanding.

"You look a little tired, Ernie," Grandma Caliburn said. "Did you stay up late last night?"

Ernie yawned. "I'm not really a morning person." He

was dressed in his Agent Thunderbolt costume in hopes that it would earn instant respect from his fellow students, though Harley had warned that Ernie was more likely to end up with an atomic wedgie.

"Here we are," Logan called as he pulled up to a towering iron gate. Beyond lay an impenetrable wall of trees. Two men dressed similar to Logan manned the guardhouse, and when they saw the Scotsman, they opened the gate and let him through. Logan waved and pressed on.

Looking out the window, Max caught faint glimpses of a building through the thick foliage. With most of the school still under reconstruction, Iron Bridge was only offering grades six through eight this year. As new buildings were finished, the academy would be opened to more students. That meant that most of the kids would be about the same age as the Griffins.

As the building came into view, Max was disappointed. Even though it was part of a depot, nothing about it looked like an elite military academy. It was just...well...schoolish. There was a playground where everything was painted in red and yellow. Max couldn't imagine why they would need slides or merry-go-rounds if they were supposed to learn how to protect the world from evil.

"Remember, not everything is as it seems," Logan said, catching Max's sigh of discontent. "Once you are inside, you'll feel different."

"Wait a minute," Ernie said, fidgeting. "You're coming with us, right?"

"First I have to park the car. I'll catch up with you in a bit," the Scotsman said. "Just stay out of trouble. I don't want to hear stories about you getting yourself into fights, got it?" He looked over at Harley, who ignored the comment.

Ernie eyed the swarm of unfamiliar students milling around the entrance, and his stomach churned. "Can't you just stand in line with us?"

"You've fought witches and werewolves. I think you can handle a few students."

"Just relax and enjoy your time here," Grandma Caliburn added softly. "And remember, you're the Grey Griffins. You're practically famous...."

Logan helped the Griffins unload before he drove off to find a parking spot, leaving Max, Harley, Ernie, and Natalia surrounded by a crowd of complete strangers.

STICKING OUT
IN A CROWD

"Well," Max sighed as he pulled on his backpack, "I guess we should get in line with everyone else."

"I don't feel so good," Ernie announced. "Maybe I should call my mom."

"Some superhero you are," Natalia muttered, grabbing him by the sleeve. "You're coming with us."

Though Max smiled at a few of the passing students, no one seemed interested in the Griffins. Everyone else had transferred to Iron Bridge from Templar academies around the world. They were too busy catching up on the latest gossip about what had happened over the summer.

That suited Max just fine. He despised being the center of attention.

Max was about to tell Ernie that there was something caught in his braces when he caught sight of a woman helping her son out of a car. Their skin was a warm sienna brown, and their accent had a Latino flair.

"You're going to be fine, Robert," his mother consoled as she handed him a backpack. "Besides, you aren't alone—some of your old friends transferred here as well."

"I just want to go back home, Mom," Robert begged. His eyes were filled with terror.

"This *is* our home now," she said, and kissed him on the forehead. With that, she climbed back into the car and drove off down the lane. Dejected, Robert turned and trudged up the sidewalk, where dozens of students watched him with great amusement.

"Now, *that's* embarrassing," commented Ernie.

Natalia rolled her eyes. "You were just complaining that you wanted your mommy to pick you up because you have a tummy ache."

"Oh, please. I was just kidding."

"Check it out!" Harley exclaimed as a black-and-cream roadster pulled up. "That's a '29 Mercedes Gazelle." The passenger door opened, and a boy with mahogany skin jumped out. He wore a loose trench coat with the collar flipped up, and his watch had a yellow dial. Long dreadlocks were swept back from his face by a pair of flight goggles with amber lenses.

"Hey, Xander, over here!" a girl called out, waving him over.

With a smile, Xander walked to the front of the line and promptly cut in. A horde of students surrounded him, each positioning for a chance to get his attention.

"Who the heck was that?" asked Max, as he watched them all disappear into the depot.

"I don't know, but did you see that car? His family must have some serious money," Harley said.

There was money, and then there was *money*. Max's family had the latter, complete with jets, multinational corporations, and even private islands that would one day be his. It wasn't Xander's wealth that had impressed Max. It was the way he seemed to be at ease with it. There was no doubting that this Xander had style — at least until he cut the line.

Ernie sighed as he walked through the double doors of the red brick building. "This place is lame. I thought Iron Bridge was going to be a castle or something. Where's the moat?"

As they moved along the squeaky hallway, the line of students was directed toward an escalator that disappeared into a dark hole in the floor. Max couldn't see through the darkness, but the echoes from the students ahead indicated that they were in for a long ride.

"Is that Brooke?" Ernie asked a few moments later,

pointing to a girl with long brown hair who was about to disappear in the darkness.

"Where?" Max asked.

"In case you hadn't noticed, I'm not a changeling," Natalia reminded Ernie. "Just because you can see for a hundred yards in the dark doesn't mean the rest of us can."

"Oh yeah, sorry," Ernie said.

"Besides, if you must know, Brooke came to school with her father early this morning," Natalia went on.

"How do you know?" Harley asked.

"Because I talked to her on the phone last night, that's how," she retorted.

"Seriously?" Ernie asked as reached into his backpack to pull out a bottle of Plumples. After a rash of cavities, the carbonated fruit juice was the closest thing to soda that his parents would let him drink.

"What's wrong with that?" Natalia wanted to know.

Ernie shrugged. "Nothing, I guess. So are you two best friends now? Because if you are, maybe we can finally make Brooke an official member of the Grey Griffins."

"I'm not sure we're ready for that yet," Natalia replied. "Besides, we have more important things to discuss."

"Like what?"

"For starters, I haven't been able to find much on those Round Table cards," Natalia said. "The Templar Library must have had at least a thousand books on the subject. It would take weeks to go through them all."

"And the other stuff?"

"There was nothing on mechanical beetles, Clockwork Kings, or the Brimstone Key. But I'll keep trying."

The rumbling escalator finally emptied into an underground foyer, and a short man greeted them. He was smiling broadly under a shabby derby, and the tips of his pointed ears could just be seen beneath the brim.

"This way, ladies and gentlemen," he announced, like the ringmaster at a circus. He led the students into what looked and smelled like an abandoned subway station. "Step lively, and mind the platform. Don't get too close."

"Did you notice how everyone is dressed?" Natalia asked, turning to the boys. "It looks like they're auditioning for a Charles Dickens play."

A girl carrying a black parasol with red roses pinned around its edge walked by. She wore a matching silk dress and pointy-toed boots. The boy next to her was dressed in leather pants, jackboots, and a gold waistcoat, with a pair of aviator goggles pushed up on his forehead. They weren't as intricate as Xander's, but they still looked expensive.

"Yeah," agreed Max. "Is there some costume party we weren't aware of?"

"You must be newbies," a girl in a safari ensemble observed as she stopped to look disapprovingly at the Griffins. "And look," she said, turning to her friends. "They're all dressed in civilian clothes. Aren't they precious?"

"Civilian clothes?" Max asked, shocked by the intrusion. "What are *you* supposed to be dressed as?"

The girl's smile faded. "My name is Hera, from the Third House of Argos. And you, little boy, are in *way* over your head."

Her friends laughed as they all disappeared into the crowd.

THE TOAD BROTHERS

"That was rude," Natalia commented. "We've met plenty of people in the Templar society, and they don't all dress like that."

"We've never met any our age, though," Max pointed out. "Maybe it's just the fashion around here."

"Well, I hope the fad ends soon. I already bought all my school clothes, and I don't have the money to update my wardrobe with corsets and ball gowns."

Ernie looked up at the ceiling, where water was dripping from deep fissures. "All I know is that we're in serious trouble if this roof comes crashing down."

"Shows what you know, civilian."

Ernie turned to see two boys smiling at him with eerie grins. The one who had spoken was thin, with square glasses and rabbit teeth. His pudgy companion looked disheveled and dirty. He had a spectacularly thick head of hair that looked rather like an overgrown hedge. Both were dressed in strange clothes, like everyone else, though their ensembles were faded and a bit threadbare.

"The dripping water is a side effect of the MERLIN Tech, that's all. Nothing to worry about," the first boy said.

His companion agreed, folding his arms. "Our great-great-great-grand-uncle Tobias helped design this place. If a Toad builds something, it ain't coming down." Max had no idea what the boy meant by "a Toad" but didn't want to risk a stupid question this early on his first day.

"*Ain't* isn't a word," retorted Natalia.

The two boys didn't pay her any attention. Instead, each extended a hand to Max.

"My name's Todd," said the boy with the rabbit teeth. "This here is my brother, Ross. They call us the Toad brothers." He beamed with pride.

"Because you have warts?" Natalia asked, eyeing their dirty hands.

"Because that's our *name*," Ross replied.

"Well, *this* is Max Sumner," Natalia announced just as proudly. "And we're the Grey Griffins."

Their jaws fell open.

"Seriously?" Todd Toad exclaimed, turning to his

brother. "This is incredible luck! Can you imagine what the year is going to be like with Xander Swift *and* Max Sumner at the same school? Who do you think will become the alpha male?"

Ross paused to look at Max carefully. "Definitely Xander," he replied. "I'd give four-to-one odds on it, maybe higher."

"Four-to-one?" Todd nodded, scratching his chin. "Well, Xander *is* the reigning Round Table champion. Still, Max is the Guardian of the *Codex*."

"Wait, how did you know I'm the Guardian?" Max interrupted.

"You also won the Medal of Arthur," Todd continued. "Plus, you've been trained by legendary mentors like Olaf Iverson, Logan, and Cain Lundgren."

"And your dad stole the Spear of Ragnarok. Look, we've got all your stats," Todd explained, patting a small book in his hip pocket.

"Do you have anything on Agent Thunderbolt?" asked Ernie, eagerly stepping closer.

Todd nodded. "Not much. No offense, but you're not exactly A-list. Don't worry about it, though; nobody expects much from changelings. They're kind of..."

"What?" Ernie asked, growing frustrated.

"You know...weird."

"Oh, honestly." Natalia sighed. "This is ridiculous."

"Of course," Ross began, turning his attention back to Max, "you're going to run into a few problems, thanks to your dad. He might be one of the wealthiest men on planet, but he hasn't done you any favors."

"Yeah," agreed Todd. "You might want to look out for a kid named Angus McCutcheon. Rumor is that he has it in for you."

"You're kidding, right?" Max asked, thinking the entire conversation was surreal.

"A lot of good people died when your dad betrayed us," Ross explained. "Some of these kids lost people in their families."

"Max is the one who stopped the Black Wolves," Natalia protested. "He saved our lives."

"Sure," Todd admitted, motioning toward a group of boys. They were tall and strong, and their faces were grim. "But you don't have to convince *us*."

"Bullies don't scare us," Natalia retorted. "We're monster hunters."

The Toad brothers' eyes lit with wonder as they spoke in perfect unison. "You *are* monster hunters?"

"Of course," she replied. "Why is that so hard to believe?"

"Well," began Todd, "for one thing, you're too young. Training isn't supposed to start until you're sixteen. You have to be handpicked by the THOR Division, and there hasn't been a monster hunter our age since..."

"Since my grandpa Caliburn," Max answered.

"What do you use?" Ross began, pulling out a notebook and a pencil. "Silver bullets? Holy water? Wooden stakes?"

"Depends on the job," Harley replied in feigned indifference.

The elusive answer only set the Toad brothers into a flurry of questions until the platform started to vibrate and a whistle blared. A steady beam of light approached from the depths of the tunnel.

A dark form shot out of the tunnel at such a high speed that Max didn't think it would be able to stop in time to catch the platform. Yet like a bullet caught in midflight, it did. Before Max could get a good look, a rolling cloud of steam enveloped the bystanders. Umbrellas, parasols, and hat brims were lowered.

The cloud soon faded, revealing the unmistakable form of a subway train. Max's grey eyes swept over the lines of the mechanical beast. He'd never seen a slimier piece of junk in his life. It looked as if it had been freshly pulled from a swamp. Yet he could see hints of the subway's glory days. The narrow passenger windows, now rippled with age, were constructed from leaded glass with filigree, and its doors were equally well crafted. More interesting, its corroded wheels hovered above the rail on a silvery light, which Todd referred to as a MERLIN sled.

Max watched as another jet of steam issued from the subway's underbelly and the silvery light faded. The subway lowered its wheels soundlessly onto the track.

"I can't believe they actually found the *Zephyr*," Todd declared. "I mean, there were rumors, but..."

A swirl of stories swept through the crowd, passing

over Max like a wave. Some claimed the subway had been dismantled and sold for scrap. Others were just as certain that it had been sucked into a magical vortex before disappearing with all its screaming passengers aboard.

"What is this hunk of junk?" Natalia asked.

"The history books claim that the London Underground was the first subway rapid-transit system," Ross stated. "But the Templar built the *Zephyr* way before that."

"Is it steam-powered?" asked Harley, as mist swirled about.

"Mostly MERLIN Tech."

"As in the magician?" Ernie wondered aloud.

Todd stopped and looked at Ernie sideways before correcting him. "As in *Lord Merlin Silverthorne*, the scientist."

"He harnessed energy that was a cross between electromagnetic radiation and what civilians like to call magic," Ross said. "But it doesn't have anything to do with hocus-pocus. It's real science."

"So the train runs on some kind of electrical magic?" Harley asked, intrigued by the idea.

"Not exactly," Ross replied.

"In the old days, the *Zephyr* was just a normal underground train that transported students to the school and back," explained Todd, his voice lowering to a conspiratorial whisper. "Traveling through the enchanted waters of Lake Avalon isn't safe, though. After a few years, strange things started to happen. Some say the *Zephyr* became haunted. Others claim that it was being controlled by aliens, but our dad knows the truth."

"And that is?" Natalia prompted.

"MERLIN Tech can have unintended side effects. Dad told us that in the case of the *Zephyr*, one day it was a subway train, and the next, it was *alive*."

Natalia rolled her eyes, completely unconvinced by the theatrics.

The Toad brothers didn't seem too worried about impressing Natalia. Instead, they focused their attention on Max. It was clear they considered him to be some kind of celebrity.

"Can we see it?" Todd asked eagerly.

"See what?" Max replied.

"You know, the *Codex*," Todd said.

"Yeah. Maybe you could trap us in one of those captivity orbs," Ross added. "We've always wanted to know what it would be like to get trapped inside a portal prison."

Max raised his eyebrows. "I don't think so," he said. "Besides, they only work on faeries and monsters."

The Toad brothers frowned in unison. "Are you sure?" Todd asked.

"I'm almost positive that James Moriarty was caught with a captivity orb," Ross conjectured.

"Professor Moriarty?" Natalia asked, incredulous at the absurdity of the statement. "This is the real world, not a Sherlock Holmes novel."

"Shows what *you* know," Todd said, and Ross snickered. "Anyway, have you guys been to Mad Meriwether's Gadgetry Shoppe? I heard they sell replica *Codex* Gauntlets there."

"I'm thinking about putting it on my Christmas list," Ross added. "But I have my eye on a derringer that shoots paint pellets. My parents won't let me have a real gun, so it's the next best thing."

"There aren't any gadgetry shops around here," Harley pointed out. "The closest thing was the Shoppe of Antiquities, but it's closed now."

"Mad Meriwether's isn't in Avalon," Todd pointed out.

"Yeah, it's in New Victoria," Ross explained. "On Baker Street, across from the apothecary. In fact, it isn't too far from Iron Bridge."

Harley just stared at Ross with a blank look on his face.

"I don't think these four are going to make it past the first week," Ross proclaimed.

"Agreed," Todd said. "It looks as though the undertaker is going to have a busy semester."

IRON BRIDGE

"Undertaker? What on earth are you talking about?" demanded Natalia, who had gone from annoyed to angry.

"As long as you stay on school grounds, you should be okay," Ross explained. "I just wouldn't wander into the rest of the city if I were you."

"Look, the island is big enough to hide a school; but an entire city? I don't think so," Natalia argued.

"New Victoria isn't on the island," Todd said. "Neither is Iron Bridge."

"What's that supposed to mean?"

"They're both in the Land of Mist. You know, the in-between place that separates the real world from the

Shadowlands?" he continued. "That's where dreams come from."

"Really?" Ernie asked. "Even nightmares?"

"How do you think all those monsters slipped into Avalon?" Todd asked. "They crossed over from the Land of Mist."

"But don't worry—Iron Bridge is *mostly* safe," Ross assured. "Besides, they locked the gateway to the Shadowlands a long time ago. Most of the really bad stuff got stuck on the other side."

"Wait a minute. What do you mean, *mostly safe?*" Ernie didn't like the sound of that.

"The academy is surrounded by walls that are fifty feet high and twenty feet thick," Ross replied. The only way in and out is by airship."

"Or subway," Todd added. "That's where the *Zephyr* comes in."

"What about portals?" Max asked.

"Portals are shut down inside all Templar academies," Todd replied. "They say it's a safety precaution."

"It's more like they don't want the students sneaking out for a night on the town," Ross corrected.

At that moment, the doors to the subway creaked open. Max thought he could see Brooke enter one of the cars behind them, but the cloud of steam, the crackle of MERLIN Tech, and the rush of students made it a confusing scene.

"Ladies first." Ernie bowed to Natalia. Harley couldn't

wait, though. He was too excited to see what was inside, so he slipped past her as she scowled.

The *Zephyr* had been a marvel of comfort and luxury in its heyday. It was tastefully appointed with dark mahogany, brass accents, and leather hanging straps for anyone who chose to stand. For those who sat, there were deep leather benches set like parlor couches, some facing one another, some with their backs to the windows. The whole of the carriage was illuminated by the warm glow of Tiffany lamps mounted on the side walls. Whoever had built the subway had spared no expense.

"Too bad the train was left to rot," Natalia remarked. The seat beneath her was split and covered in mildew.

"It's not so bad," Harley replied. "A little elbow grease and a bit of varnish, and this baby could be as good as new."

After three whistles, the doors to the *Zephyr* closed, and the carriage rose into the air on its silvery sled. An instant later, the subway shot into the darkness.

"Wait a minute," Natalia said, glancing over her shoulder. "Half of these people weren't on the platform with us."

"There are lots of stops between here and the Twin Cities," Ross explained.

"The students at Iron Bridge don't have to live in Avalon?" Ernie asked.

Todd laughed. "This is my first time in this boring town, and I bet it's the same for most of us."

"Avalon most certainly isn't boring," Natalia said defensively.

"Give me a break," Ross chimed in. "It's just a tidal pool that was left over from the old world. And trust me, there is a big difference between a pool and the ocean."

"You have to understand, most of us live either in the Land of Mist or in major cities like New York and London," Todd explained. "Compared to those places, in Avalon you barely have your toes in the water."

"So when are you going to give us a tour?" Harley asked, hopeful for a chance to visit Mad Meriwether's Gadgetry Shoppe.

"I wouldn't count on it any time soon," Ross explained. "I'm sure there will be restrictions on students entering the city."

"How long is this ride supposed to last?" Ernie asked. The bumps in the rails were making him feel nauseated, and he didn't want to vomit in front of everyone.

"Time and distance are completely different in the Land of Mist," Ross explained. "You might as well get comfortable, because we're going to be in here for a while."

As he spoke, the subway train cut into swirling fog. Max noticed everything around them start to shimmer, and then the subway changed. The rotted interior became sleek and polished. Gone was the smell of mildew and the bumps in the rail. Once it entered the Land of Mist, the *Zephyr* had returned to its former glory.

"That was incredible!" Harley said, marveling at the transformation.

"Not bad," Todd agreed. "Just watch out for the rogue portals and bottomless pits."

"Don't forget the sea monsters," Ross reminded him. Ernie gasped.

"Don't worry," reassured Todd, with his nose pressed against the window. "The *Zephyr* will know what to do."

The subway emerged into a glass tunnel deep under the shimmering water. Max watched in awe as they sped past sunken ships, schools of exotic fish, and a forest of plants that were as tall as skyscrapers.

"It's amazing down here," Todd remarked.

"As long as you don't mind the threat of drowning or being eaten by sea monsters," Ross added as he pointed toward a large, lumbering shadow in the distance.

"What in the world was *that*?" asked Ernie. He felt his throat constricting.

"Probably a Megalodon," Ross observed, and Todd nodded his agreement. "Prehistoric sharks like that could bite this subway in half." He followed up with a crunching sound.

"You can stop the theatrics," Natalia scolded. "If this subway wasn't safe, the Templar wouldn't have put students on it in the first place."

As she finished her sentence, the sound of metal twisting and snapping reverberated throughout the subway carriage. With a lurch, the *Zephyr* jerked to the side before it slammed to a stop. Students flew to the floor as the lights flickered and died. The car was bathed in murky light that emanated from the lake bottom.

The monstrous shadow drew near.

Most students stared in wide-eyed awe as a few others started pounding on the doors to get out. Robert, the frightened boy from the depot, was among them.

Then the intercom system crackled to life.

"Please remain in your seats. We have encountered a minor problem with the aft turbine engine. We should be on our way shortly."

"Aft *turbine*?" Todd repeated in puzzlement. "There's no turbine on the *Zephyr*. It's run by MERLIN Tech!"

There was another ominous rumble, as if the subway train were shaking itself like a wet dog. Windows began to fracture, and the dead lights overhead swung back and forth. Suddenly the shark wasn't their only concern.

"It's the Big Squeeze!" Ross proclaimed as he stood up on the seat. "The water pressure! It's gonna squish us like bugs."

"There *are* worse ways to die," Todd said casually. "Uncle Seymour was sucked into a black hole at the Celestial Cyclotron, and Great-Grandpa Daanon was skewered by a rhinoceros in British East Africa."

"Look, just because this junky train has been *grimthorped* doesn't mean that I have to sit and listen to you two psychopaths read through the encyclopedia of death," Natalia scolded.

The Toad brothers looked at her blankly. "Grimthorped?"

Harley pulled Natalia back into her seat. "She means that whoever restored the *Zephyr* screwed it up. And yes, she always uses annoying words like that."

As Harley spoke, everyone could hear a low growling emanate from beneath the floorboards. The next moment, Natalia's seat upended, throwing her into the aisle.

"What in the world?" she exclaimed, looking around in confusion. She was the only one on the floor.

"I think you made it angry," Todd warned. "You better be careful."

"Made *who* angry?"

"The *Zephyr*. I told you that the train was alive."

"Are you kidding me? This piece of..." Natalia began, but she quickly found Harley's hand clamped over her mouth.

The next moment, the lights reignited and the subway train resumed its course. Max looked around, but the cracks in the windows had been mysteriously repaired, and the floorboards were back in place.

Todd laughed and elbowed his brother. "I bet the *Zephyr* planned this all along. It was just testing us...you know, having some fun at the expense of the newbies."

Natalia rolled her eyes at the preposterous notion of a living subway. She didn't buy it for one second. Still, she kept her mouth shut for the rest of the trip, just in case.

The *Zephyr* raced through several stops in New

Victoria, and a few minutes later it pulled into Iron Bridge Depot. Natalia's book bag was promptly launched out the window by the train, where it landed in a puddle.

The subway platform wasn't in much better condition than the depot they had left behind, but it was certainly busier. A flock of teachers in hard hats guided the students through a maze of yellow caution tape. It looked like a disaster zone after an earthquake.

"I wonder who built all of this," Max mused, looking up at a cavernous ceiling.

"Faeries, of course," announced the sharp voice of a nearby teacher. She was thin, fitting into her clothes like a blade into a starched scabbard. Her eyes were bright, and her white skin was flecked with small red veins near her temples—possibly from too much thinking. She smelled of cats, and her hands were arthritic rakes with glassy nails. "Though I daresay machines are more reliable. Now, which one of you is Tweeny?"

"Um...I am," Ernie admitted, his voice faltering. The teacher's narrowed eyes peeped out from two wrinkly bags, and Ernie squirmed under the scrutiny.

"I am Dean Nipkin," she said. "And I believe that we'll be getting to know each other quite well, my little changeling friend. Yes, I've heard a great deal about you...." Her voice trailed off as her eyes fell on another student of interest. "Ah...the impertinent mongrel has shown up," the dean said to no one in particular. She turned on her heels and clicked toward her new target.

A Cloud of Smoke

The escalators leading to the surface were elegantly appointed, but like the *Zephyr*, that elegance had been brutalized by neglect. The wood floorboards were rotten, and the leather handrails had been nibbled away by a hundred years' worth of hungry mice. Worse yet, the escalator was pitched at a murderous angle.

"This thing should be condemned," Natalia stated as she listened to the floorboards moan beneath her feet. Steam rolled out from the cracks as invisible engines worked to move the students up to an impossible height. "It's a giant lawsuit just waiting to happen."

"Look at that," Max announced, pointing back to the

bottom of the escalator. Dean Nipkin was arguing with a boy whose blond hair was spiked at impossibly sharp angles. He was dressed in jeans and leather boots, and his goggles were pushed up on his forehead like those of most of the other boys and more than a few of the girls.

"Maybe that's the 'impertinent' kid she was talking about," Natalia thought aloud.

As the argument escalated, the boy shook his head and, in a burst of black smoke, disappeared. An instant later he reappeared behind the Griffins, but only long enough to smile mischievously at the dean. Then he disappeared again, leaving another cloud of smoke. Up where the escalator ended, there was an explosion of books and papers, followed by a scream. Then the boy was gone.

"He's a teleporter!" Ernie shouted with joy. "That means he's a changeling, too. Holy cow! You were right, Natalia. I'm not the only one after all!"

"I wonder how many changelings are here," Harley mused.

"They pretty much keep to themselves," Ross explained. "It's the rule."

"Rule?" Ernie exclaimed. "What do you mean?"

"Welcome to Iron Bridge Academy!" Todd announced suddenly as they reached the top of the escalator.

Soaring above a cobblestone courtyard were buildings as varied and wondrous as Max could ever have imagined. Tall towers and gabled peaks rose above the mist, as walls of ornately arched stone bridges and hundreds of stained-glass windows peered out over a thick green court of flowering trees, hedges, and fountains. Each structure was an architectural marvel of intricacy, and the buildings reflected the majesty of each subject taught within.

Max looked over his shoulder to see the massive walls that concealed any possible view of the city of New Victoria. The Toad brothers had aroused his curiosity about what the city might look like, not to mention who lived there.

"This path is called the Green Corridor," explained Ross, gesturing to a grassy lane that led to the school grounds. "It'll take you straight to De Payens Hall. That's where all the offices are. Everything to the left is controlled by the Sciences Council, which means it's off-limits. The right-hand side is for students."

"How do you know so much about the school?" Ernie asked.

"We have our sources," was all Todd would admit to.

They followed the mass of students into a wide courtyard where colorful hot-air balloons floated overhead. Strange vehicles slipped along white gravel lanes that connected the various buildings, while airships hovered high above.

The school was still under construction, and most of the buildings were cocooned within scaffolding. "Once they're done with this place, Iron Bridge is going to be the jewel of New Victoria," Ross proclaimed.

They followed the Toad brothers through a set of

double doors and into the three-storied brownstone that was called Apprentice Hall. Max looked for Brooke, but he couldn't find her in the crowd.

When they got to the second floor, they could hear the sounds of cogs turning and holes being punched in paper. Lines of students were waiting in front of a console as Max watched Xander walk over and place his hands on an opaque ball. It lit up, and then a brass punch card emerged from a nearby slot.

"Is that his schedule?" asked Natalia.

"It's more than that," Todd replied as he pushed his glasses back onto his nose. "That's a student ID. It has everything on it, from what doors you can open to what you're having for lunch."

"Meaning what?"

"The card knows you better than you know yourself," Ross explained. "Diabetic? Vegan? Low on iron? The card can sense it and ensure you get the food you need."

Harley whistled in appreciation. "It sounds like it reads your biochemical, or maybe your electrical, signals when you touch it. That's pretty high-tech."

Ross yawned. "The Cheiromantic Scheduler is an out-dated piece of junk. Stirling Academy has the Scheduler XT."

Max watched as Xander entertained a throng of admiring girls before inserting his card into a second slot farther down the wall. As he did, a green light flared before a brass door opened, releasing a stack of books tied together with a leather belt. Xander picked them up, along with the books of a beautiful girl, and together they strutted down the hallway.

Max decided right then that he didn't like Xander. He reminded Max of someone, but he wasn't sure who it was. At first Max thought it might be his old nemesis, Ray Fisher, the superpowered freak who nearly blew up the Griffins in a cornfield. That wasn't it, though.

"Why do you keep staring at Xander?" Ernie asked, catching Max's gaze.

"What are you talking about?"

"We saw it, too," Ross added. "Look, maybe you guys will be friends."

"Who knows?" Todd said with a shrug. "Stranger things have happened."

"What makes Xander so special?" asked Natalia.

"Oh, I don't know," Ross said sarcastically. "He's brilliant and athletic, and girls think he's handsome."

"Most important," added Todd, "he's the highest-rated Round Table duelist in the world. Well, for the junior division anyway."

"Max nearly beat a Round Table Grandmaster last year," Natalia noted. "So Xander better watch out."

Todd pulled out his little black notebook and jotted something down. His facial expression said it all, though—he liked what he had heard.

Max was the first of the Grey Griffins to approach the

console. He placed his hand on the globe, and a shock like static electricity shot up his arm. The light flashed, and Max took his card before making room for Ernie.

"What the heck is Transformational Science?" Ernie asked as he pored over his schedule.

"If you kept reading, you'd see that it's a special class for *changelings*," Max said. "Who knows, maybe you'll end up in the same class as that kid who can teleport."

Ernie broke into a smile. "That would be supersonic."

"I have a class called Runes and Ciphers, and another called Forensics!" Natalia announced with enthusiasm.

Max scanned his own schedule. Physical Training. Arithmetick. Latin. Grammar. History. Lunch. Then it was Natural Science, followed by rotating electives — Bounder Care and Portaling. Not too bad, he thought... well, except for the Arithmetick part. Then his eyes went back to the Bounder class. He looked around at the students nearby, wondering if any of them had Bounders, as well.

"Why are you so happy?" Natalia asked when Harley's eyes lit up.

"I got into MERLIN Engineering," he answered.

"You can thank me later," Logan said. Harley spun around to see the Scotsman smiling down at the Griffins.

"You got me in?"

"*You* got you in," Logan corrected. "You already have the knack for engineering; I just let them know."

"So you're going to stay with us the rest of the day?" Ernie smiled hopefully.

Logan shook his head before scratching at the stubble on his cheek. "If I stay with anyone, it's the young man whom I'm paid to protect."

Max's stomach sank. He loved Logan like an uncle, but having a bodyguard shadow him all day was going to draw the wrong kind of attention. He didn't want everyone to think he was a wimp.

"Don't worry, Grasshopper," Logan said, catching Max's discomfort. "I'll be out of sight most of the time. Just let me know if you need anything, got it?"

Then a voice called over the intercom...

"All students are to report immediately to the Grand Auditorium. Repeat: All students report to the Grand Auditorium."

A LESSON IN FASHION

The Grand Auditorium was in the heart of Apprentice Hall, and when Max walked in, he could hardly believe his eyes. Unlike the subway stations, there was no mildew, stench, or crumbling statues. Everything was rich and luxurious. Flanked by three levels of balconies and hundreds of plush leather seats, a central aisle proceeded toward a stage draped with a velvet curtain. The walls were brilliant gold, filling the room with a warm glow. Soaring nearly seventy feet above their heads, the ceiling was alive with interlocking designs and five of the largest chandeliers Max had ever seen.

Xander Swift and his flock of admirers were blocking the aisle as they waited for the assembly to begin. Max paused, knowing he'd have to cut through the middle of them. All he wanted to do was find Brooke and sit down.

"Hey, that's the Sumner kid, right?" someone asked.

Max cringed.

When he turned around, Xander was standing there staring at him. The older boy was at least a head taller than Max, and it was obvious that he spent a lot of time in a weight room. He had green eyes, and his dark skin was flawless.

"Welcome to Iron Bridge," he said, offering his hand to Max, as though he were welcoming Max to his personal residence. "I'm Xander Swift." Max took it reluctantly. "Just transferred here from Stirling. Which academy are you from?"

Max looked around uncomfortably. "King's Elementary," he mumbled.

Xander looked puzzled for a moment. It was as though the idea of attending anything other than a Templar academy had never occurred to him.

"Nice work with that Medal of Arthur," he said.

"Thanks," Max replied as he stared at the ground. Xander's charm was so contagious that Max was struggling to maintain his disdain.

"I hear you're a pretty good duelist," Xander continued. "Playing Round Table against a Grandmaster is crazy. You must have had some serious moves."

Max sighed. The Toad brothers evidently couldn't keep their mouths shut. The Grandmaster in question was a gargoyle named Throckmorton, and Max was convinced that Throckmorton had been toying with him.

"Hey, there's Brooke," Harley said, catching Max by the arm before he pulled him through the crowd.

"Sorry...got to go," Max offered in relief.

Xander shrugged and turned back to his friends.

Max felt his face flush as he wound his way to where Brooke was sitting. They had been neighbors ever since Max could remember. He had even asked her to marry him when they were five. Thankfully, she hadn't mentioned it since.

"I was wondering if I would get to see you," Brooke said as she stood up to give Natalia a hug. Moments later the two girls were comparing class schedules.

"We really needed you the other day," Natalia said as they sat down.

"What happened?"

"I almost drowned!" Ernie declared.

Natalia went on to explain the details of their adventure as Max pulled out his share of the mysterious Round Table cards from the bunker. "Look at this."

He handed Brooke a card with a hideous monster called a Reaper painted on the front. The thing had long fingers, iron nails, and skin the color of coal.

Brooke shivered as she looked at it. "I don't remember Round Table cards looking this creepy."

"No kidding," agreed Max. "The whole deck was full of monsters just like it."

"Don't forget about the Clockwork King," Ernie added.

"Really?" she replied with curiosity. "My dad was just talking about clockworks the other day. Maybe he'll know where the cards came from."

"I was kind of hoping to keep this quiet...at least for now," Max said, lowering his voice. "I'm not even sure we're supposed to have them. Do you think you could help us find out where they came from? You know..."

"Without telling my dad?" Brooke slipped the Reaper card into her purse. "I'll see what I can do."

"What about you?" Max asked. "Do you know anything about clockworks?"

"Not really," she answered. "I mean, they're all over the school, of course. You'll see some in the dining hall at lunch. They serve the food."

"You're saying a robot is fixing my dinner?" Ernie asked incredulously.

"They aren't really robots. Anyway, after a few days, you won't even notice that they're there." Brooke laughed.

"You wouldn't say that if you'd been thrown into a nest of those things, as we have."

Natalia rolled her eyes. "Good grief, Ernest. That was just a pile of junk!"

"A pile of killer robot junk," Ernie maintained. "And what about those blueprints?"

"Excuse me," apologized a boy in a bowler derby as he

slid past the Griffins to reach a group of his friends. Max studied the hat thoughtfully, wondering if it would be as comfortable as his Twins cap.

"So why aren't you dressed like everyone else?" Natalia asked, turning back to Brooke.

"I guess I didn't feel like it," Brooke said. "Besides, I was running late and I didn't want to miss the *Zephyr*. This was just easier."

"I don't get it," Max said. "Why does everyone wear stuff like that?"

"It's all the rage," Brooke explained. "It's sort of a mix of Goth, punk, and nineteenth-century England all rolled into one. You'll see girls with pink hair and combat boots wearing crinoline and corsets. You get used to it."

"What's the point?"

Brooke shrugged. "Templar kids have their own sense of fashion. It's a different culture than we're used to. They borrow their style from different eras and mix them together to make it their own. It's edgy, and I kind of like it."

"What about the goggles?"

"You definitely need to get some," she advised. "They're critical. Besides, they come in handy if you ever ride in an airship with open windows."

Harley snickered. "Yeah, that happens to me all the time."

Natalia's eyes roved across the auditorium. "Are all the rooms going to be this extravagant?"

"Eventually."

Just then the lights dimmed, and a distinguished man with an elegant walking stick strode across the stage. Despite a slight limp, his heels clicked in perfect cadence as he stepped to the lectern.

"Can you believe your dad is the director of the academy?" Natalia whispered.

"It's weird," Brooke admitted as she regarded her father. "I just hope the other kids won't hate me because of him."

Baron Lundgren was discussing something with Logan, who was standing just offstage. The two men seemed to reach an agreement, and then Logan disappeared.

FAIR WARNING

Between his military posture and the streaks of noble grey around his temples, Baron Cain Lundgren looked positively regal. He might have been forty. Or he might have been two hundred. No one seemed to know for sure. His goatee was meticulously groomed, his suit was custom-tailored, and his eyes were filled with dark secrets.

Though the Baron did not hold an official membership in the Templar Knights, the Grand Council had unanimously selected him to direct Iron Bridge Academy. He accepted on the condition that he would maintain his role as Max's mentor—a position he had inherited from Olaf Iverson, and one he took with deadly seriousness.

"Before we begin," Baron Lundgren commenced, "I would like to take a moment of silence to remember our friends and family who fell at the hands of our enemies. This has not been an easy year, and as you can see, there are many empty seats in this auditorium—seats that should have been filled with bright minds. Let us remember them now."

As the room fell silent, a knot formed in Max's stomach. He considered looking around to see if anyone was glaring at him because of his father, but he decided it was better not to know.

"Our survival was fortunate, but it cannot be taken for granted. Every moment that passes gives our opponents an advantage, and I expect each of you to consider that as you approach your studies. Those who fell to protect your freedom would expect nothing less."

Determined faces filled the auditorium as the Baron continued.

"Our sister schools in Stirling and Antioch, Carthage and Novgorod, Rome and Jerusalem, have all sent us their well wishes. Many of you have come to Iron Bridge from those academies. Know that you were hand-selected to be a part of this historic launch. Welcome, and well done!"

There was a wave of applause.

"As you can see," the Baron continued, "much of our campus is still under construction. Though you may be curious to gauge the progress, the Construction Zones are strictly off-limits to students."

He let his words sink in before continuing.

"Also, I do not recommend that you leave the safety of our campus without an escort. For those who haven't been to New Victoria before today, sections of the city can be a bit dangerous. However, the mayor has offered his full support to our endeavors, and for that, we thank him."

"Lastly, you will be expected to behave with discretion when you are in civilian cities, such as Avalon. Templar matters are meant for the Templar only. Guard your tongues as you walk in their streets. The less they know, the more freedom we will have to protect them."

Max had never been comfortable with all the secrecy surrounding the Templar. Whatever they did and wherever they went was shrouded in mystery. Getting a straight answer was almost impossible, and it didn't look like that was going to change anytime soon.

"Now on to a more pleasant topic," the Baron continued. "As you know, each spring the Templar academies come together to crown the Round Table champion and—" Before he could finish his sentence, the crowd erupted in cheers. The Baron seemed to enjoy the enthusiasm, and he let it play out before continuing.

"The varsity qualifying tournament will take place in December. Sixty-four of you will compete for eight positions, as well as the traditional four alternates. But I must confess"—he paused with a grim look, though his eyes had a mischievous light about them—"the other academies are skeptical of our ability to challenge them…"

Cheers quickly turned into boos and foot stomping.

"I, for one, share your opinion," Baron Lundgren said, calling the assemblage to quiet as he raised his hands. "We may not be at full strength, but with the highest-rated junior duelist in the world, we have a legitimate shot at the title."

He motioned to Xander Swift, and the crowd erupted in cheers. Frustrated, Max watched as Xander stood and waved to the crowd. And that's when he realized who Xander reminded him of... his own father, the notorious Lord Sumner!

Xander had that same easy way with people, entrancing them with his charm. As Max connected the two, his dislike for Xander grew.

"Lastly," Cain said as Xander sat down, "I want to tell you how proud I am of each of you. You have earned your place at Iron Bridge, an institution that has graduated some of the most gifted men and women in our history. I have no doubt that you will uphold their legacy as you study to become our future leaders and heroes—and our world has never needed heroes as much as it does today. Congratulations and welcome."

CHANGELING QUARANTINE

"Look at that," Harley called out as the Griffins left the auditorium. He had stopped at a picture window that allowed a full view of New Victoria beyond the walls. Airships hovered over what looked like a sprawling replica of nineteenth-century London. There were spires that shot up to dizzying heights, ringing bell towers, bristling smokestacks, and cobblestone streets that wove like spidery veins through a cluster of dark roofs that seemed to go on forever. The sidewalks were packed with strangely dressed figures hurrying to their destinations.

"Who lives there?" asked Ernie as he watched an airship slip overhead, casting the window in shadow.

"Humans, faeries, and everything in between," Brooke replied. "It's a port city, so it gets a lot of strange visitors — and some of them aren't very friendly. Unless you know what you are doing, you could end up getting stuffed in a sack and hauled away to scrub the decks of a pirate airship."

Ernie's mouth fell open.

At that moment a trail of sparkling dust flittered across the hall before coming to rest near Brooke's shoulder. Like Max, she had a Bounder Faerie. The pixie was dressed in a gossamer gown of orange and adorned with gaudy jewelry. Though she was six inches tall, Honeysuckle could be vicious. The pixie folded her arms in annoyance as several giggling girls walked by and pointed at her. If it weren't for Brooke, Max had no doubt that Honeysuckle would have turned them into slugs. With the exception of Brooke, Honeysuckle didn't appear to be terribly fond of humans.

"So where's Sprig?" asked Brooke.

Max shrugged. "As far as I know, she could be off chasing a butterfly in Kansas or snorkeling in San Diego."

Natalia sighed. "You really need to discipline her, Max. She's supposed to watch over you, but she can't do that if she's never around."

"You can't discipline a faerie." Brooke laughed. "They aren't pets. You just have to take them as they are."

"Are there other kids here with Bounders?" asked Max, looking down the hall.

74

"A few," Brooke replied.

"Look," Natalia said, pointing to her watch. "We have to hurry, or we're going to be late for homeroom."

With that, the five of them set off with books in hand, heading around a corner and down a long hall that was lined with busts of past instructors atop marble pedestals. Ernie stopped at one that had shoulders and a neck but no head. "Who is this guy supposed to be? The Headless Horseman?"

Brooke shrugged. "I think his name was Strife, or something like that anyway. The teachers don't like to talk about him for some reason."

As they neared their homeroom, they found two instructors locked in a dispute. The tall one was none other than Dean Nipkin. Her bony finger was pointing in accusation at her colleague who, as Brooke informed them, was their homeroom teacher, Ms. Merical. The dean was clearly the aggressor, but Ms. Merical didn't look like she was ready to back down.

The Griffins moved behind a statue to watch the argument from a safe distance. As they did, Max caught sight of a boy hiding behind Ms. Merical's skirt.

"Hey, that's Robert!" Ernie exclaimed in a hushed tone. "But what's wrong with his legs?"

It looked like Robert's shoes had somehow become a part of the floor. He was literally rooted to the spot.

"He must be a changeling, too." Ernie smiled.

"...and I am telling you that boy cannot be allowed

into your class!" Dean Nipkin continued. "He's not like the others, and you can't treat him as such. There are rules here, Ms. Merical. Changelings belong under my supervision, and I would *appreciate* it if you could ensure that Robert Hernandez is escorted to Sendak Hall in due haste."

Ms. Merical offered a cherubic smile. "Fortunately for Robert, his schedule dictates otherwise." She held out Robert's papers as incontrovertible evidence.

The dean snatched the schedule from Ms. Merical's hand. After a moment of study, she stuffed it into her pocket. "I can assure you this was a mistake. At Iron Bridge, we don't mix humans and changelings. Not anymore. There have been incidents, *Elaine*."

Ernie's mouth dropped open. "What's that supposed to mean?" he whispered.

"I am well aware of our history," Ms. Merical countered. "However, Robert's schedule puts him under my care. Unless Baron Lundgren instructs otherwise, he is going to stay right here."

At that moment, one of the instructors ran up to the dean and began whispering in her ear.

"What do you mean, one of the changelings disappeared? Is this some kind of practical joke?" she asked with fury. "Stephen was under constant supervision. *Your* supervision, I might add. How did this happen?"

The discomfited man wiped at his brow. "One minute he was in his room, the next he was gone. The guards never saw him leave."

"What about the Quantum Cameras?"

"Nothing. I've scoured the video. Perhaps he portaled out?"

"Nonsense! All portals have been shut down on campus. You know that. There has to be another answer..." The dean's veins flashed red against her temples. She turned to Ms. Merical. "It seems we have a runaway, Elaine. We'll have to continue this discussion later."

Robert flashed a relieved smile, but he didn't budge.

"Happy hunting," Ms. Merical offered cheerily as Dean Nipkin hurried down the hall. Then she turned to wink at Robert. "Why don't you go ahead and take your seat?"

Robert's shoes uprooted from the floor, and he bounded into homeroom.

"Welcome," Ms. Merical said, turning to greet the approaching Griffins. "It's quite an honor to have the Secret Order of the Grey Griffins and the fabulous Miss Lundgren in my classroom."

"You know who we are?" Ernie asked, astonished.

"Of course, Agent Thunderbolt."

Ernie blushed all the way to the tips of his ears.

"What happened with Robert?" Natalia ventured.

"Oh, just a little mix-up with his schedule, that's all," Ms. Merical explained.

"It doesn't sound like Dean Nipkin cares for changelings very much."

"I'm sure that's not true," Ms. Merical countered with

a cheerful expression. "She is one of the leading authorities on the subject of changelings. If she has a fault, it's that she cares too much."

Just then, a terrible crash shook the hall.

"There goes another ceiling!" Ms. Merical exclaimed as she ushered everyone into the safety of her classroom. "That makes three in the past week."

The intercom system crackled to life, and the voice of Baron Lundgren's secretary filled the halls: *"Due to unforeseen circumstances, class will be dismissed early today. All students are to make their way to the* Zephyr *depot in an orderly fashion."*

CAUGHT IN THE ACT

Ernie spent the rest of the day drawing up a roster of potential changeling recruits for his superhero team. Natalia decided to use the spare time to log in to the Templar Library with her remote-viewing card. She was hoping for a breakthrough in her investigation. There was plenty of information on Round Table cards and clockworks. In fact, if anything, there was too much. Despite reading everything from game strategy guides to manuals on clockwork protocol, she wasn't finding any useful information. Meanwhile, Harley and Max waited for nightfall before heading over to the Shoppe of Antiquities.

"Maybe we shouldn't do this," Max whispered as they snuck down the alleyway behind the stores on Main Street. He wasn't worried about getting caught. The sheriff was at the diner having a cup of coffee, and all his deputies had the night off. Max just didn't want to face the fact that Iver was really gone. An empty store would only underscore that depressing fact.

When Max had heard that Iver was caught in the explosion on the island of Malta, he felt as though he had lost his grandfather all over again. And when Max found out that his own father was responsible for Iver's death, his entire world fell apart.

"Look, I don't mind going in by myself," Harley assured Max. "I just want to take a quick look around. It'll be five minutes, tops."

Max shook his head. "If one of us goes, we both go."

Harley reached up to unscrew the lightbulb hanging over the back door of Iver's shop. Then he tested the knob, and the door creaked open.

"That was easy," Harley said as Max pulled out a flashlight.

"It looks like somebody was already here," Max remarked, sounding concerned.

Books and papers were scattered everywhere. Filing cabinets were half open, and picture frames lay broken on the ground. The haunting smell of Iver's pipe tobacco still lingered in the room, but most of the knickknacks had been packed away. All that remained were some shredded boxes and overturned cabinets.

"Wait a minute. Did you hear that?" Harley whispered, pointing up at the ceiling.

There was a soft scraping sound followed by a muffled thud. Max instinctively twisted the ring on his finger, and the enchanted metal flowed over his hand to form the *Codex* Gauntlet. The blue flicker of Skyfire lit on his fingertips, and he moved past the BEWARE OF DRAGONS sign that still hung by the staircase.

The knotted door at the top of the steps was ajar, but they couldn't see anything. The hall beyond was draped in shadow. Harley nudged the door open with his foot, and the boys prepared for an attack that never came. As they stepped into the hallway, the sound of a rapidly ticking clock filtered from a room down the hall.

"It sounds like that brass beetle," Max whispered.

They traced the sound to a spare room in the back that had been ransacked like the shop below. Chairs were overturned and the contents of boxes were strewn everywhere.

Then Max saw it.

A mechanical creature no larger than a raccoon knelt on the table in the center of the room. It was methodically slashing its metal claws through one box after another, ignoring the boys entirely.

Max lifted his gauntlet and released a torrent of blue

flame. The Skyfire shot across the room, enveloping the machine in a nimbus of enchanted energy. The blast would have been enough to drop a Tanker Troll, but the machine wasn't even fazed. Instead, it simply turned to Max and its eye flashed. Then it leaped through the windowpane in an explosion of glass.

HARLEY'S SECRET

It wasn't long before the sheriff's sirens were screaming down Main Street. Avalon didn't have much in the way of crime, and those sirens were going to draw unwanted attention. Max and Harley were in no mood to stick around and answer questions. Besides, who was going to believe that a machine had broken into the Shoppe of Antiquities?

They raced down the stairs, out the back door, and down the alley to a comic-book shop called the Spider's Web. Max was hoping the owner had stayed late. He was sure that Monti would let them hide out until everything died down. Harley pounded on the door, but unfortunately nobody answered. So the boys hopped on their bikes and tore off down the alley just as an officer with a flashlight rounded the corner.

Max and Harley stuck to the back streets until they hit the long stretch of gravel road that led to the outskirts of town. Thankfully, the moonlight was blanketed by thick clouds; a few minutes later they were safely inside the barn loft behind Grandma Caliburn's house.

"What was that thing?" asked Max. He was still breathing heavily as he peered through a window to make sure that they hadn't been followed.

"I have no idea," Harley admitted. "I've read a lot of stuff about robotics, and we're supposed to be years away from anything that can move on its own like that. Someone must have been controlling it remotely. It's the only thing that makes sense."

"So what was it doing in Iver's shop?"

"The same thing we were," Harley replied. "Looking for something that it didn't find."

Max sighed as he sat back. "Do you think our lives will ever be normal again? I mean, if I'd never found the *Codex*..."

"You were going to find it eventually, Max."

"I don't know," Max said with a sigh. "Sometimes I feel like this is just a dream, and that I'll wake up and everything will be the way it used to be. I mean, Iver is dead because I gave that stupid spear to my dad. I might as well have killed him myself. After my grandpa died, Iver looked out for me like I was his grandson."

"I know," agreed Harley. "He did that for all of us."

"Saturday mornings used to be my favorite time of the week," Max lamented. "I couldn't wait to go to his shop. And it wasn't just about playing Round Table. I miss his stories—" Max paused as he reached back for memories. "Even when it seemed like the world was falling apart, as long as Iver was around, I felt like everything was going to be okay. I'm not so sure anymore."

"Well, I miss those caramel rolls and the fresh-squeezed orange juice he would give us," Harley said with a smile.

"And the smell of his pipe."

"Don't forget those plaid shirts and his suspenders."

"And his laugh," Max added. "I really miss his laugh."

Harley frowned. "Your dad killed Iver. Period."

"But—"

"Look, so you've messed up a few times...who hasn't? You were trying to do the right thing. That's more than a lot of people can say."

Max regarded his friend closely. Harley had a rough life, but no matter what happened, he never complained. Max wished he could be like that, too.

"What about you?" Max asked. "Do you ever think about your dad?"

Harley shrugged as he chewed a piece of straw. "He's never coming back, so what's the point?"

"Did you know him?"

"I haven't even seen a picture of him. I guess it used to bother me, but when your mom cries every time you mention someone, you learn to shut up."

Max plucked a strand of straw from the bale behind him and twisted it around his finger. "I don't know... maybe it would have been better if my dad had disappeared like yours did. But even after all he's done, I still kind of miss him."

"It's because you have a heart. Look, you can try to be as tough as you want, but the reason the Griffins would follow you into a nest of dragons is because we know you'd do anything for us. That's what makes a great leader."

Max heard his grandmother's voice from outside. "Logan just called," she announced. "He said to get some sleep. You have a training session tomorrow morning before school."

"What time?"

"Four A.M."

Max sighed. "If mechanical monsters don't kill us, it looks like Logan will."

SWAMP FIEND

Logan had been taking the Grey Griffins on monster-hunting expeditions for nearly a year now. Any complaining was met with extended training, so the Griffins learned to take their lumps. On this particular morning, they were knee-deep in the chilling waters of a marsh in the Old Woods. The moon was still out, and they couldn't see more than a few feet in front of them. Worse yet, Max felt his boots sinking into the silt. He tried not to think about what might be lurking beneath the surface.

Charles Butterman, a local farmer, had complained that something had been dragging his livestock into the marsh behind his barn. He thought it was just a black bear, but Logan had a hunch. THOR scans reported the presence of a Swamp Fiend, and it was up to the Griffins to capture it before the monster did any more damage.

"What's with all the textbooks?" complained Ernie as they trudged along. "I'm going to need a chiropractor after carrying them around."

"Nobody said it was going to be easy," Natalia reminded him.

Overhead, Sprig buzzed along in the form of a large dragonfly. She joined the Griffins on their monster-hunting expeditions from time to time, mostly out of curiosity. She could become distracted easily and disappear. Today, Max had made her promise to stay close.

"If you're my Bounder, I need to know I can count on you," he had told her, to which her reply had been: "Max doesn't need to hunt silly monsters. Max doesn't need his silly friends. We will be his only friend, if Max wants." Still, she had promised.

Natalia turned to Max as they sloshed along through the swamp. "Have you heard anything from Brooke about those cards?"

"Too much chatter," Logan said through the voice transmitter. The Griffins couldn't see where he was, but he'd be there in case they got in over their heads. *"You're nearing the target. Look lively."*

Max held his fist in the air, signaling everyone to stop. Then he turned to Sprig. "Okay, just like we planned.

You're the bait, so give the Swamp Fiend something tasty to go after."

"This is silly," the spriggan maintained. "If Max wants to capture the Swamp Fiend, we will turn into a dragon and eat it."

"You can't. We need the practice," Max answered.

"As you wish." The spriggan yawned. With a flash, she turned into a butter-brown cow. Her great belly dipped low into the water as Max directed the rest of the team to take up a position behind her left flank. They settled in and waited.

It didn't take long.

Just a few yards away the reeds rustled.

"Steady," Max said, patting Sprig on the back. He reached down to activate his *Codex* Gauntlet. Iver's mechanical intruder may have been immune to Skyfire, but Swamp Fiends were not.

"Get ready," he called.

Harley nodded and set his weapon against his shoulder. For his latest invention, he had replaced the barrel of two rifles with lengths of oversized piping. Swamp Fiends were especially vulnerable to salt, so he converted them to fire salt charges the size of soda cans. He gave one to Natalia and saved one for himself.

A moaning figure rose from the swamp, just a few feet away. Made from muck and rotted weeds, it looked like a corpse and smelled worse. With its hooked hand, it reached out toward the rather deliciously presented cow.

In a flash, Sprig shifted back into a dragonfly and buzzed away. At the same time, Harley and Natalia fired their weapons. Mud flew as the salt struck home, sending the Swamp Fiend backward. Max raised his gauntlet to fire, but before he could take aim, the creature melted back into the swamp.

"That was a lot easier than I expected," Ernie said. Then a muddy claw reached up from the water and took hold of his leg. With a yelp, Ernie was pulled under, leaving only a few bubbles behind.

"Go after him!" Logan shouted over the communicator. *"I'm on my way!"*

Max dove in after Ernie as Sprig took the form of an otter. She slipped under the surface to help her master. Max groped for his friend, but all he found were tangles of weeds.

He surfaced for air as Natalia screamed. Ernie was dangling from the Swamp Fiend's grasp like a puppet. Then it opened its jaws to swallow him whole.

"Help me!" Ernie begged. His arms flailed wildly.

"Don't move!" Harley shouted. Weapon in hand, he raced toward the terrible scene. Harley jumped out of the water, leapfrogging onto a rotten stump to bring the power of his salt cannon to point-blank range. As the crack of his launcher rang out, the fiend roared. Then the beast's head exploded in a spray of glop that showered the Griffins.

Ernie plummeted into the water. The Swamp Fiend

grasped at the place where its head used to be. Then Max watched tendrils of sludge start to expand around the fiend's shoulders, quickly piecing together a jaw, then an ear.

"You have to be kidding me," Harley shouted as he reloaded. "Its head can grow back?"

"Captivity orbs, Max!" Logan shouted as he splashed onto the scene.

Max lifted the gauntlet to release a crackling sphere of light from his palm. The ball of energy exploded across the creature's chest, expanding until it swallowed the monster whole. With a blue pulse, it contracted to its original size, taking the Swamp Fiend as it returned to Max's gauntlet. Then it disappeared.

"You cut that one a bit close," Logan said, "but it was nice work. We'll debrief later. Right now I need to get the lot of you back home so you can shower up before the *Zephyr* leaves the station."

"Do you think we can make a quick stop at Hasty Hamburgers?" Ernie asked. He sat on a stump and emptied his helmet of swamp water. "They have the best egg, cheese, and bacon croissant."

"Aye, you've earned it."

"Ouch!" Natalia stumbled in the water, catching her fall at the last moment. "What was that?" She reached into the muck and pulled up a piece of twisted metal that was coated with rotting weeds.

"Let the swamp have it," Logan advised.

"But what is it?"

"Something better left alone." Logan's voice was gruff as he started toward dry ground.

Natalia did as she was told, and the metal arm sank to the bottom of the marsh. As Max watched it disappear, he decided it was time to come clean.

"I know you're going to get mad, but I have something to tell you," Max said before launching into the story about finding the bunker.

"Have you told anyone else?" Logan asked after Max finished.

Max shook his head.

"Good. Keep it that way...at least for now."

"I just wish we would have grabbed those blue-prints," Natalia lamented. "That Brimstone Key looked interesting."

"What did you say?" Logan asked, turning toward her.

"The Brimstone Key? Why...have you heard of it before?"

Logan's jaw clenched. "It's classified, and so was that bunker. I don't want to hear another word about it, under-stood?" With that he stormed ahead of them, leaving the Griffins in confused silence.

GUILT BY ASSOCIATION

The Griffins raced into the Apprentice Wing and down the main corridor toward their lockers. Having worked the combinations on the mahogany doors, they stuffed their coats inside, grabbed their books, and headed up the three flights of stairs toward their Arithmetick classroom.

A stream of boys in grey uniforms jogged through the crowd of students at the same time. Xander Swift was in the front, and every time he called out a cadence, the rest of them echoed his words.

"What the heck is going on?" Ernie asked.

"Drills," Natalia replied. "Don't forget, this is a military academy."

"Out of my way!" one of them shouted before he slammed into Ernie.

As Ernie fell to the ground, Max saw that the assailant was Angus McCutcheon, the same kid the Toad brothers had warned him about. As the rest of the uniformed boys disappeared down the hall, Angus remained, glaring down at Ernie.

"What's your problem?" Harley called, catching Angus by the arm.

"I don't have a problem," Angus answered, pulling away from Harley's grasp. He wasn't tall, but he was thick as a bulldog. Angus also had a reputation for starting fights just for the fun of it. "Your little friend should pay attention to where he's walking."

"Actually, you were in *his* way," Max said, stepping in front of Angus. "I think you owe him an apology."

Ernie shook his head vehemently, declining any such need.

Angus turned to Max and snarled as a crowd began to gather. "Well, if it isn't the Black Wolf pup."

Max recoiled. "What are you talking about?"

"Like you don't know," Angus said as he stepped close enough for Max to smell his rank breath. "This is a Templar academy, not a werewolf training facility. Dog soldiers aren't allowed. So how did *you* get in?"

"Leave him alone!" Natalia warned. "Max didn't have anything to do with the Black Wolf Society."

"And he has the Medal of Arthur to prove it, right?" Angus sneered.

Max caught sight of Logan from the corner of his eye. Then he saw Brooke, who was pushing her way through the crowd.

"Why don't you turn around and walk away while you still can," Harley warned.

Angus snorted. "This isn't the minor leagues, Eisenstein. You don't scare anybody here. Or can you turn into a werewolf, too?"

The bell rang, and the crowd reluctantly dispersed.

"Don't worry, Sumner. We know how to handle dogs like you." With that, Angus shoved past the Griffins to his next class.

"Does somebody want to tell me what that was all about?" Ernie asked as he rubbed his shoulder.

"Angus McCutcheon's brother was killed by the Black Wolves," Brooke explained. Then she grabbed Max by the arm. "Let's go to class."

THE DIFFERENCE ENGINE

The Arithmetick classroom was not particularly large, with enough desks to seat twenty students. Gold filigree bordered the leather surface of each desk. The windows were tall but narrow, and it was insufferably warm inside.

"Did you guys see what happened out in the hall?" Ernie asked as he took a seat next to the Toad brothers.

"Everybody did," Todd replied, admiring a pencil that he had been sharpening into a stake. His theory was that you never could tell when you might run into a vampire.

"Look." Ross turned to Max and lowered his voice. "Everybody knows Angus is a jerk."

"I can't really blame him." Max sighed. "I'd be mad, too."

"That's ridiculous," Brooke countered. "When my dad hears about what happened, Angus is going to get suspended."

"Don't say anything," Max urged. "It's only going to make things worse."

Brooke hesitated before she sighed. "Fine, but it better not happen again." Then, switching topics, she smiled. "By the way, I found a set of books in my dad's office. They are called *The Van Wyck Guide*, and they catalog just about every Round Table card that was ever made."

"Did you find any of our cards?" Max asked.

"Not yet. The only time my dad leaves his office is when he's at school. I don't even think he sleeps anymore. I'm nervous he might start asking questions if he finds me snooping around."

"You see," Ernie said, a little too loud for Max's taste. "That's why we need to make Brooke an official member of the Grey Griffins. She can be our spy on the inside."

"On the inside of what?" Max asked, confused.

"You're so funny," Brooke said, winking at Ernie. "And whether or not I'm an official member of your secret organization, I'd spy for you any day."

Ernie blushed.

The final bell rang, and Max turned to the front of the room as their Arithmetick instructor came in. Dr. Archimedes Thistlebrow was an odd-looking man. Shorter than Natalia, he had a ring of wild white hair, woolly eyebrows that seemed to have a life of their own, and pointed ears. His rectangular spectacles perched at the end of his long nose as he looked out over his new students.

"If you would allow me, I would like to begin today's lesson by attempting an illusion for you," he announced. "I've been practicing it for quite some time. I hope you don't mind."

Without waiting for a response, he pulled out a single sheet of white paper. "As you can see, there is nothing terribly extraordinary about this paper. But if you have vision..." In short order he had created an origami dove with wings that flapped when he pulled the tail. The class clapped politely. "As in life, if you aren't careful, you can lose everything you've worked for in the blink of an eye." In a flash, the dove burst into flames. "But we never give up hope," he explained as he calmly clapped his hands together. Then, when he opened them back up, a living dove appeared. He walked over to release it out the window. "I've always liked happy endings."

The class cheered.

"Now, before we begin today's lesson, I have something I'd like to show you," Dr. Thistlebrow announced. He pulled a sheet away from a table in the corner of the room, revealing several cases stacked up like gold bricks.

"For those of you who are not familiar with this particular machine, it is called a Babbage Difference Engine Tablet. If you prefer, you can simply call it a DE Tablet."

Dr. Thistlebrow lifted one of the cases and placed it on his desk. It resembled a small suitcase, padded in rich leather and adorned with brass fittings and scrollwork. He flicked a button, and four brass lion feet swung out to support it. "This device will be your primary tool for completing homework and conducting research here at Iron Bridge. With it, you will be able to communicate with fellow students and instructors, as well as a host of other possibilities. Treat it well."

Dr. Thistlebrow motioned for the students to form a line. Max took one of the DE Tablets back to his desk and examined it. The screen was framed in brass, and the keyboard buttons were round with raised letters, like an old-fashioned typewriter. There were several toggle switches on the right-hand side of the screen, and a few dim lights flickered beneath small lenses.

Robert raised his hand sheepishly from the back of the room. "I think my Tablet is missing the power cord."

Some kids snickered, and Dr. Thistlebrow offered an enthusiastic smile. "We haven't used cords in over a century. Instead, we use Tesla Vaulting, a form of MERLIN Tech." He went on to describe the technology in mind-numbing detail. Harley seemed to be the only one paying attention.

At the end of class, Dr. Thistlebrow let them have a few minutes to figure out their DE Tablets. Ernie was just pulling up his syllabus when the classroom grew quiet. Dr. Thistlebrow was standing over him.

"Mr. Tweeny, is it?"

Ernie gulped and nodded slowly.

"Dr. Trimble would like to see you after class. Apparently you're in need of an examination."

"What?" Ernie exclaimed. "I already had my physical."

Dr. Thistlebrow only smiled politely. "Be a good boy and find your way down after class."

"I'm sure it's nothing," Natalia said, as Ernie's face turned pale.

"Yeah...nothing." Ernie swallowed the lump in his throat.

Doc Trimble

The medical office wasn't easy to find. It had taken Ernie nearly ten minutes to navigate the arching bridges, not to mention the maze of stairs and corridors. Ernie held the examination request with the tips of his fingers. He was certain that Doc Trimble was going to harvest him for spare parts.

A worn voice spoke before Ernie could knock on the door. "Please come in."

Ernie stepped into a laboratory that smelled like turpentine and peppermints. The ceiling was low, and sturdy shelves encompassed most of the wall space. They were loaded down with glass jars filled with strange powders and tiny creatures suspended in formaldehyde.

"How do you do. My name is Dr. Jonah Trimble," a man said, reaching to shake Ernie's hand.

Ernie hesitated. Dr. Trimble was seated in a wheel-chair. His skin was sallow, and it sagged from his skeleton, giving him the appearance of a zombie. But it was the robotic left arm that threw Ernie off.

"Um...I'm..."

"Ernest Bartholomew Tweeny?" Doc Trimble asked as he removed his stovepipe hat to reveal a thinly covered pate of grey that matched his woolly sideburns. Catching Ernie's eyes locked on his mechanical appendage, Doc snorted in amusement. "It's my lucky arm. Lost it in the Great War," he continued with a dark smile that curled at the corner of his mouth. "You should see the other guy."

Ernie shivered as the old man lifted his prosthetic limb and flexed the fingers. All Ernie could think about was the eerie pile of robotic remains that they had found in the underground bunker.

"Now I hear you've had a run-in or two with those boys in the Black Wolf Society; is that right?" Doc pulled out Ernie's chart and glanced briefly at the bottom. "Had a bad knock on your head, it appears."

"Yes," Ernie confirmed, scratching absently where his scar had been.

Doc Trimble ran his metal finger across the chart as he read. "But your friend saved you by injecting you with faerie blood? Hmm..." He set the chart aside and gave Ernie a contemplative once-over. "It's been hard for you, hasn't it?

Suddenly, everything's changed. You can outrun a train and hear whispers a mile away. You never get sick, and you never feel like you've had enough to eat. Your skin tingles, and you see flashes in your eyes at night. Sound about right?"

Ernie nodded. "Are you going to fix me?"

"Fix you?" Doc snorted again. "There's nothing wrong with you, son, except your perspective. You're a changeling now. You have different needs than you used to, and that's why you're here. We're going to start by addressing your accelerated metabolism and your consumption-to-weight ratio."

"You mean, why I eat all the time?"

"Couldn't have said it better myself. My goal is to help you stop worrying about where your next meal is coming from, so you can concentrate on your schoolwork. How would that sound?"

With that, Doc Trimble pulled back a curtain to reveal a strange contraption that looked a lot like an electric chair. It even had leather straps for the wrists, ankles, and head. Ernie almost wet his pants.

"Old Bessie here is a Model Sixteen Phrenologic Scope with a nutrient induction system. Why don't you go ahead and have yourself a seat."

Ernie sat down before he even realized that he had moved. His vintage helmet was removed, the straps were secured, and a lens was lowered over his right eye. Next came a breathing mask. It was connected to a clear tube and it smelled like the trunk of a car.

"How does that feel?" Doc Trimble asked as he started flipping a series of switches. Even if Ernie had been able to speak, his voice would have been drowned in the rumbling of the engine. A series of meters lit up, and Ernie watched out of the corner of his eye as the needles jumped back and forth.

"Now if I'm not mistaken, you're one of them Grey Griffins," Doc Trimble said as he picked up a tablet and started jotting down notes.

"Yes, sir."

"I bet you miss old Iverson something fierce," the doctor said. "He was a right fine man, he was."

"You knew Iver?"

"Of course I did. We served in the war together, along with that scoundrel William Caliburn. My, but he was a prankster."

Doc Trimble's eyes glazed over for a moment as he recalled a distant memory. Then he asked Ernie a few questions about his medical history. Ernie's vision grew hazy, and before he knew it, he was asleep.

When he woke up, the examination was over. The doctor had shut down the main switch and flipped off all the toggles. "Am I dead?" mumbled Ernie.

Doc Trimble laughed and handed Ernie an updated ID card. "Just take this with you to the cafeteria. It's been programmed with a prescription for something called Boom Food. You'll be eating in style in no time."

BOOM FOOD

The floors of the dining room were marble, and wood panels covered the walls. The tables were already filled with students chatting away over fine china, sipping from crystal, and wiping their mouths with linen napkins. Many of the students at Iron Bridge would become soldiers in a war against unspeakable evil, but others would become diplomats and ambassadors. Poor etiquette would not be tolerated.

"So Doc Trimble programmed a prescription into your ID card and that was it?" Natalia asked as they joined the lunch line.

Ernie swiped his card over a reader and placed it back in his pocket before he grabbed a tray and headed down the line. "I guess it's some special diet or something. He called it Boom Food."

"Boom Food? That doesn't sound very good," Max pointed out.

"Either that, or it gives you gas," laughed Harley. "Remind me not to sit behind Ernie in Natural Sciences this afternoon."

"Very funny," Ernie said. Then he stopped when he saw the machines that were serving lunch. Covered in brass and steel casing, they looked like robots. Unlike the schematics the Griffins found in the underground bunker, these machines were equipped with spatulas and ladles, not weapons. And they moved along efficiently on wheels and treads rather than legs.

"What's wrong?" asked Max as Ernie stood there staring.

"It's just that...well...I know this is going to sound stupid, but what if Doc Trimble is a clockwork machine?" Then his eyes shot wide. "Or what if *he*'s the Clockwork King?"

"Doc Trimble isn't a clockwork," Todd said from nearby. "He's just an old man with a metal arm."

Ernie was unconvinced. He turned his gaze to the clockworks behind the counter, wondering if they might be planning a robot uprising.

"They aren't going to hurt you, Tweeny," Ross insisted.

"Clockworks usually have only one function, and these make food. The only thing you'll have to worry about is getting too many vegetables."

Ernie relaxed, if just a bit. As he made his way down the line, the clockwork chefs served him a tower of pasta doused with rich tomato sauce and spicy sausage. Next came four magnificent ham-and-Swiss sandwiches on marbled rye, followed by a dozen tomato slices topped with mozzarella cheese, basil, olive oil, and balsamic vinegar. The machines completed the task in seconds, wielding knives and plates with precision.

"This is supersonic!" Ernie exclaimed.

Famished, Ernie started to eat one of his sandwiches as the Toad brothers and the rest of the Griffins waited for clockworks to serve their food. The line moved quickly, and soon they headed off to find a table with enough empty seats so they could sit together.

Most of the students were engaged in animated conversations about everything from dating rumors to their favorite music. Apparently a band named the Gilded Dolls had a big following in the Templar academies.

"What's going on over there?" Harley asked, pointing to the back of the room. A group of boys had moved some tables, and it looked like they were sparring as some of the teachers watched with interest.

"Those are MERLIN swords," Ross explained.

"In the dining hall? We would have been suspended for doing something like that at King's Elementary."

"You better get used to it," Todd said. "We're all expected to train if we have free time."

Harley smiled. "So where can I get one of those swords?"

Max recognized one of the kids from their Natural Sciences class. Dean Lorey stood out from the crowd. He was shorter than Natalia, thinner than Ernie, and he shaved his head with a razor, leaving a gleaming scalp. What he lacked in size, Dean made up for in speed and determination. In seconds, he had disarmed a much larger opponent, before turning to wave at Max.

Dean had dubbed Max the "Wolf Killer," which wasn't technically accurate. Max hadn't killed anybody. Still, Max appreciated the support. Thankfully, most of the students at Iron Bridge either respected the Grey Griffins or just left them alone. Angus, however, was another story.

"There's a spot over here," Natalia called out, pulling the boys away from the sword fight. She had been hoping to sit by Brooke, but there weren't enough seats for everybody. So Natalia led the Griffins to a table where a single student sat eating her lunch. Max immediately recognized her as Erica Harkness, Xander's girlfriend. He tried to steer Natalia away from the table, but it was too late.

"Hi," Natalia greeted the other girl. "Would you mind if we joined you?"

Erica looked up, her smile fading when she saw Max. "These seats are taken," she announced before promptly turning back to her magazine.

"There're some chairs right here," Ernie called, heading to the next table.

"Those are taken, too," Erica said without bothering to look up.

"What's your problem?" Natalia asked.

Erica raised her eyebrows. "I'm sorry. Perhaps I didn't make myself clear. You aren't wanted here."

"Why? What did we do?"

Erica's eyes never left Max. "We worked hard to get to the top, and you're not going to come in and ruin it for us."

"What are you talking about?" asked Max.

"I've heard about what you've been saying behind Xander's back."

Max stood there, dumbstruck. "I think this is just a misunderstanding."

Erica turned away, signaling the conversation was over. "Please leave."

"How dare you!" Natalia shouted. "You don't know anything about any of us."

"Forget it, Natalia," Max advised, grabbing her by the elbow.

Natalia yanked her arm free, but the force sent her juice glass flying. It shattered on impact, sending a spray of liquid all over the table's sour occupant.

"You little freak!" Erica seethed as stains from the juice spread across her dress. Just as she was about to rip Natalia's braids from her head, Erica caught sight of

Ms. Merical walking toward them. Logan was also watching from a doorway.

"Watch your back," Erica warned through a saccharine smile. She stormed out of the cafeteria.

"Looks like a table just opened up," Ernie announced as he took his seat and attacked his meal.

THE SIM CHAMBER

The Grey Griffins hadn't been able to choose any of their electives. In fact, none of the students at Iron Bridge had that privilege. Everything at the academy was based on aptitude, not choice. If a student scored high in math, he or she might be sent to Rift Geometry; or if someone was a gifted athlete, there were combat classes. The exam results determined the future for each of them.

While the rest of the Griffins were looking forward to their "elective" classes, Ernie had been shipped to Sendak Hall. Each afternoon he had to study alongside the other changelings. On his first day, he met Hale, a petite girl with antennae. Then there was Denton. He looked more like a lion than a twelve-year-old boy. Some of the other changelings had gone through various stages of metamorphosis, but most of them seemed normal enough — at least until Ernie got to know them.

There was a girl with a frog tongue, another who could walk through walls, and a boy who disappeared whenever he sneezed. If that wasn't enough, Sendak Hall had all the charm of an insane asylum. It was depressingly grey, the grass was rotten, and it seemed to sit under a perpetual cloud. The guards stationed at the doors were supposedly there to keep the uninvited out, but Ernie had a feeling they were more interested in keeping the changelings locked inside.

As Ernie went to open the front door, it burst open. A horde of changelings streamed out, nearly running him over. Apparently they had been awarded some rare time outside Sendak Hall.

"Watch out, Tweeny," a boy named Aidan Thorne warned. Nicknamed Smoke, he was the changeling who could teleport.

"You're late!" Denton called out as his lion tail accidentally hit Ernie in the back of the head.

"Where are we going?" Ernie asked.

"It's SIM time. Didn't you read the syllabus?"

The only things Ernie read without coercion were comic books. With a shrug, he followed Denton, hoping that Dean Nipkin wouldn't notice that he was late.

The SIM Chamber was a hyper-real holographic

training room located in the Master's Wing of the academy. That's where Romulus Wolfhelm, a retired Templar military commander, used scenario-based battles to mold his students into soldiers.

Over the summer, Baron Lundgren had used a similar device to put the Grey Griffins through a series of custom training sessions. Ernie knew how frightfully real things inside a SIM Chamber could feel, and he wasn't looking forward to it.

Coach Wolfhelm was standing on an observation deck, with Dean Nipkin at his side. The room was domed, with metal grating on the floor. The walls were clad in iron. The iron was poison to faeries, but it only dampened the powers of the changelings.

Ernie made his way to where Denton was standing. "Hey, Shannon, on the first day of school, I heard Nipkin talking about a runaway."

"I told you not to call me that. The name is Denton. Period," he said. "And the kid's name is Stephen. They never found him. Not even a trace."

"Did you know him?"

"Are you kidding? He was a cryo—a frost elemental changeling. And he sucked at it. A couple of kids had to go to the hospital to get thawed out because of him. How does a kid like that disappear without a trace?"

A whistle blew, nearly startling Ernie out of his shoes.

"We're going to start with something simple," Coach Wolfhelm explained. "Dodgeball."

"Piece of cake." Ernie sighed with a relieved smile. "Super speed and dodgeball go together like peanut butter and jelly."

Coach Wolfhelm smirked. "Don't get ahead of yourselves," he warned. "When the ball hits you, you'll be paralyzed until the end of the game. Trust me, it's going to hurt."

"What if we catch it first?" Ernie called out.

"The person who threw the ball will be paralyzed instead," Coach Wolfhelm explained. "The last one standing wins."

There was a nervous tension as they waited for the game to begin. Most of the changelings had never been in the SIM Chamber before, and they didn't know what to expect. In particular, Robert Hernandez looked like he was about to vomit.

"What's wrong?" Ernie asked.

"I'm a transmuter," Robert explained, staring at his hands. "I can turn into just about anything I touch, but if everything in here is a hologram, I don't think it's going to work. Besides, I'm not that good with my power anyway."

"How long have you been a changeling?"

Robert shrugged. "My whole life," he said. "My mom had a Bounder Faerie that could transmute. The doctor said it affected her pregnancy."

"If you've been a changeling that long, how come you don't look...you know—"

"Like me?" Denton interjected. "Look, it doesn't hurt my feelings. Besides, girls like my fur."

"Yeah, right," Ernie said, laughing loud enough to get Dean Nipkin's attention.

"My mom gives me some kind of experimental inhibitor," Robert explained. "I guess it works. What about you?"

"I've only been a changeling for a few months," Ernie replied. "I got my power from a blood transfusion, and now I'm a speedster." Ernie struck a heroic pose. "I'm thinking about starting my own superhero team. Maybe we could all team up."

"I don't know," Denton said. "It sounds kind of weird."

Robert looked interested, though. "But you're one of the Grey Griffins. Why would you want to start a new team with someone like me?"

Before Ernie could answer, a horn sounded and the atmosphere shimmered. Soon the SIM Chamber was twisted in a whirlpool of light. An instant later, the changelings were standing in an abandoned city of crumbling concrete and steel. Some just stood there in awe, but Denton leaped to grab one of the rubber balls that dropped from the sky.

In less time than it took to blink, Ernie sped off and scooped one up before taking cover inside a Dumpster. He watched from relative safety as a heavyset boy with thick fingers and narrow eyes grabbed one of the other balls. The boy was looking for his first victim when a puff of smoke exploded over his head. Then a rubber ball crashed into his face like a pile driver, paralyzing him on the spot.

"Smoke..." Ernie whispered.

By teleporting, Smoke could pop in and out before anyone else could react. Ernie's only chance was to sneak up on him, and even with his super speed, that wasn't going to be easy.

Smoke went on the attack. He zapped into view beneath a broken streetlight. Nearby, a girl with eyes that glowed a brilliant green spun around just as Smoke threw the ball at her. His aim was true, but the ball passed right through her. It bounced into the front window of an abandoned delicatessen, shattering the glass. As though it was a normal thing to do, she phased right through the wall to retrieve the ball. Then, like a ghost rising from the grave, she shot up from the street directly behind him.

"I got you!" she shouted, but Smoke disappeared through a portal before she could throw the ball.

That's when Coach Wolfhelm released more rubber balls. In a flurry, five more changelings were knocked out of the game. There were only a few left, and like Ernie, Robert was one of them. Ernie could see the timid boy crouched in the shadows of a doorway across the street. He tried to wave him over, but Robert didn't see him. Then Ernie spotted a girl hovering overhead. Her wings were made of magical energy that looked like stained glass, and her hair was bright pink. But just as Ernie was

116

about to sneak out of his hiding place to nail her with the ball, Smoke opened a portal and hit her.

"Have a nice nap, Laini!" Smoke laughed as he disappeared. Paralyzed, the winged changeling dropped like a rock. Luckily a giant mattress shimmered into view, softening her landing.

Figuring there was safety in numbers, Ernie made a dash to Robert's hiding place. "Don't worry," he said, as Robert looked nervously at the ball. "I'm not going to knock you out. Actually, why don't we team up? When we're the last two left, we can duel it out just like those old cowboy movies that my dad likes."

Robert nodded before turning back to look out the doorway. There was a girl with black hair standing out in the open. Her arms were folded as though she was agitated, but even though she was an easy target, nobody had knocked her out of the game yet.

"What's her deal?" Ernie asked.

"That's Raven Lugosi. Nobody messes with her... not even Smoke."

"Why?"

"Because she knows everyone's secrets," Robert explained.

"I don't get it," Ernie said. "Does she read minds?"

"Look out!" Robert shouted.

Ernie turned in time to see Yi Lu racing toward them. He was running from Smoke, who was taking aim at Yi's shoulders.

"Out of the way!" Yi cried. He was a fire elemental, and his body was shrouded in flames. He burst through the doorway and leaped over their heads, knocking Ernie and Robert to the ground. The fire singed Ernie's helmet, but Robert's back smoked as flames erupted across his jacket.

"Get away!" Robert shouted to the others.

"What's happening?" Ernie called. He wanted to help, but the air around Robert already felt like a furnace.

"I must have absorbed Yi's power, but I can't control it!" Robert shouted. "I can't hold myself together…"

"Emergency, evacuate!" came Wolfhelm's voice over the intercom. The holographic world disappeared, and the sprinkler system opened up a torrent of water.

"That's not going to help!" Yi shouted as he leaped on top of Robert. "I have to suffocate the fire."

Smoke rolled out from Robert's mouth as his veins lit with volcanic fire. Ernie watched in horror as the flames grew stronger. He wanted to help, but there was nothing he could do. Just as Ernie reached the exit, Robert exploded.

POPPING IN

The blast of heat that shot from Robert's body had rocked the SIM Chamber, scorching the walls and melting the glass in the observation deck. Luckily most of the changelings were able to get out in time.

"Everyone is saying that Yi saved your lives," Natalia mentioned as they rode home in the *Zephyr*. "He could have been killed."

"I was there, Natalia. I know," Ernie replied tersely. "Everybody thinks he's a hero, but Yi is the one who scorched Robert with his flame. It caused a chain reaction that Robert couldn't control. What was he supposed to do?"

"Don't worry, Doc Trimble will fix them up," Harley said. "They're in good hands."

"That's not the point," Ernie lamented. "People already think we're freaks, and now they're going to be scared of us, too. It's not fair."

With that, Ernie reached into his backpack and pulled out a sketchbook, signaling that he wasn't in the mood to talk about it anymore. At the same time, a spark of light flashed, and suddenly Sprig popped into Max's lap. She was wincing in pain. Her spiked fur was damp, and her paws were slick with mud. She looked exhausted.

"What happened to you?" Max asked.

"Iron..." she hissed. "The machines have returned, and they are hunting faeries. Collecting them and..." Her gaze roved to Ernie.

"What?" he asked. "Why are you looking at me like that?"

"The faeries are afraid, but changelings should be as well," Sprig replied. "You must get away.... Not safe!"

"What do you mean?" Ernie shouted, his skin alive with goose bumps. "Who is looking for me? You have to..."

There was a sudden commotion in the back of the subway car.

"I'm talking to you, freak!" someone shouted.

The Griffins turned around to see Angus McCutcheon standing in the aisle, glowering at Smoke. The changeling seemed unperturbed as he sat by himself in the back of

the subway car. His goggles were flipped up on his forehead, and he was staring straight ahead.

"Everybody knows this is my bench," Angus barked.

Smoke didn't even bother to blink as Angus's face
turned red. The bully reached out to grab the changeling
by the arm, but all he got was a fistful of air. An instant
later, Smoke reappeared, locking his arm around Angus's
neck.

"I wonder how tough you'd be if I teleported you out
the window right now? Or better yet, maybe I'll just take
your head with me instead."

Angus's shoulders slumped, but his eyes continued to
burn.

"That's what I thought," Smoke said. Then he pushed
Angus into the bench and disappeared.

"Does anyone else think that Smoke kid is a little
extreme?" Natalia ventured.

When the Griffins turned back around, Sprig was
nowhere to be seen.

MAX GOES ON A DATE

Logan dropped Max off at Grandma Caliburn's house an hour later. The bodyguard hadn't said much after hearing the news about Sprig, but he didn't look very happy. As soon as Max had jumped out of the car, he started hunting for the Bounder. She wasn't in his bedroom, the barn loft, or even the greenhouse where she liked to sleep now and again. He decided to distract himself with homework, but he couldn't stop looking out his bedroom window, hoping that the spriggan would show up.

She never did.

When Grandma Caliburn came home from the market, she decided to treat Max to a night on the town. So they got in the car and headed to the Prairie House Café down on Main Street. Max wanted to wait at home for Sprig, but he couldn't turn down his grandmother's invitation. It was a quiet night, and most of the tables were empty when they got there.

"I haven't been on a date in I don't know how long," Grace Caliburn said with a smile. "What looks good?"

"I hear they've got great apple cobbler."

"They better! It's my recipe." She laughed before turning back to the menu.

Down the street, a crew hammered away, boarding up the broken window above the Shoppe of Antiquities. Max had seen the police tape stretched across the back door in the alley, but the investigation had already been closed. The local paper had reported that the sheriff's office was out of leads. There weren't any eyewitnesses, and with so many customers over the years, dusting for prints had been useless.

"I don't understand why someone would break in to Iver's shop," Grandma Caliburn remarked. "I remember a day when we didn't even have to lock our front doors. What is this town coming to?"

Max cleared his throat uncomfortably. "Do you ever wonder if Iver is still alive?" he asked. "I mean, he packed up his whole store before he left. It was almost like he expected not to come back. And they never found his body."

Grandma paused a moment, her eyes sad. "Max, I know it's been hard, but you need to let this go."

Max looked down at his menu.

"You know," Grandma Caliburn continued after a few uncomfortable moments, "not a day goes by when I don't wish your grandfather was still here. He was such a teaser, and the stories he could tell? Oh my." She laughed to herself. "Yes, I miss him very much. I understand what you're going through."

The restaurant was starting to fill up when the waitress returned to take their orders. Max went with the meatloaf, and Grandma Caliburn selected the chicken pot pie with a side of green bean casserole.

"So tell me," Grandma Caliburn said. "How is everything going for you and your friends at Iron Bridge?"

"It's okay."

"Just okay?"

Max sighed. "It's just that there's a kid named Angus. The Black Wolves killed his brother, and he's blaming me for it." Max paused before taking another sip of milk.

Grandma Caliburn placed her hand on Max's arm. "Honey, you are *not* your father."

"But he's half of who I am," Max countered. "I doubt he woke up one morning and decided he was going to destroy the world. How do I know I won't turn out like him?"

"You have a lot to learn about your father. He wasn't always the way you see him now." She sipped her tea thoughtfully. "You're handsome and charming, like he is. And both of you are very giving. I couldn't tell you how much money your parents have donated to charities, or

124

how many children's hospitals your father has commissioned in third-world countries."

"He also divorced Mom and betrayed the Templar."

"Before his fall, your father was the best sort of man," she replied. "Yes, he has certainly committed some terrible acts, but I know there is good inside his heart. It might be hidden away, but it's in there somewhere."

"What if I make the same mistakes he made?"

"Nonsense. You might have your father's blood flowing through your veins, but there's more than a little bit of your grandfather in there as well. Every time I hear your laughter, I can see his face. Oh, Max, he would be *so* proud of you."

Max played with his straw, too uncomfortable with his feelings to reply. The adventures of William Caliburn were legendary, and living up to them wouldn't be easy.

"Children can be cruel," Grace continued. "Trust me, in time Iron Bridge will be everything you dreamed that it could be."

CIRCLE OF
CONFUSION

The Transformation Sciences classroom in Sendak Hall was unusually somber when Ernie entered. Laini, the girl with the pink hair and wings, was crying—and she wasn't the only one.

Confused, Ernie took his usual seat next to Robert. They sat alone in the back of the room like lepers. Since the accident in the SIM Chamber, the only person who would talk to Robert was Ernie, and that made him a social outcast, too. Denton wouldn't even talk to them, and he was friends with everybody.

"Did you hear the news?" Robert whispered. "They found what happened to Stephen."

"The kid who ran away?"

"He didn't run away," Robert corrected. "He was kidnapped...or at least, that's what the other kids are saying. The teachers won't tell us anything, but apparently THOR agents found a rift echo in his dorm room."

"A what?"

"You know, the signature that's left behind when a portal is opened? Somebody teleported into his room and grabbed him."

Ernie paused. "I thought portals didn't work here?"

"Except for Smoke, they aren't supposed to. That's what has everyone worried."

As the warning bell rang, Raven Lugosi ducked into the room. As usual, she was dressed like a vampire, with lug boots and a black trench coat. She didn't talk to anyone, and no one talked to her.

Ernie found himself staring at her hypnotic violet eyes, but when she caught him, he turned away with a blush.

"Are you crazy?" Robert whispered, pulling Ernie away. "Don't even look at her, okay? I told you what she could do."

"No, you told me she knows everyone's secrets. You never told me how."

Robert shook his head. "Look, you need to forget about her. Besides, I've been thinking about what we talked about the other day...you know, about forming a superhero team. Even if Denton doesn't want to join, I'm in."

"Seriously?" Ernie asked, beaming. "That's so

supersonic! Now all we need is an arch-villain…" Ernie pulled out a sketchbook that contained illustrations of superhero costumes that he had drawn.

"You're kidding, right?" Smoke asked as he teleported into his desk. "Do you have a thing for leotards or something?"

"This is a private conversation," Ernie announced, closing his sketchbook.

"Then don't talk about it in public, dork," Smoke replied, and pushed his goggles up on his forehead. "I bet you've got superhero underwear, too. Pathetic. You know, life isn't like a comic book. In the real world, people die."

"All I know is that we were given powers for a reason," Ernie said. "We can make a difference!"

"So what are you going to do when you catch up to some guy with a gun? Run around in circles until he gets dizzy? Your power is worthless."

"And yours is better?" Ernie glared.

Smoke disappeared in a burst of black vapor, only to reappear next to Ernie, who nearly fell out of his chair in surprise. "I can go anywhere I want, anytime I want. I could even teleport you a mile into the sky where all of the super speed in the universe wouldn't do you much good. Nobody can stop me. They can't even touch me, and that goes for the teachers, too."

Smoke teleported back to his desk. The door opened and a round woman with a cheerful smile entered.

"Please, everyone, come sit on the pillows at the front of the room," she invited warmly, motioning to a collection of overstuffed cushions that were arranged in a circle. She was the first to take a seat, right smack in the middle of the circle. The students soon took their seats in orbit around her. Without another word, she snapped her eyes shut. She took in a series of deep breaths, and a euphoric smile painted her face. Then, just as suddenly, her eyes shot open again.

"My name is Frances Burrows, though you can simply call me Fanny. I am going to be your Transformation Psychology coach. After the accident in the SIM Chamber, Dean Nipkin thought it would be a nice idea if we got to know one another."

There was a smattering of uncomfortable laughs.

"Today we're going to discuss some of the worries that a changeling can experience. It can be about anything: the day you first discovered you were different... what happened with Yi... or, if you like, we can just talk about the weather. We're going to explore our thoughts as a group."

"I don't need a shrink," Smoke grumbled.

A small-framed Finnish girl named Astrid was the first to speak. "Sometimes I can hear what people are thinking, and I can't shut it off."

"How does that make you feel?" the psychology coach coaxed.

Astrid looked around at her fellow students, who were

looking back at her with curiosity. "It's not a very useful talent. And sometimes, when I'm around lots of people, it can hurt. I just wish I could shut it off."

"You can hear what I'm thinking?" asked Ernie.

The girl nodded as Ernie's eyes shot wide. "That's why my parents sent me to Iron Bridge. I just want to be normal. At least for a while."

Fanny nodded before turning to Denton. "How about you? Is there anything that you would like to share, Shannon?"

"Well, I don't know if anyone has noticed," he began with a wry smile as his tail swished back and forth on the ground, "but I seem to get better looking every day. I just feel bad for all the girls around here. It can't be easy having a guy like me around."

Most everyone laughed. Except Raven.

Robert raised a shaky hand. "I can't control my power very well."

"That's the understatement of the year." Smoke laughed. "Hothead Hernandez nearly fries us. And that's all he has to say about it? How about 'I'm sorry'?"

Robert's lips began to shake. Whether it was in sadness or anger, Ernie couldn't tell. He just hoped Robert wouldn't do anything rash.

"That will be enough, Aidan," Fanny instructed softly. "You don't know what it's like to be Robert. None of you do. Transmutation is one of the most difficult changeling powers to control."

130

"There are other people like me?" Robert asked.

Fanny smiled. "I've worked with several, Robert. And I think you'll be just fine. You just need a little practice, which is exactly why you are here. We want to protect you."

"What about Stephen?" Becca Paulson, the changeling who could walk through walls, asked. "You guys didn't do a very good job protecting *him*. What's going to happen to us?"

Everyone grew quiet. Even Raven's eyes were locked on Fanny.

"What I can tell you is that there is nothing for you to worry about," the transformation psychology coach said after a deep breath. "We've found little evidence to form any conclusions. If anything, it is still very likely Stephen ran away. We can only hope that he will miss his friends and come back soon."

"What friends?" Smoke snorted. "That kid was a freak."

"Have you looked in the mirror much?" Raven said in a dark voice. Her eyes cut right through Smoke, and he shut his mouth. Then Raven looked around at the others. "We're all freaks."

With that, she stood up and left the room.

There was a long stretch of quiet before anyone dared to talk.

The final changeling to participate was Tejan Chandra, who came from the ruling class in Bengal. He was intensely brilliant, with a hawkish nose and a playful smile, and his English was absolutely flawless. Every vowel. Every syllable. It was so perfect that Ernie had the sense Tejan hadn't so much learned the language, as he had downloaded an English translation program into his head.

"...and I daresay it was a bit of a tricky situation for my family," Tejan concluded. "Me, being a changeling with the ability to cause others to forget. My parents would constantly misplace me, or worse, forget that I was their son. That changed once I enrolled at Carthage Academy, of course. They trained me to control my abilities. In fact, I can even reverse the memory loss in others. It really is a gift, just as Ernest Tweeny believes so passionately. We were given this power to help others. I, for one, am looking forward to a wonderful future."

"A future where the teachers keep us incarcerated like convicts?" Smoke mocked. "If you think there's a happy ending for any of us, you're deluding yourself. Have you ever seen an adult changeling?"

No one answered.

"It's because we all die young. That's what Sendak Hall is...a place where kids like us go to die."

PART TWO

THE
CLOCKWORK
CONNECTION

CAUGHT IN THE SPIDER'S WEB

The Spider's Web was the only comic-book store in Avalon, Minnesota. After the Shoppe of Antiquities closed, it also became the local place where the Grey Griffins could buy Round Table cards. With Iron Bridge finally opening its doors, there was a whole new crop of customers waiting to buy Round Table expansion packs and custom knucklebones. The owner, Montifer McGuiness, had never been busier.

Like Olaf Iverson, Monti was more than a simple shop proprietor. He was also part of the secret Templar society. Though Max and the Grey Griffins knew Monti's role had something to do with technology, they weren't exactly clear on his specific function.

Many of the Templar who lived among the civilian population had covers to hid their true identities. Since Monti had been a fan of comic books as long as he could remember, he decided to open his own shop. His personal favorites were the classics — Golden and Silver Age superhero comics. Behind his cash register hung an original Fantastic Four page drawn by Jack Kirby.

"Has Sprig turned up yet?" Harley asked as the boys waited for Natalia on the sidewalk outside the comic shop.

Max shook his head. "No, and after everything that Ernie told us about Stephen, I'm starting to worry that someone out there is collecting faeries, too. What if she got caught?"

"I'm sure she's fine," Harley offered. "Besides, I'd rather face another werewolf than fight a shapeshifter like Sprig. She can take care of herself."

"I hope you're right."

"Hey, did you see this?" Ernie asked. He lifted his goggles to read a flier that had been posted in the front window. "Monti is going to host Round Table tournaments every Friday night. There's going to be prizes for the winners and everything."

"When do they start?" Harley asked, joining Ernie at the window.

"Next week," Natalia said, as she walked up to join

the boys. "Don't you check your mail? Monti sent us the flier a few days ago."

"There's going to be a blind tournament, where we have to play with cards from unopened packs," Max added. "The winner gets a whole case of the Darkling Scourge expansion pack that comes out next month. And look at this, Ernie, there's going to be a tournament where you can only use gargoyles."

"You can count me out!" Ernie stated. "I don't care what you say about gargoyles protecting people. Once you've nearly been eaten by one, you'll change your mind, too."

The door to the Spider's Web opened, and the Toad brothers bounded out carrying bulging bags of new comics.

"Don't tell me you two collect comic books, too," Natalia complained, rolling her eyes.

"Of course we do," Todd said.

"What do you have in the bag?" Ernie asked, already peeking inside Todd's.

"Just part of a little project that we're working on," Ross replied proudly. "Our goal is to own every appearance of Benjamin J. Grimm that's ever been printed. I created an application for my DE Tablet that tracks all the details. I'll get you a copy if you want to use it for your collection."

"Who in the world is Benjamin Grimm?" asked Natalia.

Ross and Todd frowned in unison. "Is she kidding?"

"Unfortunately not," Ernie said, clearly embarrassed by Natalia's ignorance.

"They call him The Thing," Ross explained, as though Natalia had come to Earth from another planet. "You know, the big guy that looks like he's made out of orange rocks."

"He sounds ridiculous," Natalia groused.

"So are unicorns, but you don't hear us making fun of your hobbies," Ernie retorted.

"Anyway, you're looking at the owners of seventeen percent of that legendary collection, my friends," Todd said proudly.

"Seriously?" asked Ernie. "That's supersonic!"

Todd turned to Natalia and smiled like a fox in a hen-house. "Any more fights with Erica Harkness?"

"It wasn't a fight," Natalia objected.

"What made you pick her, anyway?" Ross asked. "Was it strategic or something? You know, knock off the most popular girl so you can take her spot? That was pretty risky, but you sure have the whole school talking."

"Yeah," agreed Todd. "You aren't the only one who wants to knock Erica off her high horse, but she has some powerful allies, too."

"Look, we just wanted a place to sit down and she started treating us like we were pond scum. What was I supposed to do? Let her walk all over us just because..."

The Toad brothers didn't bother to listen to the rest of her explanation. Instead, they turned around and rushed into a limousine that looked more like a hearse than anything else.

"Can you believe that?" she asked, turning back to the other Griffins. "The entire school thinks that I started a fight?"

"Well, you *were* yelling at each other," Ernie pointed out.

"We were *debating*," Natalia clarified.

"Whatever," Harley said, as he walked through the front door.

Inside, the Spider's Web overflowed with stacks of comic books, walls of action figures, and wrinkled T-shirts on display.

"Look who's here," Monti greeted the Griffins as he polished a glass counter that held boxes of Round Table cards and a knucklebone display just like Iver used to have. "I was starting to think you had forgotten about me."

Montifer McGuiness's spiked hair stood on end as he gazed through a pair of glasses that looked just like the horn-rimmed pair that Ernie used to wear before he was a changeling. The only difference was that Monti's glasses had a strange armature with a crystal lens that was attached to the frame, allowing him to see in different spectrums.

"I kind of forgot my wallet," Ernie said. "Can I pick up the comics from my box later this week?"

"No worries." Monti handed him the comic books anyway. "Just pay me for them next week."

"Thanks!"

"By the way, what's this I hear about the Harvest Festival? Are they really going to host a party on campus for the students?"

"Don't remind me," Ernie complained.

There was no record of when the Harvest Festival officially began. The local museum had a picture of the mayor leading the parade in 1905, but it was much older than that. Avalon started as a farming community, and each year the entire town would gather to celebrate the bounty of the harvest. It began as a small picnic, but it wasn't long before party organizers got involved, and the celebration became a spectacle of parades, music, dancing, funnel cakes, and caramel apples.

So when Baron Lundgren announced that Iron Bridge was going to host a mandatory celebration the same night as the festival, it came as no surprise that the Griffins were upset. It was the most spectacular night of the year, and they feared that they were going to be stuck at school drinking stale punch and eating dry cupcakes with those sprinkles that tasted more like paste than anything else.

"You know why Cain is doing it, don't you?" Monti asked.

"To keep us safe, blah, blah, blah," Ernie said, throwing his hands in the air. "I think Dean Nipkin is the one behind it. She loves to torture us."

140

"They have a point," Monti reminded them. "Don't forget, Stephen is still missing. The THOR agents would have a difficult time tracking all of you at a block party. Keeping you isolated makes sense."

"I guess," Ernie lamented. "I'll just have to bring my sketchbook so I have something to do."

"That reminds me," Monti said. "When am I going to get the first issue of *The Amazing Adventures of Agent Thunderbolt*?" Monti was referring to the comic book that Ernie was writing, drawing, inking, coloring, and lettering on his own.

Ernie sighed. "I was hoping to have it done for the Christmas rush, but I don't know if I'm going to make it. I have the first issue written, but I haven't started drawing it yet. Plus I need to find a way to add a Transmuter, but homework keeps getting in the way."

Monti was a graduate of Stirling Academy, so he understood what Ernie was talking about. "Don't worry, it's only going to get worse."

"Great," Ernie moaned before disappearing to the back of the store. Harley and Natalia wandered off as well, leaving Max alone with Monti.

"You used to play Round Table, right?" Max asked.

"I was on the varsity team at Stirling, just like Iver and your grandfather. I wasn't too bad, if I do say so myself. Why? Are you thinking about trying out for the team at Iron Bridge?"

"Actually," Max began as he pulled out the mysterious

deck of cards they'd found in the underground bunker, "I wanted to get your opinion about these."

"Let me take a look." Monti adjusted the armature on his glasses and thumbed through the stack several times.

"Where did you say you found these?"

"We're not supposed to talk about it," Max admitted after a long pause.

"I see," Monti said with a smile. He looked back at the clock. "I know it's getting late, but if you have some time, I might have something that could help. We have to hurry, though. The *Zephyr* leaves for New Victoria in a few minutes, and it won't wait."

New Victoria

"New Victoria?"

"That's where my workshop is," Monti explained. "Just give me a minute to clean up." With that, he tapped a sequence of numbers onto the screen of a small hand-held device. A blue beam shot out of the ceiling and spread across the room. There was a puff of mist that smelled like lilacs, and then it was gone.

"It's a dust atomizer and furniture polisher," Monti explained.

"Where did you get it?" Harley asked with admiration as he rejoined the group.

"I built it." Monti tapped another code, and armored shades dropped over the doors and windows. The lights dimmed, leaving the store bathed in the red glow of an exit sign.

"Pretty heavy protection for a comic-book shop." Harley nodded appreciatively.

"After what happened at the Shoppe of Antiquities, you can't be too careful."

Twenty minutes later, the *Zephyr* dropped them off at the Farringdon Street platform in the heart of New Victoria. Monti led the Griffins through the empty underground and up the tiled steps to a busy street corner. Draft horses pulled massive carts laden with wares as elegant motor carriages and MERLIN Tech hovercycles zipped past strange steam-powered tricycles. Men and women strode down the wide sidewalks in top hats and bustled gowns. Others wore faded jeans and derbies. There were pixies that carried on conversations on windowsills, hobgoblin fishmongers, and just about every assortment of strangeness that Max could have imagined.

As they moved through a throng of charm peddlers, Monti pointed out a few landmark sites. The Griffins were too entranced by the city to pay much attention. Most of the people they passed seemed entirely uninterested in the Griffins, but Max still had the feeling that they were being watched.

"Welcome to the warehouse district," Monti said as he turned down Walpole Road. The street looked like a nest of warehouses and factories. Men with thick arms sat on steel girders high in the air, eating their sandwiches as others unloaded copper cable from the back of a wagon.

"New Victoria isn't so bad," Ernie said as he watched an airship lift off with a load of goods.

"You haven't been here after dark," Monti retorted, stopping in front of a green door with a polished brass knob in the center. He pulled out a device that looked like a pocket watch and wound the stem. Suddenly a series of eight brass legs extruded from the casing until it sat in his hand like a mechanical spider. Natalia's eyes shot wide as she thought about the scarab they had found in the tree house. She was about to say as much, when she caught Max shaking his head at her.

Like the beetle, Monti's clockwork spider was elegantly designed. There was a series of floral designs that came together in the form of a magnificent ship that was etched on the back. The design was flawless, right down to the smallest coil and articulated joint.

"I made this, too," Monti said. "If somebody other than me tries to use it, it's programmed to inject a serum that will paralyze them until the authorities come."

The strange mechanism crawled across his palm

before leaping onto the wall. It skittered across the bricks until it landed on a brass plate with an indentation that was just about the size of its body. The spider lowered itself into the groove and spun in a combination of directions that was followed by a click. Then it hopped back into Monti's hand and returned to its original form. "Wait until you see what I have inside."

THE VAN WYCK GUIDE

Monti's workshop was bigger than a warehouse. The monstrous structure was a symphony of steel and glass that stood over a floor of polished stone. There were hoists, cranes, metal tables, hissing machines, and an array of amazing contraptions in various stages of construction.

As the Griffins followed Monti across the floor, they had to duck away from flying sparks that shot out from mechanized welding machines.

"Is the whole place automated?" Harley asked.

"For the most part," Monti responded, as they passed a beat-up automaton that was testing a rocket pack. "This is kind of like a jet pack, but it's run by MERLIN Tech.

The clockwork running the tests is one of my oldest models. They don't make them like that anymore."

"I can see why," Ernie commented. "That thing is a hunk of junk."

"I don't know," Monti said. "The pack he's wearing has exploded three times this month, and he withstood each hit. That's pretty impressive."

Everywhere the Griffins looked, they could see other automatons working tirelessly under the flat glass roof.

"You make weapons here, too?" Ernie called as they neared a movable wall filled with dangerous-looking contraptions.

"Someone has to keep Logan and his THOR agents on the cutting edge if they're going to take the fight to all the bogeymen that go bump in the night," Monti noted proudly. He patted the stock of one of his rifles. "This is Logan's MVX. It's a pulse rifle, and he requested some upgrades."

Monti motioned toward a palm-sized pistol with a filigreed barrel and an ivory handle. "This model is the Peapod 7000. It's a concealable six-shot plasma pistol with a fairly big bang considering the size of the weapon."

Monti went on, describing the rest of the weaponry with obvious pride.

"We're also developing specialized armor and advanced field science over there," he said, pointing to the far end of the workshop. "That's where you'll find the Magma Manacles, jump boots, and a few other toys."

"What about this?" Harley asked, picking up a small device that looked like a remote control for a television.

"It's a hologram projector," Monti said. "I'm still beta testing, but we've had good results. Here, watch this." He took the control and punched in a series of numbers. Suddenly a Tundra Troll appeared next to them. It was nearly twelve feet tall and covered in thick white fur. Horns jutted out from the sides of its head and tiny black eyes scanned the room as it growled.

Ernie ducked behind a table as Monti walked right up to the monster. He was laughing as his hand passed through the troll. "See," he said, "it's just a three-dimensional projection. I can only make it last for a few seconds, but we're working on it. Not bad, huh?"

"This place is amazing," Harley said, relaxing. "I'd give just about anything to work here."

Monti shut the projector down. "I've been thinking about bringing you on as an apprentice this summer. Maybe we can work something out. I've got an airship I'm working on, and I could use the help."

"What's with the killer robot?" Ernie asked, as he gawked at a towering clockwork that looked an awful lot like the war machines from the schematics the Griffins had found in the bunker.

"That, my friend, is a Grimbot," replied Monti. "In fact, it's one of the few complete war machines that still exist."

The tarnished clockwork was propped up like a museum piece in a glass case. Its general shape was humanoid, with armored shoulders, a Gatling gun instead of a forearm, and legs that were outfitted with propulsion units. Its face was narrow, and its eyes were nothing more than slits in the metal casing.

"Did it belong to the Clockwork King?" Ernie asked.

As soon as the words left Ernie's mouth, Max wanted to throttle him. Logan had told them to be quiet about that stuff, and here Ernie was blabbing again.

"Now there's a nickname I haven't heard for a while," Monti replied. "From what I hear, Von Strife didn't care for it very much. He felt it was pejorative."

"It means derogatory," Natalia said, as she caught the confused look on Ernie's face.

"Wait a minute," Max said. "That's the name on the statue with the missing head over at Iron Bridge."

Monti laughed. "They still haven't fixed that? Well, I guess I shouldn't be surprised. He was a demanding teacher, which meant he wasn't very popular with the students."

"What did he teach?"

"Advanced MERLIN Tech," Monti replied. "But after a few years he took a position leading a controversial research and development team for the Sciences Council. They designed advanced hybrid systems that combined traditional clockwork mechanics with molecular engineering and MERLIN Tech."

"That sounds incredible," Harley remarked.

"It was," agreed Monti. "The Templar Grand Council

asked Von Strife to use his findings to create advanced weapons systems like this Grimbot. The entire world was at war. Millions of people were dying, and the Templar wanted to send a message that decimation on that scale would not be tolerated.

"Von Strife understood that his machines would need to react to complex battle scenarios," Monti continued. "So he perfected something called Systemwide Turing Intelligence."

"You're telling me that Grimbots could think on their own," Harley said with stunned admiration.

"Exactly," Monti replied. "The artificial intelligence he developed was so close to human consciousness that many people believed that the machines were capable of actual emotions. Some even conjectured that the clockworks were able to feel pain. An ethics committee was formed, and once the politicians got involved, the program ground to a halt. Then they shut it down."

"What's this?" Harley asked. He had found a manual on Monti's desk that was faded and cracked. Inside was a series of schematics for all kinds of clockworks, from insects to war machines.

"Please be careful with that," Monti pleaded. "It's one of the last known collections of Von Strife's work. I shouldn't have left it sitting around."

"This is incredible," Harley said, as he thumbed through the pages. "It's basically a how-to guide for making your own clockworks. Can I borrow it for a couple days?"

Monti looked stunned. "I'm afraid that would be impossible," he said. "If something happened, I would never be able to replace it."

"Do you think that the school has a copy?"

Monti's face turned white. "I doubt it. Unfortunately, owning a copy falls into a bit of a grey area."

"You mean it's illegal?" Harley pressed.

"Yes," Monti agreed reluctantly as he moved to retrieve the manual. "It's not exactly a secret that I have a copy. I'm just supposed to keep it discreet. You have to promise me that you won't tell anybody."

Harley smiled coolly. "You owe us one."

Monti paused. "If I make you a copy and you get caught, you didn't get it from me."

"Deal!"

"That reminds me," Max said. "Harley and I were at the arcade the night that Iver's shop was broken into. We saw something."

Monti stopped shuffling the papers on his desk. "I don't understand."

"We think it was a clockwork," Harley said. "We could hear the thing ticking."

Monti removed his glasses and rubbed the bridge of his nose with his thumb and forefinger. "Are you sure?"

Max nodded. "Its eyes kind of looked like camera lenses, and I think it took a picture of us before it ran off."

Monti was listening so intently that he put his elbow in a full cup of coffee. He seemed flustered as he mumbled something unintelligible and pulled out his pocket watch. "If we're going to get you back to the shop before your parents start looking for you, we better get to work. Can I see those cards again?"

Max handed them over, and Monti strapped on a pair of strange multi-lens glasses. Then he pulled a book from a nearby shelf titled *The Van Wyck Guide: A Complete Guide to Round Table Cards, 1860–1920*. It was from the same set of books that Brooke had found in Baron Lundgren's study.

Max smiled, thinking that he might finally get some answers.

"We might not find these cards in *The Van Wyck Guide*," Monti said as he thumbed through pages filled with images of Round Table cards. "Van Wyck didn't track custom decks."

"How can you be sure the deck is custom?" asked Natalia.

"For starters, each of these cards is hand painted," Monti explained. "That means one of two things — either they are original works that were used as a template for mass production, or some wealthy collector commissioned his or her own deck. Either way, they won't be in here, but I'm fairly certain that I've seen this artist's work before."

He turned back to the book. "Ah yes, this is it," Monti said, pointing to a collection of cards titled *The Jewel Dragons*.

"Supersonic!" Ernie proclaimed, practically drooling over the illustrations. "I've never seen an entire set of dragon cards before. If I had that deck, I'd be unstoppable!"

"Sure you would," Harley said. The sarcasm wasn't lost on Ernie.

"It looks like this particular set was released in October of 1915," Monti explained. "The artist was Oswald Chinnery. Look there," he said, pointing to a small squiggle that was barely perceptible. "You can see his mark on the cards from your deck. It's the same mark in the book, so it looks like we have a match."

"Now what?" Max asked. In the back of his mind, Max wondered whether there was a set of the *Van Wyck Guide* at the Shoppe of Antiquities. Thinking the books would come in handy, he made a mental note to check the next time he went there...if there was a next time.

"Give me a couple of days to look into it," Monti replied, taking out a small camera before snapping several pictures of the deck. "In the meantime, it's getting dark. Logan will kill me if I don't have you back soon."

TRANSFORMATION

The night of the academy's Harvest Festival dance finally came. Natalia's mother dropped her off at the Lundgren estate so the girls could get ready. Embarrassed by the minivan, Natalia waited until her mother drove away before she rang the doorbell.

Brooke answered, and the two of them rushed to her bedroom. "I think I have an outfit that you're going to love," she called to Natalia from a closet that was nearly as big as Natalia's entire bedroom. A moment later she emerged holding a black collared dress with plumed sleeves in one hand, and a pair of boots that tied all the way up the knees in the other. "What do you think?"

Natalia bit her lip apprehensively. All students were expected to attend the dance, and she was completely at a loss on what to wear.

"Black is all the rage right now," Brooke explained as she watched Natalia start to hedge. "I have the most incredible corset and a parasol that will go with this. Add a brooch, some lace gloves, and then a little eyeliner and lipstick, and I'm telling you, the boys won't know what hit them when you walk in."

"I don't know," Natalia said, looking at her pale skin in the mirror. "I'm afraid that I'm going to look like a vampire if I wear all that black. Maybe I should try something a little more conservative."

"You worry too much about what others think," Brooke told her. Then she paused to study Natalia's face and hair.

The last time Natalia let her guard down with another girl, she had been hurt. Athena had turned out to be a double agent, spying on the Templar for Vlad Dracula's Order of the Dragon. Natalia had looked up to Athena like an older sister, and when Athena had betrayed all of them, the wound had cut deep. Since then, trust hadn't come easy. It wasn't that Natalia didn't want to trust Brooke, too...she just didn't want to get burned again.

Brooke didn't have any reservations about Natalia's friendship. She promptly directed Natalia to sit in front of the mirrored vanity where she set to work unraveling Natalia's braids. Then Brooke pulled Natalia's long

156

tresses into a regal updo, allowing two spiraling locks to cascade against her cheeks.

"Do you see what I see?"

Natalia stared at herself in the mirror just long enough to start feeling self-conscious. "It's not my style."

"But it *could* be," Brooke returned quickly. "Our secret is that girls can be a hundred different people if we want. But if it's going to make you uncomfortable, I have something else. Just a second." Brooke disappeared back into her closet, quickly returning with a flowing silver dress made out of taffeta and a green crushed-velvet jacket that went over the top.

Natalia took the ensemble from Brooke and held it up to the light. The jacket felt scrumptious to the touch, and the hand stitching on the dress was remarkable. "What if I get a stain on it?"

Brooke pushed Natalia toward the bathroom. "Why don't you just go and change. We'll let the dry cleaner worry about the stains. Now hurry up or we're going to be late."

A few moments later, Natalia was smiling as she admired herself in the mirror. "Max told me that your dad found out about the Round Table cards from the bunker," she said through the bathroom door.

"Logan told him," Brooke said. "I asked if he knew where they came from, but he wouldn't tell me anything. Anyway, he left on business the next day, and I haven't heard from him since."

"Do you think he left because of the cards?"

"He's always going somewhere."

The bathroom door swung open, and Natalia nearly tripped over the dress.

"You look amazing," Brooke said "Now come try these boots on."

She handed Natalia a pair of mid-calf black boots with pointed toes and a heel. "These will give you a little boost. You won't be as tall as Harley, but you'll definitely get his attention."

"What? I don't care what Harley thinks…"

"I'm just kidding," Brooke replied. "Now we need this," she said, holding up a necklace that she tied around Natalia's neck. She followed up with a touch of lip gloss and some eyeliner for good measure. Then came the goggles.

"There." Brooke admired her work. "What do you think?"

"I don't even recognize myself," Natalia admitted. "And I love your outfit, too."

Beneath a brown riding jacket, Brooke wore a white linen shirt with the cuffs hanging out from under the jacket sleeves. Her brown skirt was loosely pleated, and it met at the top of her tall leather boots. She was also wearing a pair of aviator goggles on top of her forehead.

"It's kind of fun, isn't it?" Brooke giggled.

"Maybe," Natalia admitted, trying not to sound too excited. The smile gave her away, though.

THE MENAGERIE

"Let's just make an appearance and then sneak out of here," Ernie whispered as he crossed the Green Corridor with Max and Harley. "I bet we could get back to town in time to watch the jousts."

Ernie had begged his parents to let him stay home so he could go to the Harvest Festival parade, but they wouldn't lie to cover for him.

"I don't like it any more than you do," Max replied, "but they shut down the *Zephyr*. We're stuck here, so we might as well make the best of it."

As the boys walked down the tree-lined path, lanterns swung lazily in the cool autumn breeze as the smell of damp leaves filled the air. The boys passed through a series of arches that led to their destination—the Menagerie.

"By the way, what the heck is a Menagerie, anyway?" Ernie asked, as the sounds of music and laughter started to get louder.

Max shrugged. "It's kind of like a zoo."

"This doesn't look like a zoo to me," Ernie replied as they passed through the expansive doors of a glass palace.

Max looked around, drinking in the splendor of the amazing room. The upper balconies were filled with exotic birds.

"Did you see that?" Harley called as he pointed at a green bird with orange feathers and a long, fan-shaped tail. "I think that's an archaeopteryx, but that species has been extinct for millions of years."

The archaeopteryx was only the beginning. Strange beasts roamed freely among the students. There was a pair of okapis, which looked like a cross between giraffes and zebras. Exotic monkeys with long coats the color of butterscotch swung from the branches, and Max thought he spotted an ocelot lounging in the shadows.

There were faerie creatures, too...Bluebell Bonnets, Peapod Pixies, River Sylphs, and a gaggle of gold-laying geese. Ernie even spotted a Nipper Drake, which looked like a tiny dragon, but instead of eating damsels, it preferred frogs and mice.

Then a scream rang out nearby. Max turned in time to

160

watch a girl grasping her hat as a magnificent parrot with a spiked tail attacked the headpiece. Someone shouted, and the bird took off, but not without the prized hat.

"Oh my gosh, do you guys smell that?" Ernie asked. He closed his eyes and took a deep breath. "Caramel rolls…apple crisp…and rhubarb pie! Maybe this party isn't going to be lame after all."

Ernie bolted to the buffet, leaving Max and Harley standing there. He heaped food onto his tray, skipping the plates altogether, before he wandered off to find Ross and Todd.

"Isn't that your changeling buddy?" Todd asked between mouthfuls as Robert walked in by himself.

"Yeah," Ernie said. He stood and waved.

Robert slowly wound through the crowd to join them. His shoulders were slumped, and his eyes were on the ground. He looked like a sad puppy that had just gotten dropped off at the pound.

"I thought your mom was going to let you stay home tonight," Ernie said.

"So did I," Robert replied as he pulled off his goggles and threw them on the table. "All I want to do is go home and play video games. This is lame."

"I know what you mean," agreed Ernie. "Besides, someone told me that Angus wanted to stuff my head in the toilet. So if you see him, let me know."

"He couldn't catch you if he wanted to," Robert pointed out.

Ernie cracked a smile. "That's true."

"You should get some food," Ross suggested between mouthfuls. "It's amazing."

"Thanks, but I'm not very hungry," Robert replied. Then he picked up a saltshaker, and his hand took on the properties of the crystal. Light reflected off the surface of his skin as the Toad brothers watched in awe.

"How did you do that?" Todd asked.

Robert shrugged. "I don't know." He put the saltshaker down, and his skin returned to its warm brown color.

"You know, we've been thinking," Ross said. "Maybe we should join your superhero team, too."

"But you guys don't have any powers," Ernie pointed out.

"Neither does Batman," Todd argued.

Ernie thought about it for a minute and then shrugged. "I guess you're right," he admitted. "What do you think, Robert?"

"It's fine with me."

As the Menagerie buzzed with excitement around them, the boys entered into a deep discussion about secret headquarters, roles and responsibilities, and everything else you'd need to know if you were starting a superhero team.

Meanwhile, Max and Harley decided to get some food.

"Hey, Wolf Killer," Dean greeted as he walked by.

"What happened to your eye?" Max asked. It was bruised and swollen shut.

Dean shrugged. "I was training with Xander, and he caught me with my guard down. It happens."

"Look who just walked in," Harley said, nodding to the door.

Max and Dean turned to see Honeysuckle flying in circles around Brooke and Natalia.

"What the..." was all Max could say when he caught sight of Natalia.

"So are you guys dating them?" Dean wanted to know.

Harley nearly spit his punch all over Dean's shirt. "Are you kidding me?"

Gone in a Flash

"You look amazing," Dean said, smiling broadly as the girls walked over.

Harley elbowed him in the ribs.

"What? They do," Dean said, absently rubbing his shaved head.

"Thank you," Brooke offered with a curtsy. Natalia, however, simply stared at her shoes. She wasn't used to compliments from boys.

"Well, I agree with him," Max said, handing each of the girls a plate as Honeysuckle glared at him.

"You three look very handsome, too," Brooke said.

Dean walked over to join his buddies while the rest of them got some food. As they walked through the buffet line, Max filled Brooke in on the conversation they had had with Monti in his lab.

"So do you think there's any connection between the cards and those clockworks?" she asked.

"I don't know what to think," Max admitted. "Monti mentioned that Von Strife used to run a clockwork program here at the academy, but we haven't been able to connect the dots."

"Hey, isn't that Smoke?" Harley asked as they joined Ernie, Robert, and the Toad brothers.

"Unfortunately," Ernie grumbled. The changeling who could teleport just about anywhere was standing by himself next to a banyan tree.

"What's his deal?" Harley wanted to know.

"There is a rumor that his parents don't want him," Todd explained as he chewed on a buttermilk biscuit that was dripping with butter and raspberry preserves. "Other people say that he grew up on a pirate airship somewhere in the Durban Sea."

"Well, I heard that he might be Dean Nipkin's nephew," Ross added.

"I think we should ask him to join us," Brooke announced to everyone's surprise.

"Please tell me that was a joke," Ernie complained. "And if it was, it wasn't funny."

"I bet he's just lonely," she argued. Brooke dabbed at the corner of her mouth with a napkin, and then she walked over to talk to Smoke.

He didn't look very happy about it, but before long, Brooke was leading him over to their table. Robert was quick to excuse himself as the rest of the table fell silent. Smoke scowled, but he took a seat next to Brooke.

"I hope that they announce the pairings for the Round Table tournament soon," Brooke started. "Did everyone enter?"

"Not us," Ross said, sliding a slice of venison into his mouth. His jowls were already covered in gravy. "We're businessmen."

"Well, I signed up," Ernie answered sullenly, "but I'm not very good."

Todd turned to Smoke. "How about you?"

"Oh, I'll be there," he responded coldly.

"I didn't think you played," Ross continued.

"Are you spying on me, frog boy?"

Ross recoiled.

Smoke snorted. "What's the deal with you two, anyway? You call yourselves brothers, but you don't even look alike. Are you sure your parents aren't lying to you?"

Neither of them said a word.

"I hear that you can teleport," interrupted Brooke, hoping to break the tension.

Smoke folded his arms smugly. "All I have to do is see the target, and I'm as good as there. It's the same with any

166

place I've ever been before. I just picture it in my mind, and bam, I'm there! And nobody can stop me...not even Nipkin."

"If you use your powers that much, why haven't you started to morph yet?" Natalia asked. "I thought the more times that changelings tapped into their abilities, the quicker they're supposed to turn into faeries."

Smoke glared at her for a second, but then he smiled. "There are ways to slow it down; you just need the right connections.

"Anyway," he continued after standing up, "this is the worst party ever. Does anyone want to go to the Ward Forest to look for Water Sprites?"

No one said a word, but Brooke's eyes were shining with wonder. Water Sprites were extremely rare. To see one was considered the best of luck.

Smoke smiled mischievously and leaned closer to Brooke. "It's not that far away, you know. I can take you there. I mean, if you want."

"Right now?" Brooke asked, her cheeks flushed.

Max was about to protest, but he didn't know what to say.

"It's not like your dad is going to kick you out of the academy if he catches you," Smoke said, trying to entice her.

"You don't know her father," Max said.

Smoke ignored him, keeping his eyes on Brooke. "Come on. He'll never even know that you were gone."

To everyone's surprise, Brooke took Smoke's out-stretched hand. "Okay," she said.

In a flash, they were gone.

"Please tell me that didn't just happen." Max jumped up.

"What's wrong?" Natalia smiled. "Are you jealous?"

"No!" Max exclaimed. "But we have to tell somebody. It's too dangerous out there."

"I'll get Logan," Ernie said.

In a flash, Agent Thunderbolt was off, but before he returned, Smoke was already back. Brooke wasn't with him.

"Where is she?" Max asked as he grabbed Smoke by the collar.

"Right where I left her," Smoke replied, snorting as he pushed Max away. "I didn't have enough juice to take her with me, but she can handle herself."

Max saw a small flash of blue light flicker behind Smoke's ear. Smoke winced and reached back to scratch his neck. "Somebody just turned my power off!"

"That would be me," Logan said, stepping out of the shadows. "You've got exactly five seconds to tell me where you left Brooke Lundgren before I reach down your throat and pull the words out of you."

Don't Fear
the Reaper

Max struck his head against the side of the carriage as
Logan slammed on the air brakes. The force sent the
vehicle drifting through a cobblestone turn before the
carriage raced under the gate that separated Iron Bridge
from the rest of the island. Then, like a comet, the carriage shot toward the Ward Forest.

The vehicle looked like the hybrid of a nineteenth-
century carriage and a sleek bullet, but there were no
horses. Instead, Logan guided two hovering spheres of
light that pulled the carriage, while Max rode alone in the
coach below. The rest of the Griffins were back at Iron
Bridge, being debriefed by an outraged Dean Nipkin.

That Smoke had managed to teleport outside the school was both a shock and an outrage.

Max's stomach felt like a sack of spiders as he thought about Brooke. She was alone out there, in a dark forest that could very well be inhabited by monsters.

"I need you to stay focused," Logan said. "Don't let your emotions take control. We need you on this one... Brooke needs you."

No pressure, Max thought. He wished that Iver were here to keep him calm and focused.

Soon they entered a section of the forest known as Gimble Eaves, and when Logan hit the retro-engines, the carriage slid to a frictionless stop. Max could see several hovercycles parked on the edge of the wood, white steam rising from their idling tailpipes. THOR agents had been called in to locate and, if possible, rescue Brooke Lundgren.

"Miss Lundgren has taken shelter in the cottage," one of the THOR agents relayed over the communicator. *"She's safe for now. But she's afraid to come out. Says there's something outside waiting for her. She's asking for her father."*

Logan shook his head as he replied. "He's five thousand miles away and unreachable. Just tell her I'm on my way. Max is with me." The Scotsman growled. "I've got a bad feeling about what we're walking into, Grasshopper. You better activate your gauntlet. Whatever happens, stay close."

Max twisted the silver ring on his finger. It shimmered

before spreading over his hand to form the *Codex* Gauntlet. As Max flexed his fingers inside the metal glove, a spark of blue flame ignited on his fingers. He was ready.

It wasn't long before they found the cottage, but an ominous stretch of moonlit grass lay between them and Brooke. As Max ventured a foot onto the meadow, a chill crept over him. Something very evil was near. He backed into the safety of the trees.

Logan looked down at a handheld device and tapped on the screen with his gloved finger. "The temperature just dropped thirty degrees," he whispered, his breath visible in the night air. "Stay sharp."

Max saw several figures emerge from the foliage like wraiths. Some wore ski masks, and others had grease paint streaked across their faces. They all wore black uniforms, Spectral Vision goggles, and a hammer insignia on their shoulders. Logan's THOR agents had arrived.

"Status?" Logan asked.

"Sensors confirm that she's inside," answered a stoic soldier named Søren. "Vitals are normal, and the cottage, a temporal rifting nest, is currently providing adequate defense against the assailant. She's lucky she found it."

"Our baddie?"

"Delta Class Reaper."

"Options?"

"The Baron's gargoyle has a theory, sir," Søren said, and he fell back.

A figure draped in a dark overcoat stepped forward.

His skin was limestone grey, his eyes were smoky orbs of yellow, and his hands were like finely chiseled rock.

"Evening, Throckmorton," Logan greeted the creature.

The gargoyle was Baron Lundgren's personal Bounder Faerie, sworn to serve the Lundgren family until the end of days. Apart from his imposing fangs and colossal strength, he was a Round Table Grandmaster, as well as a renowned expert in the fields of Faerie Biology and Ancient Ciphers.

"This fiend is a relative of the Djinns of Arabia." The gargoyle spoke in a soft German accent. "They feed on fear before they feed on their victims."

Logan took a deep breath. "I thought Reapers were supposed to be extinct. In fact, didn't the boy's grandfather lock up the last one during the war?" He nodded toward Max.

The gargoyle stared back at Logan with his yellow eyes, unblinking.

"That's what I thought you'd say." The Scotsman sighed. He unzipped his duffel bag and began to piece together a cylindrical metal rod, spinning a handle onto the back end, before popping a scope on the top rail. "Look lively, gents. This one isn't going to be easy."

Then Throckmorton pulled a card from his jacket and handed it to the Scotsman.

Logan growled as he looked at the empty face on the card. He turned to Max. "You gave her one of those cards you found in the bunker, didn't you?"

Max gasped. "Yeah, but why is it blank like that? Do you think whatever attacked her came out of the card?"

Before Logan could answer, a shadowy form dropped from the tree above them, crushing Max to the ground. Max tried to fight back, but the Reaper had pinned his gauntlet. It was a shadowy beast with ghostly eyes and silver teeth, but there was something else. The creature had been modified, like the boy in Max's dream. Mechanical bits and whirring clock gears were fused with its dark flesh. The cyborg monster gripped Max's neck with a hand of cold steel.

The THOR agents responded with a barrage from their MVX pulse rifles, but the Reaper dissolved into mist faster than they could pull their triggers, only to reform after the barrage had ceased, keeping Max pinned to the ground.

"Delta Class. We have a lock!" a soldier called out.

Max managed to open his watering eyes to see a metal ball hit the ground next to him. A small green light blinked, followed by the disembodied voice of a Scottish woman: *Sonic grenade detonation in T-minus three… two…one…*

The explosion rattled Max's teeth, but it had done the trick. The Reaper released its grasp and fell to the ground, convulsing. Another weapon fired. In an instant, the flailing Reaper was enmeshed in a net of sparking electricity, meant to short-circuit its ability to phase. Unfortunately, the net had been designed for Gamma Class monsters, and the Reaper wasn't going to give up so easily. With a roar, it ripped the net apart and phased into the ground.

The clearing grew deathly quiet. The agents quietly spread out.

"Shhh..." the Scotsman warned Max. He pointed to the ground. "It's waiting for us to make a mistake."

As Logan spoke, the air in the clearing seemed to crystallize. Max watched helplessly as a wave of frost shot up, rooting everyone to the ground. There were shouts, but no matter what they seemed to do, the ice only latched on more tenaciously. It continued to sweep up their bodies.

Max was the first overcome by the cursed frost. It constricted his chest and wrung its icy fingers around his neck. As he opened his mouth to cough, the frost swept inside and down his throat. He coughed and gagged, unable to move. His heart thudded. It was difficult to breathe. Then Max felt something move inside his jacket. A moment later, one of the Round Table cards from the Chinnery deck managed to wiggle its way out of Max's pocket and onto the ground. It was a red dragon known as Shadowbane.

Max watched through watery eyes as the image exploded from the card and into the air. Crimson particles swirled in the night until they coalesced into a menacing dragon the size of a truck. Its armored tail pounded the earth and its mouth glowed with fire.

Belowground, the Reaper snarled.

Shadowbane roared its challenge, gliding through

the air under the power of its great wings. The dragon circled the clearing, its radiating heat melting the frost. Max could breathe again. Logan quickly scooped him up and carried him to safety.

Seeking the Reaper like a hawk hunting after a field mouse, the dragon struck the ground in a tumult of fiery earth. With a roar, it plunged its armored head through the soil and plucked the Reaper out like a weed.

The monster lashed at the dragon's eyes, frantically trying to break free. There was no escape. In three short bites, the Reaper had disappeared into the dragon's molten jaws.

With a roar of victory, Shadowbane shot into the air and made a triumphant pass over the battlefield before finally dissolving into a red mist that was sucked back into the Round Table card in Max's hand—the same card with Oswald Chinnery's mark on it.

After examining Max for wounds, Logan stood back. "Two cards from that deck of yours have come to life now. That means you're going to help me track them down before someone else gets hurt. Understood?"

Max nodded slowly.

Throckmorton passed over the clearing and ripped the cottage door from its hinges. Brooke raced out and into his arms. Max started after her, but Logan held him back. "Give her some time, Grasshopper. She's had quite a scare. Besides, you've got work to do."

Consequences

The Griffins walked off the *Zephyr* and onto the platform below the school. It was October, and the subway's eccentricities had become commonplace to everyone except Natalia — it hadn't forgiven her in the slightest. It would often remove the springs from her seat or ensure her window was covered in smelly slime.

"This thing hates me," she complained.

Max laughed. "Well, at least you have the three of us."

"I'd prefer a ride to school where I didn't have to worry about getting tossed into the bottom of the lake. I can feel it watching me all the time. The other day I ended up stepping in a bucket of fish heads that hadn't been there until I walked into the compartment. Fish heads!"

Max swallowed his smile. "So, Harley, did you find anything in that clockwork manual?"

Harley whistled. "Monti was right; Von Strife was a genius. If you gave me a hundred years, I still don't think I could replicate half of the machines he designed...even with the blueprints. He was way before his time."

"Does the manual mention anything about artificial intelligence?"

"Not a word," Harley replied. "But I found a chart in the back with a bunch of names I didn't recognize," he said. "I think they're all changelings, but I'm not sure."

Ernie took the book and scanned the list. "Oh my gosh. Flight...molecular restructuring...transmutation.... These are definitely changelings. I wonder why he wrote all this down."

"Who knows," Harley said, before he put his copy of the manual back in his bag. "He was a teacher. Maybe those were some of his students."

"Does anyone know what's going on with Brooke?" Natalia asked. "I haven't heard from her since Smoke dumped her in that forest."

"She hasn't been answering her phone." Max sighed in worry. "Logan said she's going to take a break from school for a while..."

"I hope Smoke gets what's coming to him," Natalia

muttered as the Griffins passed through the pillared gates and into the Green Corridor.

"Baron Lundgren shut his powers off," Ernie said. "I guess Dean Nipkin had him locked up somewhere in Sendak Hall."

The Griffins fell into silent thoughts as they passed through the halls of the school. As they neared homeroom, they found Dean Nipkin and Ms. Merical locked in another heated discussion. The difference was that Dean Nipkin won this time. She was holding Robert's arm in her bony fingers as she turned to leave.

He reached out to fuse himself to the wall, but his power disappeared like a dead battery.

"No!" Ernie shouted. In a burst of speed, he tore down the hall, placing himself in front of Dean Nipkin. "Where are you taking him?"

The dean looked down at Ernie with tired eyes. "You know very well where he's going. You of all people should understand that Robert needs special attention until he can control his talents."

"I don't want to go!" Robert complained. "I want to stay here with all the normal kids."

"What would happen if you blew up in the middle of a classroom? Do you really think we should put the entire student body at risk because you prefer to roam around the campus unfettered? Do you really want a repeat of our tragic history?"

"What about Ernie?" Robert maintained. "Why does he get to stay?"

Ernie felt exposed as the dean turned to eye him carefully. "I'm working on it." With that, she brushed past Ernie and disappeared through the doors with Robert in tow.

Ms. Merical placed a hand on Ernie's shoulders. "As much as I hate to admit it, Dean Nipkin is right. Robert needs to learn how to control his abilities, or we're all at risk."

"Am I next?"

Ms. Merical shook her head as she smiled at Ernie. "I don't think you need to worry about it."

"Dean Nipkin mentioned a tragedy," Natalia began. "What was she talking about?"

"Naomi…" Ms. Merical answered after a sigh.

"Who?"

"Many years ago, a young girl named Naomi attended this academy. She was a fire elemental like Yi, and she had extraordinary potential. In fact, she might have been one of the most powerful changelings in recorded history."

"Why haven't I heard about her before?" Ernie wanted to know.

"Because something went very wrong…" Ms. Merical's voice trailed off. After a moment she blew her nose, wiped her eyes, and continued. "As difficult as it may seem right now, the rules are here to protect us. One day you will understand."

"No. I won't," Ernie said flatly.

An Important
Announcement

Ernie stewed through the rest of the morning, refusing to talk to anyone unless it was on the topic of food. He always ate a lot, but when he was depressed, his appetite went into overdrive. He was lucky that he never gained weight. When the bell announced lunch, he shot out the door. A stack of papers swirled behind him as he raced to his locker, where he opened the small refrigerator door that the maintenance team had installed. He grabbed a stick of summer sausage and bottle of Plumples before slamming his locker shut.

"I thought you weren't supposed to use your super

speed unless it was an emergency," Max said, placing his books in the locker next to Ernie's.

"I was hungry," Ernie grumbled before turning to walk to the dining hall.

"I'm sure Robert is going to be fine," Max said, trying to catch up.

Ernie stuffed half the sausage into his mouth before tearing a chunk off. "Look, I know you're trying to make me feel better, but you don't get it," he said as he smacked his lips. "Eventually I'm going to turn into some kind of a freak all covered in fur, or feathers, or who knows what. It's the same for Robert, and all the other changelings. Instead of trying to help us find a cure, they want to lock us away like we're criminals."

"Maybe we could talk to Brooke's dad," Max suggested.

"Yeah, right," Ernie said. "He probably gave Dean Nipkin permission to take Robert away. I bet you anything that I'm next. Besides, what's going to happen when they see this?" Ernie pulled up his shirtsleeve to reveal a series of faint spots on his arm.

"Have you shown that to Doc Trimble?" Max asked.

"You're kidding, right?" Ernie said, rolling his sleeve back down.

By the time Harley and Max grabbed their lunches, Ernie had already rushed through the line. He was sitting with the Toad brothers, eating with the rest of the social outcasts. The room was packed with chattering students.

"What the heck is going on?" Harley asked as he wove through the crowd.

"Beats me," Max replied.

"You're just the two we were hoping to see," Todd said, as Max took a seat next to him. "Where's Romanov?"

"I don't know. She told me that she would meet us here before class started," Max replied. "It's usually better not to ask. Why? What's going on?"

Ross finished scribbling something into his little black notebook. "They just released the pairings for the Round Table tournament."

"You aren't going to believe this," Todd said, looking at Ernie. "You're dueling against Smoke."

"Smoke?" Ernie asked, nearly choking on his macaroni salad. "I thought he was locked away."

"Apparently he's still eligible for the tournament," Ross replied indifferently.

"Who am I dueling?" asked Harley.

"Cricket Willoughby," Todd answered. "You two have a similar style, but you should be in good shape if you don't do anything stupid."

"How do you know what my dueling style is? You haven't even seen me play."

"Honestly," Ross began, tucking a pencil behind his ear, "have a little faith. We do this for a living. How else do you think the *Toad Reports* have become world famous?"

The Griffins looked at one another blankly.

"The *Toad Reports* are only the best scouting reports that money can buy. We can tell you everything from what kind of cards your opponent plays with to what he had for breakfast on his seventh birthday."

"Speaking of which," Todd said, flipping to a chart in the back of his notebook, "what kind of Kinematic goggles do you guys duel with? Salvino Technohancers? The Tesla Recoil?"

"I don't have a clue what you're talking about." Max sighed.

"You're serious, aren't you? Look, you have to keep up with the times if you want to be competitive, Sumner. Kinematic goggles work kind of like the SIM Chamber. They allow you to duel in three dimensions, just like a real battle. It can get pretty intense, but it's the only way to play."

"Besides, you can't play in an officially sanctioned tournament without them," Ross added. "And you've got enough to worry about. You're going up against Yoshino Takamori."

"So do you have a scouting report on him?" Max asked.

The Toad brothers smiled at each other. "Of course," Ross proclaimed. "But first we need to work out the business side."

"We want to give you free *Toad Reports* for the first round," Todd added.

"What's in it for you?" Harley asked with a healthy dose of skepticism.

The Toads smiled in unison. "If you win, you promise to buy a report for every round until you're knocked out," Todd replied. "And when you get interviewed for the school paper, you need to give us a plug."

Max turned to the other Griffins, but nobody said a word.

"All right, we're in."

THE INVITATION

Natalia showed up a few minutes later wearing a new outfit. She was sporting a ruffled blouse with a brooch fixed to the collar, khaki pants, and a pair of button-up boots.

"What are you so happy about?" Max asked.

Natalia looked around to make sure that no one was listening. Then she leaned over and whispered, "Someone is throwing a party in one of the Construction Zones, and we're invited."

"The Construction Zones are off-limits," Harley objected.

"Since when have you ever worried about the rules, Harley Eisenstein?" she countered quickly. "Besides,

Stacy Bechton said they do this all the time. The teachers just pretend not to notice. What could possibly go wrong?"

"Who the heck is Stacy Bechton?" Ernie wanted to know.

"It's this way," Natalia said, motioning for the rest of the Griffins to follow. She broke away from the crowd of students loading onto the *Zephyr*, before disappearing into a crumbling passageway marked off with yellow tape. She reached into her bag, pulled out a flashlight, and set off down the lonely hall.

"I checked some of the records in the library," she continued as they picked their way over the rubble-strewn floor. "This passage should lead us directly under Sendak Hall."

Ernie sighed. "Sendak Hall isn't really a place to party. Trust me."

"Well, we're going under it, not into it," Natalia returned crisply.

As they wandered down the cramped tunnel, Max couldn't stop thinking about Baron Lundgren's warning. He knew they shouldn't be here. The last thing he needed was to get suspended. How was he going to explain that to his grandmother? Still, Natalia was so excited about being invited to an exclusive party that he couldn't say no.

"So has anyone heard from Brooke?" Max asked, trying not to sound too interested. He didn't want Harley to start teasing him about having a crush on her.

"I've been chatting with her on my DE Tablet," Natalia said, leading them deeper into the darkness. "She says she's ready to come back to school, but her dad won't let her."

"Why not?"

"She thinks he's overprotective, I guess," Natalia replied. "I'm supposed to go to her place after school, so I should know more tonight."

"This looks like an abandoned mineshaft," Harley noted as he stepped over a pile of fallen masonry. "Are you sure we're going the right way?"

"Of course," Natalia replied. "The girl who invited us described it perfectly. They leave it like this so the teachers won't get suspicious."

"Wouldn't they notice the footprints?" Ernie asked. "I mean, you're the detective and everything, but there's a lot of dust down here."

Natalia ignored him.

After a few minutes, they found themselves at the top of a shadowy staircase blackened with soot and grime. "Down we go," Natalia directed.

"Are you kidding?" Ernie asked as he looked over the edge with trepidation.

"Nobody forced you to come with us," Natalia said. With that, she stepped over a broken gargoyle and began the descent.

"If Sprig were here, she could turn into a giant firefly or something and light the way," Ernie suggested.

Max's stomach turned. His attempts to find his Bounder had failed. She'd never been away this long before. If it was true that faeries were hiding from someone, maybe she was fine and just waiting until things were safe again.

"I told you there was nothing to worry about," Natalia said as she moved quickly down the stairs.

"Shhh...I hear somebody following us," Ernie warned.

Natalia turned her flashlight back up the stairs, but nobody was there. "It's probably more people coming to the party."

When the Griffins finally got to the bottom of the stairs, they found themselves in a long hall. The floor and walls were damp, and Max had a strange sense that he had been there before.

"There's no one here," Harley said, turning to Natalia. "Someone pulled a prank on you."

"Wait a minute," Natalia said. She saw someone move in the distance, the tail of her dress fluttering as she disappeared down one of the passageways. "That's her. That's the girl who gave me the invitation!"

"What are you talking about?" Harley pressed.

"Come on." Natalia took off after the girl, and soon the Griffins found themselves facing a sheet of tattered plastic that had been strung across the abandoned hallway.

"Where did she go?" Natalia asked, frantic to find her.

"I know this place," Max whispered. "It's from my dream..."

His nightmare had sprung to life before his eyes. It was the same hallway. The same smell. The same everything. What was next, the bicycle? The newspaper bag? Would Johnny Geist be waiting for him in the room beyond?

"Maybe we should get out of here," Ernie suggested, but Max didn't hear him. Before Max knew what was happening, he pushed aside the plastic sheet and walked down the hall until he came to a doorway.

"*Help me...*" a voice echoed inside his head.

Max walked over the threshold and into a chamber that reeked of death. There was a rusted metal table with thick straps, broken drill bits, curved saws, forceps, and knives scattered on the floor where a tray had been overturned. Max had indeed been here in his dream, but it had been a different time. Ages ago.

Ernie skirted as far away from the wicked tools as he could. Across the room, Natalia spotted shackles big enough for her to wear around her neck. "I wonder what these were supposed to hold."

"I don't know," Harley said. "But this whole room is lined with iron. Maybe they were doing experiments on faeries."

"Or changelings," Ernie mumbled.

"But we're on school grounds," Natalia countered.

"Why would the administration have allowed a place like this to exist?"

Harley walked over to five grimy cylinders that were affixed to the wall. Peeling away the layers of decay, he uncovered round gauges. "Check this out. We have some of these up in the MERLIN Tech labs," he explained. "They're kind of like batteries, but they measure plasma watts. Whatever was going on down here required a lot of juice."

"Look at this." Natalia shined her flashlight on a plaque hanging over the door. It read:

METATRON
PROF. VON STRIFE
EST. 1883

"Von Strife?" Harley whispered. "So it was true..."

Max ran his hand along the surgical table where he was certain that Johnny Geist had once lain. A shiver washed over him. He pulled away, but his arm bumped a metal tray filled with wicked tools. Pain flashed, and Max realized that he had cut himself. He looked down and saw the rusty scalpel. The same one from his dream...

Then a flood of light blasted through the doorway.

SUSPENDED

Max raised the *Codex* Gauntlet, and Skyfire erupted over his fist.

"Lower that weapon or you will face expulsion!"

Dean Nipkin emerged from the shadows of the doorway. Max could just make out her silhouette through the glare of the sodium light she was carrying.

"Do I dare to ask what you were doing here?" the dean asked, looking at each of the Griffins in turn. "I don't suppose this was one of your little monster-hunting expeditions."

"There was a party..." Natalia began.

"In a Construction Zone?" Dean Nipkin asked, looking around the dismal setting in disbelief.

"Here's the invitation," Natalia explained, handing over the paper.

Dean Nipkin pored over the invitation. "Who gave this to you?"

"Stacy Bechton," Natalia muttered, her eyes on the ground.

Dean Nipkin stepped back, as if she had seen a ghost. "Stacy Bechton?" She paused, composing herself. "There is no current student by that name. What game are you trying to play, Ms. Romanov? Where did you hear that name? And this invitation...it must be a hundred years old."

For the first time, Max noticed that the paper was faded and rippled. He wondered how he hadn't noticed it before.

Natalia sighed and lowered her eyes under Nipkin's scrutiny. Not only had Natalia fallen for Stacy's prank, but *Stacy* wasn't even the girl's real name.

"No answer? I see..." the dean continued. "Then you leave me with no alternative. From this moment, you are all hereby suspended from Iron Bridge Academy. You will be required to attend a formal hearing where you can present your case. If you are found guilty, you will face expulsion."

"I want to talk to the Baron," Max announced, stepping protectively in front of Natalia.

192

A hint of a smile traced the corner of Nipkin's paper-thin lips. "Of course you do. But don't assume that your status as Guardian of the *Codex* provides you some level of immunity. The Templar can drop you back into the real world just as easily as they plucked you out. Now follow me." With that, Dean Nipkin spun on her heels and headed down the hallway.

An Unusual Guest

The next week passed like a fog. While Grandma Caliburn was no fan of Dean Nipkin, she wasn't happy that Max had broken the rules. Still, she let him continue his monster-hunting training with Logan. Harley spent most of the week working at Monti's lab. He was only allowed to sweep the floors, but at least it was a start.

As for Natalia, she was grounded. She spent her days watching the telephone, hoping that the school would call and tell her the suspension was all just a silly misunderstanding.

The call never came.

Ernie passed the days flipping through his comic-book

collection or sketching superheroes. When he got bored with that, he stayed in contact with his friends through his DE Tablet. And he worried about Robert.

When Natalia's phone finally rang, it wasn't the call that she had been hoping for. Instead of an invitation to come back to class, the Grey Griffins had been summoned to a disciplinary hearing with Baron Lundgren.

The next morning, all four of the Griffins found themselves sitting in the Baron's office. A circular room with a glass dome, it sat atop De Payens Hall. It overlooked both the Master's and Apprentice's Halls, commanding a 360-degree view of the island. Inside, every grain of wood was polished to a shine, and the books on the surrounding shelves were perfectly placed. Conspicuously absent, however, were any pictures of his wife or daughter.

The Baron seemed to take no notice of them as he pored over a stack of yellowed papers. After several tense minutes of waiting, the Baron set aside his work and screwed the cap onto his feathered pen.

"It's all my fault," Natalia blurted. She couldn't stand the silence. "Expel me if you want, but they didn't do anything wrong..."

Cain raised his hand, and she fell silent. He continued his work for a few more minutes, then sat back in his chair, regarding them closely.

"Dean Nipkin had every right to suspend all of you," he began in a calm voice. He reached into a drawer and pulled out a set of notes. "I confess that I am disappointed that you, of *all* students, were found in a restricted area," he said, looking directly at Max. "My role as your mentor is well known here among the faculty. Not only is your defiance a slap in my face, but it also erodes my authority. You have placed me in a very difficult position. Now," he continued, glancing at the paper in front of him, "you claimed to have received a party invitation from a girl by the name of Stacy Bechton?"

Natalia nodded.

Cain studied her closely. "Then, you will no doubt be saddened to hear that Stacy is dead."

. "Dead?"

"Yes, for nearly a century, in fact. Which makes her appearance somewhat suspect. Please describe the girl you saw."

Natalia looked at her friends, unsure how to begin. "Um...I guess she was a little taller than me, with curly brown hair. Her eyes were blue, and there was a freckle just above her right eyebrow."

"I see. Had you seen her previously?"

Natalia nodded. "A few times. Always in the dining hall, near Xander's table."

Cain turned to the boys. "Have you seen the girl whom Natalia is describing?"

They shook their heads.

"But I swear I saw her!" Natalia argued. "I'm not the type to make up stories. You know that!"

Cain nodded. "Of course. Or perhaps you saw something that looked like her. Your description matches Stacy's well enough, but why would Miss Bechton's ghost invite you to a party in an area that is strictly off-limits?"

"Maybe she wanted us to find the Metatron," Natalia conjectured. "What is that place anyway? It looks like a torture chamber."

Cain shook his head. "I am afraid that information is classified. Now as to your hearing, I will admit that Miss Bechton's alleged participation is troublesome. So until this matter is cleared up, I am postponing my judgment. In the meantime, I will allow you to resume your classes so long as you behave yourselves. Is that clear?"

"Yes, sir," Natalia replied, and the boys nodded their acceptance in turn.

"What about Brooke?" Max asked as the Baron prepared to return to his work. "Is she okay?"

Cain regarded Max with coldness. "It was *you* who placed Brooke in mortal danger, Master Sumner. Not Aidan. *You* gave her the card that the Reaper sprang from." He paused, allowing the truth of his words to sink in. "If you place Brooke in danger again, unknowingly or otherwise, I will not be so forgiving."

Max nodded slowly and stared at his laces. "There's something else," he said. "Sprig's disappeared."

THE CLOCKWORK KING

"Faeries are strange creatures," Baron Lundgren explained after Max told him about what had happened with Sprig. "I have no doubt that your Bounder is very much alive. You two are linked, and if anything had happened to her, you would know."

Despite Cain's assurances, Max didn't feel any better. When Saturday morning finally came around, it took all of his energy just to get out of bed. Apparently Monti had had a breakthrough about the Round Table cards that they had found, so Max forced himself to throw on a pair of jeans and his Twins cap.

"Good morning," Monti offered with a measure of

cheer that bordered on obnoxious, considering how early it was. "Would you care for some juice?"

"No thanks," Max said. What he wanted was to go back to bed.

The other Griffins were already seated at the table in the back of the comic store. They were attacking a stack of donuts drenched with icing and sprinkles.

"Since you're all here now, I can give you these," Monti said, handing each of them a sealed envelope.

"Supersonic! It's our *Toad Reports*," Ernie shouted as he pulled out a spiral-bound document with the words TOP SECRET written across the top.

"This is incredible," Natalia had to admit. "They even have a list of all the cards my opponent usually plays with, and what order she typically uses them in."

"Sounds interesting," Monti said. "Something like that would have come in handy when I was dueling, that's for sure."

"That reminds me," Max said. "What's the deal with Kinematic goggles? I heard we need them for the tournament."

"Yes, indeed," Monti said, pointing to a pair that sat on the shelf behind him. They looked like something from a science-fiction movie. The goggles had vents, adjustment toggles, and a comlink that swiveled.

"Virtual Kinematics is popular at the Templar academies," he explained. "Next to the SIM Chamber, it's as close as you're going to get to a battlefield. Maybe Iver didn't think you were ready yet," he said, pausing thoughtfully. "Give me a few days, and I'll see what I can do. In the meantime, maybe we should talk about why I asked you here."

Monti poured himself a second cup of coffee before he continued. "I think that I finally understand what caused your Chinnery deck to come to life before it attacked Brooke. You see, it's been rumored that people called Animators have been able to animate Round Table cards for centuries, but it's never been done in public, so there's no proof. If it were possible, it would have to be exceedingly rare, and in the wrong hands, extremely dangerous. I believe someone with this skill may have tried to use Brooke as bait to get at Max."

"Right, but then the dragon actually *saved* him," Natalia countered. "If those cards were supposed to kill Max, why wouldn't all of them work the same way?"

"That threw me for a loop," Monti admitted. "At least until I realized that the skill set of an Animator is similar to the Guardian of the *Codex*. What's the difference between a Reaper jumping out of a card and a spriggan popping out of an enchanted book?"

"You're saying that I animated the dragon somehow?" Max exclaimed.

"Who would go to all this effort just to attack Max?" asked Natalia.

"A dead man."

"You lost me," she said.

200

Monti walked behind the counter and took out an antique newspaper. The masthead read *New Victoria Chronicle*, and the date was January 28, 1914. He pointed to a line in a news article that read: *The new automaton project at the Foundation will be helmed by Mr. Otto Von Strife, who some are already calling the Clockwork King.*

"When the Templar shut down his clockwork program, it seems that Von Strife struck a deal to continue his weapons program with an organization known as the Foundation," Monti explained. "In turn, they planned to sell the war machines to the highest bidder."

"What does that have to do with the cards?" Natalia wondered.

"That's where it gets interesting," Monti said, pointing to a faded image of a man wearing a strange cap. "This is Chinnery, the man who created the cards you found. According to this paper, he was hired by the Foundation to run one of Von Strife's research and development projects. It doesn't say what the project is, but you can bet it had something to do with a Round Table deck. Do you think it's any coincidence that Von Strife's title as the Clockwork King ended up as a card in Chinnery's deck?"

"I don't understand," confessed Ernie.

Monti smiled and started pacing back and forth. "Fact number one...we know your cards were made by Chinnery, and that Chinnery worked for Von Strife. Fact number two...we know that Von Strife was also known as the

Clockwork King and that he was a man of considerable prowess in the area of clockwork mechanics. Fact number three... the Chinnery deck that you found was discovered in a clockwork laboratory. And last..." Monti leaned back against a bookshelf, folding his arms in confidence. "The clockwork beetle that Harley told me about a couple days ago... the one that led you to those cards was specially designed to ensure that you made it there in one piece."

"If Von Strife is alive, why did he want us to get the cards?" Natalia wanted to know.

"Because he was trapped inside one of them," Monti replied. "How he got there, I don't know. Perhaps Chinnery turned on his master at the last moment. Or maybe Von Strife was simply trying to avoid capture. Whatever the case, in order to escape, an Animator was needed. Who better than the Guardian of the *Codex*?"

"So when Max touched the Clockwork King card, Von Strife was freed!" Natalia concluded.

Max was horrified by the thought. "You mean this is all my fault?"

"I'm saying that whatever happened down in that bunker was only the beginning."

"Wait a minute, what about this?" Natalia asked, pointing to an article lost on the bottom of the page. The title read CASE FOR MISSING GIRL CLOSED DUE TO LACK OF EVIDENCE. Her eyes grew big as she scanned through the text.

"What is it?" Ernie asked, as he tried to squeeze in to get a look.

"This is an article about Stacy Bechton," she explained. "Her parents reported her missing on Halloween night in 1914, but nobody came forward with any clues to help solve the case, and the police were forced to close it. Can you imagine what her parents must have gone through?"

"Just like Stephen..." Ernie voiced quietly.

"All right, I think that's enough for today," Monti said. "I need to get ready to open the store, and you guys have some *Toad Reports* to study."

THE MIND OF OTTO VON STRIFE

As the Griffins rode along on the *Zephyr*, a burst of black smoke billowed in the subway car. Aidan Thorne appeared on a bench across the aisle. He was dressed in a beige trench coat with combat boots and, of course, his goggles.

"Long time no see," Smoke greeted the Griffins. "Did you miss me?"

"What are you doing here?" Max barked, clenching his fist.

Smoke smirked and reclined into the leather. "Probably wasting my time, but I thought I'd give you a chance to prove you aren't like all the other jerks at Iron Bridge."

"What are you talking about?" Natalia asked.

"Von Strife," Smoke replied casually. "I know all about your little trip to the Metatron."

"You were following us!" Max exclaimed, rising to his feet.

"Let's just say I have friends who know what's going on around here."

"You're lying," Natalia accused him.

"No. I am *not*. All you know about the Templar is what they want you to know."

"I suppose you know the truth?" Natalia folded her arms.

Smoke smiled as he reached into his rucksack. "This is one of Otto Von Strife's journals." He held the book up so they could get a closer look. "I found it lying around in Nipkin's office a few months ago, so I read it. That's why I know the Templar are lying."

"Oh, please." Natalia sighed. "We've heard this before."

Smoke continued unperturbed. "Von Strife was trying to save changelings, not kill us. The Templar shut him down."

"What are you talking about?" Ernie asked.

"Von Strife's daughter was a changeling."

Ernie's jaw dropped.

"He tried to get the Templar to help," Smoke continued. "That's why he came to Iron Bridge in the first place. He was trying to save her soul by putting it into a clockwork. Then, when the biotech caught up, he'd grow a new human body and place her soul inside."

"You're talking about human cloning?" Natalia scoffed. "That's impossible."

"Look around," Smoke said. "You didn't know monsters or magic existed until last year. Now you know the truth.

"Anything is possible," he continued. "Besides, you don't know what it's like to be a changeling—to have a foreign life force living inside of you, trying to take control of your soul. Von Strife is the only one who ever understood us."

Ernie sank in his seat.

"You're lying," Max said flatly.

"Are you willing to bet Agent Thunderbolt's life on it?" Smoke asked, pausing for a response that never came. "I didn't think so. Call me if you want to know more." In a rolling swirl of black mist, he was gone.

BOUNDER CARE

After their meeting with Smoke, Max had a hard time sleeping. As much as Max wanted to dismiss the changeling's claims as being utterly ridiculous, the story was just crazy enough to be true. What if the Templar Council had condemned Von Strife's daughter to death?

Max struggled with the conundrum throughout the next school day. When sixth period came around he was the only one in the Bounder Care class without a Bounder Faerie, as usual. If machines were hunting faeries and changelings, Max didn't understand why none of the other Bounders had been abducted. It didn't add up.

It had been several weeks since Sprig had disappeared,

and despite the Baron's encouragement, Max felt sure something had gone wrong. Now with Brooke absent, Max would have preferred just skipping the class altogether. He couldn't stop thinking about her. Worse, Max blamed himself for letting Smoke abduct her — although there wasn't much he could have done to stop Smoke from teleporting.

The day after the Reaper attack, Max called Brooke to make sure she was okay. When she didn't answer, he tried to chat with her on his DE Tablet. Brooke didn't return any of his messages, though. Max assumed she blamed him for everything that had happened. At least Natalia was a friend Brooke could talk to, he thought.

Akinyi Butama was the head of the Bounder Care program. She was from Nairobi, and her Bounder, Wangai, was a magnificent spriggan nearly twice the size of Sprig. His eyes were iridescent blue, and his fur ranged from golden honey to warm toffee. He usually lounged on Ms. Butama's desk with his hind leg hanging over the side and his tail swishing like a clock pendulum.

"Let's begin with a memory lesson," she began in her elegant accent. "What are the three ways that a Binding can be broken?"

Max wasn't sure if there were more lakes in Minnesota or rules governing the relationship between humans and Bounder Faeries. Most of the students tried to avoid eye contact with Ms. Butama, but Catalina Mendez quickly raised her hand. She was a thin-lipped girl with a button nose and a long black ponytail. A lumpy imp named Scuttlebutt sat next to her. It had droopy ears, a bulbous nose, and a gut that flopped over its belt like too much dough rising from a mixing bowl.

"If the human dies."

Ms. Butama nodded, then turned to a girl with a winged gremlin on her shoulder. "Yes, Faith?"

"If a Bounder is killed."

Max winced as he thought of Sprig. The Baron had told him that if something really bad had happened, Max would know. But how?

"That leaves us with the final answer," Ms. Butama prompted. "How about you, Kenji?"

All eyes turned to Kenji Sato, whose bright red drake perched lazily on his forearm. Kenji had transferred from the Templar academy in Antioch, and he had a reputation for being the class clown.

"The guy who I bought this monster from didn't say anything about Binding. Maybe I should give it back?"

"Bounders are *not* pets," Ms. Butama warned. "Though, in fairness to Kenji, the idea of Bounders as pets was a perspective that had been held for a thousand years. However, we are enlightened now, and we will treat all creatures with equal value, human or faerie."

Ms. Butama scanned her students. "There is one last answer. Can someone tell me what that is?"

"Fading!" exclaimed Brandi Stewart after quickly scanning a file on her DE Tablet. She was a thin girl with freckles and two braids that hung to her shoulders. Her catterfly, a graceful faerie that looked like a kitten with butterfly wings, was perched on the end of her desk.

"Can you be more specific?" Ms. Butama asked.

Brandi's face fell. She hadn't read that far.

"What about you, Max. What can you tell us about Fading?"

Max shifted uncomfortably in his seat as all eyes turned toward him. "Well, I...read somewhere that Bounders have to renew themselves from time to time. I suppose if they don't, they fade?"

"Impressive," Ms. Butama said before turning back to address the entire class. "Fading can be a tricky business. In fact, some Bounders have allowed themselves to fade in order to break free from humans who have mistreated them. Once that bond is severed, they are free to return for revenge." The class looked at her and then their Bounders in horror. The faeries didn't seem the least interested in the piece of trivia.

"This is, of course, extremely rare," she continued, "as the nature of Bounder Faeries is to be faithful, even if it costs them their lives." Her eyes moved to Max. "Sadly, this can happen all too often."

ABDUCTED. AGAIN.

By Friday, Smoke still hadn't shown up at school. When Max told Logan about what had happened on the *Zephyr*, the Scotsman sent THOR agents to track the changeling down. Despite all the advanced MERLIN Tech at their disposal, they couldn't find him anywhere. Smoke was simply gone, and it didn't look like he was coming back.

Since Aidan's surprise appearance on the *Zephyr*, Ernie couldn't stop worrying about the faerie essence eating away at his humanity. Luckily, Max was able to coax him out of his depression long enough to head over to the Spider's Web for Monti's first Round Table tournament. Dozens of kids milled outside the entrance. Music was streaming from the store, and there was a feast of junk food piled high on tables near the entrance.

"Remember that machine we saw in Iver's shop?" Harley asked as the Griffins walked toward the Spider's Web together. He pulled a drawing of a small clockwork from his backpack. The head looked like a pair of large binoculars, and its metal arms and legs were oddly long.

"Where did you get that?" Max asked. "It looks just like the one we saw!"

"The Rosenkreuz Library," answered Harley. "There's an entire section on Templar technology. This thing is called an Imager Bot. It's a type of spy drone, and it's highly illegal."

"It doesn't look so scary," Ernie commented.

"They aren't supposed to," Harley replied. "Imagers weren't built for battle. THOR units used to use them for reconnaissance. That's why they have camera lenses in their eyes. They're supposed to be able to record clear images from nearly a mile away."

"Who would send an Imager to Iver's?" Natalia wondered.

"Oh, there you are," Monti called, waving as the Griffins made their way toward him. "I was starting to think you weren't going to come." Monti's store was crowded with customers, and more were filing in. He had already borrowed three tables from the Coffee Rush next door, and there still weren't enough spots to place all the duelists.

"This is crazy," Ernie said as he watched kids streaming in and out of the store. Some were already wearing their Tesla Recoil Kinematic goggles, with their force feedback feature allowing a duelist to actually feel what was going on in the battle.

"I had no idea this many people would show up," Monti admitted. "But it's good for business, so I can't complain. Which reminds me. I ordered your Kinematics. They're behind the register."

"How much are they?" Harley asked, nervous about the price. He was certain that advanced MERLIN Tech wasn't going to come cheap.

"Consider yourself sponsored by the Spider's Web. Just make sure you send any business—" The Griffins raced through the front door before Monti could finish his sentence.

There was a paper bag on the counter with the words GREY GRIFFINS written in permanent marker. "Supersonic!" Ernie exclaimed as he pulled out his Kinematics. He ripped off his old goggles and threw them on the counter as he donned the new pair. "Hey, these don't work," he complained. "Everything looks normal."

"That's because you have to turn them on, genius," Harley said, flipping one of the switches on Ernie's frame. The goggles hummed quietly, but Ernie still couldn't see anything.

"What about now?" Harley asked, as he handed Ernie a Round Table card with an undead pirate on it.

As Ernie held the card to his goggles, the image melted away, leaving a pirate with rotting skin, exposed bone, and worms boring out of its eyes. The pirate raised its rusted cutlass menacingly. Ernie shrieked.

Throwing the card on the floor, he ripped the Kinematics off his head, ready to run out of the store. It wasn't until he saw everyone gawking at him that he realized it hadn't been real.

"Honestly," Natalia complained. "Could you be any more embarrassing?"

"It was only a hologram," Max explained. "Just like the SIM Chamber. It can't hurt you."

"That's easy for you to say," Ernie countered. "You weren't the one who almost got cut in half."

"Well, if it isn't the Loser Brigade," Angus McCutcheon said as he entered the store with a group of his friends. Max tried to walk away, but Angus grabbed him by the arm.

"I was talking to you."

"Let go," Max warned, looking back at Angus with cold eyes.

"Or what?" Angus chided.

"Maybe I'll turn into a werewolf and gobble you up."

Angus bared his teeth like a feral animal. "I don't think you get it, Sumner. My brother is dead because of your father."

Angus took a step forward. Harley tried to move between them, but Angus hauled back and swung. Max redirected the blow and Angus lost his balance. He crashed into a crock of apple cider, and the hot liquid spilled all over his face and arms.

"You're dead!" he shouted, launching at Max like a linebacker.

The two boys crashed into a display case of cards before tumbling to the ground. Max struck his head, and his mind swam as Angus overpowered him and pinned him to the ground. Max recovered enough to shift his weight, sliding his arms upward. Angus lost his leverage, and Max spun the boy onto his pudgy stomach, fighting to lock Angus's arm behind his back.

"I think that's enough," Logan called from the doorway. Monti was standing behind him, flabbergasted as he surveyed the damage.

Max let go and took a step back, allowing Angus to stagger to his feet. His face was bright red, and he rubbed at his sore arm.

"The show's over!" Logan shouted. "I want this place picked up, and I want it done now."

Everyone within earshot got to work.

"As to the four of you, you're done for the night."

"But…"

"Not a word, Thunderbolt."

Ernie grabbed his goggles off the floor and followed Logan out the door.

"I'm sorry," Max told Monti. "I'll pay for all the damage."

"I'm sure it's not as bad as it looks," Monti said. Then he walked over to the counter. "Don't forget these." He handed Max the bag with the rest of the Kinematics. "You're going to need to practice if you want to make the team."

Logan didn't say a word as he led the Griffins to his car. The stars were bright in the cold autumn sky, and the temperatures had dropped far enough that Max could see his breath every time he exhaled.

"Wait a minute..." Harley said as he was about to step into the car. "Is that Sprig?"

"Where?" Max asked, fearing the news was too good to be true.

Harley pointed to the top of a building across the street where a pair of glowing eyes looked back down on them.

"That's not a faerie," Ernie said. "It's a clockwork."

"Get into the car!" Logan commanded.

Ernie fumbled to open the door until Natalia pushed him out of the way to open it herself. But by the time they had all piled in, the clockwork was gone.

As they cruised through the town, Logan's grim look never lightened. Max wasn't sure what he did wrong. He didn't even throw a punch.

"Where are we going?" Max asked as Logan drove past Lake View Terrace Boulevard—the street where Max lived.

"Iron Bridge."

"Are you kidding me?" Ernie complained. "It's Friday night, and I haven't even spent my allowance yet."

"Another changeling has disappeared," Logan informed them.

"Who?" Ernie wanted to know.

"The girl who can phase through walls."

"Becca?" exclaimed Ernie in horror. "Becca Paulson?"

Logan nodded. "Her parents went to wake her up for school this morning, but her bed was empty. There wasn't a trace, just like the first one."

"I don't get it," Max said. "Why are we going to Iron Bridge?"

"Because it's just about the safest place in the world right now, and I don't want some maniac taking you, too."

ROSENKREUZ
LIBRARY

Understandably, Ernie's parents were upset when Logan informed them that their son needed to move to the dormitories for his own safety. Their natural reaction was to keep Ernie nearby so they could protect him. After Logan explained the dangers that were likely on their way, Dr. Tweeny and his wife relented.

Since it was only temporary, the other Griffins volunteered to stay at the school with him. The boys ended up sharing a large room with two sets of bunk beds. Logan took the room next door so he could keep track of them. Natalia ended up in one of the girls' dormitories, under Dean Nipkin's watchful eye.

When Saturday morning rolled around, all four of the Grey Griffins found themselves in the Rosenkreuz Library looking for information about Otto Von Strife and his clockwork program. Apart from some staff and the few boarding students who stayed at the academy, they were practically alone.

Outside the stained-glass windows, rain was pouring down. The cold October wind had turned the library into an icebox. If it weren't for the roaring fireplace, the Griffins may well have lost their noses to frostbite.

Laid out on the table before them were maps, old encyclopedias, school yearbooks, newspaper clippings, and a pile of books on clockworks, including *A History of Clockworks* by Benjamin Glendenning and *The Quandary of Artificial Intelligence, a Retrospective* by Joseph Boudrie.

"What do we know so far?" Max asked as Ernie thumped a pencil on the tabletop, distracted by his own thoughts. The only things on the sheet of paper in front of him were a few doodles. He couldn't concentrate.

Natalia thumbed through her *Book of Clues*, looking for her notes. "Otto Von Strife was a brilliant scientist from the Prussian Academy," she began. "He was married, but his wife died in childbirth."

Natalia paused. "It always makes me so sad to read that part."

"Keep reading," Max pressed.

"Let's see. Here we are. Von Strife started teaching Applied Magic and Technology at Iron Bridge in 1874 and, a few years later, was put in charge of a clockwork research program that lasted until 1910 or so. There's not much about him until 1914 when he is mentioned as joining a group known as the Foundation. Then, nothing."

"Isn't that about the time the old Iron Bridge was destroyed?" noted Harley.

"Wait a minute. Did you guys hear that?" Ernie asked.

"It was probably Natalia's ghost friend." Harley laughed.

"There it is again."

They fell silent. The faint sound of a gear being wound up played from across the library. Then they heard what sounded like the ticking of a clock, or rather, several clocks. Max slipped out of his chair and signaled for the others to follow. Together, they cut through the Interactive Paleontology shelves before tiptoeing through the Spectral Biology section.

Though it was dark, they could see four creatures, no more than knee high. Each was helping to set up a disk-shaped machine with a hollowed-out center wide enough to drive a small car through.

"I think it's a gateway," Harley whispered. "I saw one in my textbook. They're making a portal."

One of the creatures wandered into the firelight to

collect a few wires and a coupling device. "Oh my gosh, it's a robot!" Ernie exclaimed, as Harley clamped his hand over Ernie's mouth.

"Be quiet," Harley growled. "Those aren't robots. Can't you hear the gears cranking? They're clockworks, just like in the dining hall."

Max watched as the brass machines went about their work. Then he gasped as a new clockwork with eyes like binoculars appeared. "That's the Imager Bot from Iver's shop," he whispered.

Ernie shivered as he watched the metal creatures work diligently. "Do you think this is how they took Becca and Stephen?"

"Maybe we should go get some help," Natalia suggested.

"Uh…guys?" Ernie pointed to the ceiling. Countless telescopic eyes stared down at the Griffins. As one, the machines blinked before dropping to the ground like a swarm of locusts.

Breach

The clockworks raced toward the Griffins, toppling book-shelves along the way. Blasts from energy weapons lit up the library as Ernie took off in a blur of speed. He wanted to find a hiding spot, but they were scarce. Clockworks were everywhere. Natalia ducked as one of the machines flew overhead. Then she followed Max behind a book return bin. Harley, however, was alone.

He spotted the Imager Bot across the room. It scuttled up the wall and onto the ceiling before it crawled toward the records room. Harley watched as it dropped to the floor. Gears on its hand twisted and turned until all that was left was a key. A moment later it was inside.

A blast exploded near Harley's feet, and he dove behind a bookshelf. Books flew as bolts of energy struck. Natalia screamed, but Harley couldn't help. A clockwork burst around the corner, taking aim at point-blank range. Without thinking, Harley leaped, wrapping his arms around the machine. It fought to break free, but Harley's momentum helped him wrestle it to the ground. The clockwork fired energy bolts, but they missed Harley and ricocheted off the ceiling.

Harley loosened his grip and reached for his pocket-knife. One of the blades was actually a screwdriver. He opened it and went to work on the bolts that held the clockwork neck in place. The machine continued to struggle, but Harley was too strong. When the last bolt was loose, he dropped the knife and twisted on the head. It popped off, and the lights behind its eyes dimmed as the gears died.

"There you are," Agent Thunderbolt said as he skidded to a halt. He was out of breath and his face was drained of color. "We have to get out of here. Those things are everywhere!"

"Have you seen Max and Natalia?" Harley asked as he reached behind the machine's neck to rip out a fistful of coils.

"I thought they were with you," Ernie said, shaking his head. "What the heck are you doing?"

"There's a transponder in here," he explained. "Monti told me that it worked like a remote control. If I can find it, I think I can rig it so it will tell the other clockworks to shut down." Harley smiled as his fingers ran over the transponder. Then he pulled it out. "The only problem is that it won't have a strong enough signal to reach all the clockworks from here."

"So what are you going to do?"

Harley flipped some switches and turned a dial before handing the transponder to Ernie. "You're the superhero, not me."

"No way!" Ernie argued, trying to give the component back to Harley.

"Look," Harley said. "All you need to do is turn on the afterburners and get that thing close enough to the machines so they pick up the signal. You'll be moving so fast that they won't be able to touch you."

"You want me to run around and play tag with a bunch of robots that have death rays?"

"Either that, or we get obliterated."

Ernie rolled his eyes. At times like this he wondered whether Agent Thunderbolt should retire while he still had a head on his shoulders.

"Look, what did Iver say whenever you got nervous before a big Round Table duel?" Harley asked.

"To close my eyes, take a deep breath, and then go for it before the fear paralyzed me," Ernie said.

"Well?"

"Fine. I'll do it." Ernie grabbed the transponder, closed his eyes, and took a deep breath. Then he became

224

a streak of light, zipping back and forth through the army of clockworks. In mere seconds he had covered the entire breadth of the library. The machines buzzed in a mechanical fury, bursting blasts of energy in every direction.

"It's not working!" Ernie shouted.

"Just wait," Harley said, peering out from behind the bookshelf.

As soon as the words left his mouth, the eyes of the clockworks started to fade before shutting down. Then the machines dropped in a clatter.

Moments later, Max and Natalia emerged safely from the wreckage, surveying the damage in disbelief. The library was destroyed. Flaming papers, overturned shelves, and demolished furniture were strewn about. It looked as if a tornado had ripped through the room.

"What about that Imager Bot?" Max asked. "I don't see it anywhere."

Harley scanned the room. "It's gone."

Natalia walked over to a shattered filing cabinet. Folders were scattered across the floor, and when she saw the name VON STRIFE, her eyes lit up. She opened it and found a newspaper article inside with a headline that read CLOCKWORK CALAMITY.

"You aren't going to believe this," she said after scanning through the article. "Monti was wrong. Von Strife's clockwork program didn't get shut down because the machines had artificial intelligence. Von Strife was powering them with the souls of changelings."

"What?" Ernie exclaimed in horror.

"Von Strife created a contraption that sucked the souls out of changeling children and placed them inside his clockworks. That's how he was able to create intelligent machines that expressed human emotion."

"How did I know that the four of you would be involved in this catastrophe?" a dark voice spoke from across the library.

The Griffins turned as one to see Baron Lundgren standing among the fallen clockworks. Throckmorton, his gargoyle assistant, was standing at his side.

"We were just doing our homework, I swear," Ernie started, "and then these robots started building a portal, and—"

The Baron raised his hand to cut Ernie off. "If you could see that the gateway is dismantled and brought to the labs, that would be most helpful," he said to Throckmorton. "Also, the assembler bots can be disposed of, with the exception of one. Send that to Montifer for analysis, please. And alert Jonah Trimble as well."

Throckmorton nodded and set about the task.

"Well, then," Cain said, turning back to the Griffins. "What am I going to do with you?"

ANSWERS

Baron Lundgren led the Griffins down a lonely hall-way. They pushed past a series of double doors, passing quickly through De Payens Hall and into the Master's Hall. Before long they were deep inside the research and development center.

Choosing a doorway marked ARCHIVES, the Baron turned the knob and stepped inside. The room was typi-cal of the school, with warm wood flooring and cabinets, bookshelves stuffed with important-looking binders, and lamps powered by an ever-burning flame. He signaled for the Griffins to gather around a research table before unlocking a cabinet. The Baron pulled out a series of manila folders, each with a photo of a child attached to the top with a paper clip.

He handed Max a folder with a picture of a young boy on the cover. As Max grabbed it, a chill raced over him. He knew that face.

"It's not possible."

"You know this boy, don't you," the Baron said. It was a statement of fact.

Max nodded. "From a dream."

"His name was Johnny Geist, and he was a student at Iron Bridge before the school was destroyed."

"He was a paperboy," Max added slowly.

The Baron nodded. "In fact, he disappeared one morning while delivering his papers. No one ever saw him again. That was in 1897. There were rumors that Johnny had run away, but most suspected foul play. Unfortunately the authorities had no leads, and they were forced to close the case until a second boy, named Eugene Marks, vanished."

Natalia let out a muffled shout as she held one of the files up to the light. "This is Stacy Bechton! It's the girl who gave me the invitation to the party."

"Each of these files represents an unsolved case," the Baron confirmed. "And each student who went missing led to the mounting rumor that Iron Bridge was cursed. That is the reason why, when it was destroyed all those years ago, many felt it better to leave it in ashes."

Max glanced through more of the reports, and his

stomach started to churn. Each case had one fact in common — they were all changelings.

Cain continued. "It was only later that we found those disappearances were related to Von Strife's clockwork program and his fiendish desire to meld changeling souls with machines through the highly illegal practice known as Transference."

"Does this have anything to do with Brooke's abduction?" Natalia wanted to know.

"My daughter's disappearance has nothing to do with the matter at hand," Cain said with finality, but Max thought Natalia might be onto something. After all, Brooke had abilities, just like the other changelings. Maybe she was a changeling, too.

On second thought, Max decided that idea was ridiculous.

"Aidan told us about Von Strife's program," explained Max. "We saw him on the *Zephyr* a few days ago. He showed us a journal that he took from Dean Nipkin's office."

"Logan mentioned the encounter."

"Was Von Strife really trying to save his daughter's life?" Ernie asked.

"In part," the Baron admitted. "Sophia contracted leukemia when she was very young, and Von Strife was desperate to save her. In time, he concocted a serum that contained an unusually large dose of faerie essence. It worked, of course. But at the expense of her humanity.

As she grew older, and her changeling nature grew more wild, he grew desperate to find a way to save her. Nothing could stand in his way."

"So he began to experiment on other changelings," Natalia whispered.

"Sadly."

"I'm going to throw up," Ernie said.

THE COMPETITION

Before the Griffins left the archive chamber, the Baron made them swear that they wouldn't tell anyone about what they had seen or heard.

"You will only frighten the other students, and that may impact our ability to solve this mystery. You can talk to Logan or to me. That is all."

"Don't the changelings have a right to know if we're at risk?" countered Ernie.

"We are doing everything we can. Trust me, Agent Thunderbolt. It is for the best. If any of the changelings panicked and left Iron Bridge, they would be picked off, one by one, until none were left. No, you are safer here. And your friends are better off not knowing."

Max wasn't sure why the Toad brothers were so intent on creating a rivalry between him and Xander. It was annoying, to say the least. With the Round Table tournament looming, the entire school seemed to be buzzing about the potential showdown between Iron Bridge's top duelists.

"I don't see what the big deal is," Max complained as the Griffins stood together on the observation deck of the SIM Chamber. Below, Coach Wolfhelm was berating a group of students who had just failed their simulation test.

"People are excited. So what?" Harley said. "Everybody likes a good rivalry, so you'd better get used to it."

"But that's my point," Max said, exasperated. "Even if I make it to the final match —"

"Which you will," Harley interrupted.

"Then who cares if Xander beats me?" Max argued. "All I'm trying to do is make the team."

"I don't believe you for one minute, Grayson Maximillian Sumner," Natalia said. "I've seen the way you glare at Xander whenever he walks past you."

Max couldn't believe what he was hearing. "I do not!"

"I don't know, Max," Ernie said, piling on. "You seem kind of jealous of Xander sometimes."

Max opened his mouth to defend himself, but he shut

it again. No matter what he said, they wouldn't to believe him, so he decided to let it go.

Unfortunately, Coach Wolfhelm had other plans. "I need Max Sumner and Xander Swift in here, double time!" he shouted.

Max rolled his eyes as the room became quiet. This wasn't exactly a Round Table duel, but facing off inside the SIM Chamber was close enough. Nobody wanted to miss it.

Inside the active SIM Chamber, Max found himself standing next to Xander in a sewer. The rank water was nearly up to his chest. The stench and the thick layer of scum on the surface made Max want to vomit.

Coach Wolfhelm had sent them back more than a thousand years into the past. For this training scenario, the boys were to secure a set of knucklebones know as the Dice of Damascus. The Emir who owned the dice was said to be the first ruler to have built a clockwork army. The clockworks wouldn't be as sophisticated as Von Strife's designs, but they didn't need artificial intelligence to kill. They had dark magic.

"Just watch out for Imager Bots," Xander warned as he sloshed through the muck. "Coach Wolfhelm isn't above using modern technology to make sure we don't beat his game."

"That's cheating," Max complained, looking back over his shoulder for any sign of the spy bots.

Xander shrugged. "This isn't a history lesson. It's about survival."

The rules were clear. Xander and Max were supposed to work as a team, but they'd be graded separately. That was going to be tricky. Max wanted to stand out, but he couldn't try and score points at Xander's expense. Wolfhelm deducted for what he called "glory hounding."

"Wait a minute," Xander whispered as he came to a halt a little farther down the sewer. "I think there's something in here with us."

Max froze. "Did you see it?"

"I felt it hit my leg," Xander explained. "Could be a Sewer Serpent. The Emir used them like crocodiles in a moat. They're cheap labor—cheaper than clockworks."

Something bumped Max's leg as he grabbed the first rung of the ladder. As quickly as he could, he followed Xander up, just as the water below started to bubble. Max looked down, and a terrible face rose from the darkness.

The Sewer Serpent's eyes were covered in yellow cataracts, and its snakelike mouth was unhinged to reveal rotten teeth. As the monster lunged, Max let go of the ladder, barely avoiding fangs that were nearly as big as he was. He hit the murky water and sank to the stone floor below. His shoulder took the brunt of the impact.

Max gasped, and his lungs filled with sewage. Then his hand scraped against what he thought was a piece of driftwood. He grabbed it, planning to use the wood as a weapon. But when Max surfaced, he saw that he was holding a human femur.

"Watch out!" Xander shouted as the monster attacked again.

Max nearly tripped as he sidestepped the monster. Before he fell, he shoved the bone into the serpent's eye. Like a needle piercing burlap, the femur punctured the cataract, and the monster screamed.

As the serpent writhed in the fetid water, Max seized his chance to escape. He surfaced, dove for the ladder, and scrambled up it, thankful for the help as Xander pulled him through the opening.

Xander kicked the grate shut and locked it before pulling Max away from the opening and into the shadows next to a wood-burning oven.

"I'm impressed," he said as he handed Max a towel.

"Thanks," Max replied, smiling and panting for air. "I don't suppose you have anything to help wash this taste out of my mouth."

Xander watched Max turn a strange shade of green. "Don't tell me that you swallowed the water."

"Trust me, I didn't do it on purpose."

"Are you good enough to keep going?"

"Yeah," Max said, coughing as he stood up. "Let's just find what we came for and get out of here."

White Xander studied the map that Coach Wolfhelm had given them, Max smiled faintly. He was sure that wounding the Sewer Serpent would boost his score. Xander might be able to beat him at Round Table, but Max had plenty of experience in the SIM Chamber. There was no way he was going to lose—not even to Xander.

"The stairwell to the treasury is this way," Xander said.

Max followed him through the kitchen to a spiral staircase that was hidden behind a trick wall. After climbing nearly three hundred steps, they found themselves at a slit window. "Time to signal the cavalry," Xander said.

Max nodded and pulled a mirror out of his pack. With a series of rapid hand movements, he sent several pulses of light to the streets below. When he saw three quick bursts in return, Max knew the hidden Templar Knights were ready.

"Is it just me, or has this been too easy?" Xander asked.

"Speak for yourself," Max said. "I'm never going into a sewer again."

"We'll see."

The boys continued up the stairs until they came to a pair of double doors. Max peered through the crack and quickly pulled back. "Two guards, and they have scimitars."

"Clockworks or humans?"

"They look human to me."

With that, Xander pulled out a small crystal from his pocket and rubbed it between his hands. Max tried to get a closer look, but Xander pulled it away protectively. "It's called a Mesmero Crystal," he warned. "Trust me, you don't want to be the guy who looks at it. That is, unless you want me to carry you out of here on your back."

Max rolled his eyes. "How does it work?"

"Watch and learn." Xander smiled slyly.

He placed the crystal on the floor, just beneath the door, then gave it a push into the hall beyond. He held up his fingers and counted down, "Three...two...one..." Two heavy thuds followed, and Xander winked at Max before he pushed the door open. Both guards had fallen on their stomachs, their heads turned toward and their eyes locked onto the crystal.

"If we don't run into any surprises," Xander explained, "we should have about twenty minutes before they wake up."

Max stepped over the unconscious guards and followed Xander into the treasury. It was a round room with a forest of columns and soaring brick arches. Above it all was a metallic dome that acted as a canopy for a towering tree of pure gold. Its branches stretched all directions, filled with mechanical songbirds. Like the tree, the birds were made of gold, and Max could hear the faint tick of their gears. Clockworks.

"No time for sightseeing," Xander warned, pulling on Max's arm. "We need to find those dice."

Max's eyes widened as he looked at the mountains of treasure. It would take a hundred people a year to find anything in this room. As his eyes floated over casks of jewels and statues draped in gilded finery, he began to doubt that they could find the knucklebones.

Moving through the room, Max discovered four golden figures that looked almost human. They were dressed in robes and armor, each grasping a scimitar in perfectly articulated hands. Their empty sockets stared at a table just behind Max.

Max waved his hand in front of their faces, wondering if they were ancient clockworks. The statues didn't move. He pushed them. They teetered. He knocked on their chests. A hollow sound followed.

Turning, Max saw the table that the figures seemed so interested in. There were a number of gold plates, bowls, and pitchers, all filled with rare coins. In a small goblet, there was a faint green glow. The Dice of Damascus.

"I think I found them," Max called out.

"Wait for me," Xander warned as he made his way over.

Max wasn't interested in handing the dice over to Xander, but as soon as he touched the knucklebones, the eyes of the clockworks lit with fire.

"Get out of here!" Xander warned.

He rushed onto the scene, engaging the clockworks. Xander dodged a sweeping blow from a scimitar, then another. "Didn't you hear me?" he shouted. "I told you to go!" Somehow Xander seemed able to predict their every move. He would move just before a blow landed, each step purposeful as he sent the clockwork warriors into a spin, banging into one another in their attempt to skewer the boy.

Max watched as Xander pulled out a handful of marbles and threw them on the floor. Turning, he leaped for Max and pulled the Griffin to safety. The marbles ignited and then launched into the air like bullets. They hovered for a moment, then shot into the clockworks, punching holes through the metal. The clockworks didn't seem to notice until there was a massive explosion in each of their bellies. Their eyes dimmed, and they fell to the ground.

"Magnetic concussive grenades," Xander explained, as he rolled off Max. "I thought they might come in handy."

Max was about to say "thank you" when Xander's eyes shot wide. "Behind you!" Xander shouted. "Epsilon Class Djinn! A genie!"

Max spun to see a red cloud of mist swirl into the shape of a man. The Djinn had six massive arms, glowing eyes, and a pointed beard.

Suddenly, the only door slammed shut with a thunder-clap. The genie smashed through the treasure house as it raced toward them.

"Only one way out now!" Xander yelled. "Follow me!" He scrambled to his feet and dove out a nearby window. Max shouted in horror as he realized how high up they were. Xander would never survive the fall.

Then Max heard Xander's voice outside, calling for him.

Max made for the window, but as he jumped through, the genie roared. There was a flash, and a ray of light leaped from the genie's fingers and smashed into Max just as he cleared the window.

Max screamed as searing pain shot through his body. Everything seemed to warp around him, growing larger and stretched. His scream became a long croak and as Max began to fall, he caught sight of his body.

His arms and legs were short and stubby, and he had green skin that was slick with slime. Wings were sprouting from his back. He tried to flap them, but they were too small, and he too fat. Max sank like a sack of rocks toward the cobblestones below.

As he fell, Max imagined his guts splattered across the cobblestones. But he felt a jerk as a rope caught hold of his leg. With a yank, Xander hauled Max, now a Croaker Faerie, back to the ledge where he stood, clinging to the wall.

"You really smell awful," Xander complained, as guards with crossbows peered down from the windows above. "Time to move!"

Max wanted to respond, but he couldn't.

Xander leaped away from the wall as the first volley of crossbow bolts hammered the spot they had just left behind. Down they fell, Xander spreading his arms to slow the momentum. He somersaulted as they hit the first of several awnings. After they had plowed through the first two, the third broke their fall and they slid onto the street.

The impact sent Max sprawling, his squat legs unable to turn his body around. A woman shrieked as she saw him. Xander scooped Max up before leaping over a basket and disappearing down the alley.

The Emir's guards weren't far behind. They followed Xander as he veered down an alleyway and up a small flight of stairs. The chase sent him leaping between the roofs of several buildings as he dodged hanging laundry and shouting townsfolk.

He jumped back to the street, where a group of men in hooded cloaks waited. One caught Xander by the arm, but the boy relaxed when he saw the red Templar cross peek out from beneath his captor's robes.

"This way," the man ordered, pointing to a tunnel behind them. "We'll handle the Emir's guards."

Xander raced off as Max craned to see a horde of black-robed soldiers rush the Templar Knights. Xander ducked into a tunnel, and soon the sounds of the city streets faded.

Suddenly they were back in the SIM Chamber. As the door opened, Coach Wolfhelm walked in, with a crowd of students trailing behind. They howled in laughter as they pointed at Max. He was human again, but he was covered in a thick layer of slime.

Xander won, hands down.

RAVEN

Monday morning found the Griffins headed over to their Natural Sciences class. The room was crammed to the eaves with scientific instruments, overstuffed cabinets, and illustrations of dissected monsters. Stranger still were the glass jars filled with pickled faeries and other bizarre creatures.

"Check it out," Harley said, pointing to one of the jars. "I wonder if there are any Flying Tiger Eels or Portal Piranhas like that in Lake Avalon."

"Or those eyeball sucker things," Ernie declared.

"It's called an Optic Lamprey," Natalia corrected. She smoothed her dress, took a seat, and spoke in a hushed tone to the other three Griffins. "I think I might have a lead on the connection between Von Strife and the explosion that destroyed the old Iron Bridge. Her name is Raven Lugosi, and she's a changeling."

Ernie sighed warmly. "She's so beautiful." Realizing he had actually said that out loud, he blushed all the way to the tips of his ears.

The other Griffins looked at him curiously. Ernie had never made a comment like that about a girl before.

"From what I can gather," Natalia continued, after clearing her throat, "she can read the memories of any inanimate object, like candlesticks or picture frames. If that's true, she probably knows exactly what happened the night the school was destroyed and whether or not Von Strife was behind it."

"Why would she talk to you?" Max asked.

"I have a plan," Natalia replied, looking smug.

After the final bell, Natalia darted through the courtyard and down the Green Corridor, hoping to intercept Raven before she reached the subway. With her iridescent purple highlights, striped tights, and knee-high combat boots, Raven wasn't difficult to spot.

"Hi," Natalia offered, approaching her with a smile that was as genuine as she could manufacture.

Raven glared at Natalia. There were small gems underneath her eyes that looked a lot like colorful tears.

"I'm Natalia Romanov," she said, extending her hand like a door-to-door salesman. "It's so nice to finally meet you."

Raven raised her eyebrow.

"Sorry," Natalia offered. "I just haven't met too many people yet."

"Je le crois bien," Raven replied with a roll of her eyes.

"Oh, you're speaking French. I love French. It's so... *je ne sais quoi.*"

"What do you want?" Raven sighed as she switched to English. Her voice was husky and mysterious. She stepped onto the escalator, slinging her book bag over her shoulder.

"I'm just trying to be friendly, that's all," Natalia said, joining Raven. "You're French, then?"

"Quebecois."

"Oh. I've never been to Quebec, but—"

"Look, this may sound rude, but I fly solo, okay?" Raven said, clearly growing agitated. "I don't really need a sixth-grade sidekick, so why don't you go find somebody else to be your BFF."

Natalia bit her lip to suppress a scathing reply, but she forced herself to swallow it. "It's just that I... well, I don't seem to fit in around here. I saw you and..."

Raven rolled her eyes.

With the escalator ride about to end, Natalia decided to just jump right in. "So you're a changeling, right? Like my friend Ernie."

"The dork who thinks he's a superhero?"

Natalia stifled a laugh. "That's him."

Raven brushed her hair away from her face. As she did, Natalia noticed a small device peeking out from behind Raven's ear. It was flashing with the telltale silver aura of MERLIN Tech.

Raven caught Natalia staring, and she sighed. "It's an Inhibitor," she explained. "It keeps me from using my powers when I'm not supposed to. All the changelings have them — except your geeky friend. It's how they control us."

"That's inhumane," Natalia declared, horrified.

Raven shrugged. "It could be worse. They used to experiment on us like guinea pigs," she said, making a gesture that looked like she was cutting her own throat. "I could tell you some stories that would make your skin crawl."

"How do you know so much? The teachers don't talk about it."

"I can read memories," explained Raven, as the escalator neared the bottom. "Anything I touch, I can see whatever it has seen and hear whatever it has heard."

"Really? Anything?"

Raven's patience was thinning. She began walking down the escalator. "Anything that doesn't breathe. Trust me, I already know it's a stupid power, but it makes you think twice, you know? Especially when you realize that nothing you ever say or do will be forgotten by the chair you sit in or the bed you sleep in. Ever seen life from the perspective of a toilet?" Raven laughed as Natalia recoiled in disgust.

"I'd rather be invisible, or even fly," she continued. "Instead I can talk to my toothbrush." Raven stepped off the escalator and assumed a brisk pace that forced Natalia to jog in order to keep up.

"So does that mean you know how the first Iron Bridge was destroyed?"

"Sure, but you don't need powers to figure that out."

"What do you mean?"

Raven stopped and regarded Natalia suspiciously. "Look, what are you after?"

"Nothing, I just...I mean, this is my first year in a school like this, and it's kind of creepy. If you know something, I'd really appreciate it if you would tell me."

Raven looked at a nearby wall suspiciously, as if it might be eavesdropping. "All right, there was this changeling girl who used to go to Iron Bridge. Her name was Naomi. She was a fire elemental with amazing power. Then she disappeared.

"The history books claim nobody knows what happened, but I do. It was a teacher named Von Strife. He took her down to his lab and experimented on her. I can still hear her screams if I listen hard enough."

"What happened to the school?" Natalia asked as chills rose up her skin.

"Naomi happened," she replied. "One night, when

Von Strife was working on her, he lost control and her powers went into overdrive. The next thing you know, *ka-boom!* No more school." Raven stepped onto the subway, but not before looking back with an I-told-you-so smile as Natalia stood there, dumbstruck. "I bet you wish you never asked. Later, kid."

The doors closed and the *Zephyr* sped like a bullet into the tunnel.

LET THE GAMES BEGIN

The Griffins reported to the Grand Auditorium at six o'clock the next morning. As far as Max was concerned, that was too early for a Saturday—even if it was the opening day for the Round Table qualifying tournament. He had been up half the night, splitting his time between studying his issue of the *Toad Reports* on Yoshino Takamori and reading messages from Natalia on his DE Tablet.

Thanks to the information she had procured from Raven, they knew the name of the fire elemental whom Von Strife had successfully operated on, the same one Ms. Merical had mentioned. Naomi. Natalia had tried to find more information about her, but there wasn't much. That went for the other changelings that were abducted as well. The files Natalia found online were restricted, and she couldn't break the code.

"Good morning," Ms. Merical greeted Max as he entered the Apprentice's Hall. She was wearing an orange sweater with a giant jack-o'-lantern cross-stitched on the front. "Are you ready for the big day?"

"We'll see," he replied with a sigh.

"All duelists need to check in over there," she instructed, pointing to a long table in the hallway where Dr. Thistlebrow was seated. "Logan, you can join the rest of the audience in the Grand Auditorium."

Max hesitated.

"You'll be fine." Logan patted his shoulder. "Chin up and stay sharp." With that, the Scotsman made his way toward a gathering of other Templar security guards. To honor the return of Iron Bridge, important dignitaries, including some members of royalty, were expected to attend, so security measures had to be increased considerably. There were guards stationed at every door and gargoyle sentinels perched near the windows, and the entire campus was sealed off with a Class 6 MERLIN Tech Repulsor Field.

As Max walked over to the registration table, he spotted Catalina Mendez, the girl from his Bounder Care class with the lumpy imp. They were both sitting cross-legged on the floor, with Round Table cards spread out in front of them. Kenji Sato stood nearby with his drake. Rumor had it he'd been up seventy-two hours straight preparing for the duel. He looked terrible.

Ernie and Robert were tucked away in a corner with Tejan. Robert was showing them his new pair of Salvino Technohancers. The Kinematic goggles were an early birthday gift from his grandparents.

Erica walked by a few moments later, glaring at Max but saying nothing. A number of students shook Max's hand and patted him on the back, assuring him that he could win if he ended up having to duel against Xander. Max wasn't so sure. Besides, he had to win enough matches to even get a chance to play Xander.

As he stepped ahead in the line, Max could see Harley pacing outside in the snow. He was tweaking a pair of custom goggles that he had built with Monti's help. They looked like junk, but those Kinematics were more powerful than anything on the market—or so Monti had assured Harley.

Natalia sat on a bench next to the registration table, with a tower of notes at her side. Like Max, she had been up half the night, and now she was poring over her copy of the *Toad Reports* to keep everything fresh.

"Next, please," Dr. Archimedes called out, waving a thin finger in Max's direction. With surprising efficiency, the strange little man had checked out Max's battle deck, weighed and scanned his knucklebone dice, and tested the Kinematic goggles to make sure they hadn't been programmed with any cheat codes. Then he read Max the Pledge of Honor, which every duelist had to abide by. Max took the pledge, and he was promptly handed a thick rulebook and sent on his way.

"Hey, there you are!" Todd rushed over with his brother in tow. "We've been looking all over for you."

"How do you feel?" Ross asked, checking Max out like a mechanic eyeing a race car. "Did you get sleep? Do your exercises? Those are very important, you know. How about a well-balanced breakfast? You can't duel on an empty stomach. Here's a banana. Potassium is brain food. Also, try some honey in your tea."

Sensing Max's distraction, Todd stepped in front of him and placed his hands on Max's shoulders. "Look, whatever happens out there, don't forget the *Toad Reports*. Just stick with the game plan, and you'll take Yoshino out."

"Try some concentration techniques," Ross added. "Breathing in, breathing out. Find your center. You know, all that junk."

"If I last long enough, do you two think I have a chance to beat Xander?" Max wanted to know.

The Toad brothers shrugged. "Anything is possible," Todd admitted. "Xander is as close to a juggernaut as you can get."

"Right," Ross added. "He doesn't make mistakes, so you're going to have to play flawlessly."

"All right, I need everyone to listen up," Dr. Thistlebrow finally said. The Arithmetick professor was dressed in black pants, shiny buckled boots, and a green velveteen vest over a white shirt and black tie. "The tournament is set to begin in just a few minutes, but before we step onto the stage, I will offer this single warning. Each of you is expected to follow the rules of conduct to the letter. The slightest infraction will result in disqualification. Are there any questions?"

There were none, though there were several knowing smiles passed among some of the older players.

"Excellent. Now please follow me."

With that, the Arithmetick instructor led the duelists through a door that opened on the backstage of the Grand Auditorium. The stage had been set with thirty-two square tables that lined the floor like a checkerboard. Each had two chairs and a golden hourglass filled with white sand.

"Be ready when I call you," Dr. Thistlebrow warned.

ROUND ONE

Thistlebrow greeted the audience and bowed deeply. "It is my distinguished honor to welcome you to Iron Bridge Academy's first Round Table Qualifying Tournament in far too long!"

Applause cascaded across the auditorium, and it didn't die out until Archimedes finally raised his knobby hand. "We have lost so many years, but what you see today will astound you, I have no doubt."

He straightened his tie and smoothed his coat. "As we are playing by the King's Rules, a duelist will be declared the winner of a match after he or she is able to strike an opponent seven times. If neither combatant is able to score seven hits within an hour, then the player with the most points wins.

"As you know, the final eight duelists will be awarded a position on the varsity team and will represent Iron Bridge in the Pan-Templar Academy Championships," he continued. "And now, it is my great honor to introduce this year's impressive field."

As Max walked onto the stage, he found the auditorium lit with ornate chandeliers and draped in miles of velvet. There was a large brass scoreboard with countless pull switches and dials to track the duels. Each onlooker brought a pair of opera glasses that was linked wirelessly to portal lenses that hovered like dust mites above the stage. The tiny cameras switched angles so the audience could see what was going on at each game table.

"By the way," Natalia said before she took her seat. "I forgot to tell you that Brooke wanted to wish you luck."

Max tried to hide a smile. He wasn't sure whether his euphoria came from knowing that Brooke cared enough to send him a message — or just from a rush of adrenaline at his first official Round Table tournament.

He found his table, sat down, and started inspecting his deck before anyone could see the goofy grin on his face. A few seconds later, Yoshino walked over. He was tall, and his head was shaved clean. Someone had painted a tribal tattoo on the right side of Yoshino's face. It was supposed to make him look intimidating, and as far as Max was concerned, it had worked.

"Good luck," Max said, offering his hand, but Yoshino ignored him. Instead, he took out his own cards and placed a set of bloodred knucklebones on the table. He pulled out his chair, sat down, and leaned back.

"Get ready—" Dr. Thistlebrow announced.

The bell rang and the hourglasses turned. Max pulled his Kinematic goggles over his eyes and flipped them on. The table suddenly transformed into a life-size three-dimensional field of battle. Thanks to the MERLIN Tech, he was standing in rolling grassland under a blue sky. Yoshino stood across the field from him, sneering. Like the SIM Chamber, the Kinematic goggles made imagination a reality.

Since Yoshino won the initial roll, he went first. Without hesitation, he took a card from his hand and threw it onto the battlefield. An Inferno Imp leaped from the face of the card, burning with fury. It raced toward Max, and the grass burned beneath its feet.

It was a bold move, but thanks to the *Toad Reports*, Max was ready. Yoshino cast his knucklebones, but it was a low roll. His imp inadvertently activated the trap that Max had set. A horde of Frost Spiders poured onto the field of battle, and as Max cast his own knucklebones, the tiny monsters swarmed over the Inferno Imp. The fiery faerie exploded in a blaze of light.

Yoshino stared at Max in disbelief.

The rest of the duel went much the same way. In the end, Max won 7–2. Yoshino had been a contender to make the varsity team, but thanks to Max, he didn't even make it out of the first round.

"You cheated," he accused.

"No, I just did my homework," Max replied with a smile as he rose from his chair to stretch. He'd expected a harder game than that. Not only was it a relief, it also filled him with assurance that the next few rounds might be easy. Taking a drink of water, he could feel his heart racing in excitement. He smiled again, envisioning what it would be like if... check that, *when* he faced Xander.

Max looked at the scoreboard as he walked off the stage. Natalia had won by a landslide, and Harley just managed to squeak by. Since Smoke hadn't bothered to show up, Ernie had won by forfeit. That meant all the Grey Griffins had made it to the next round.

"Nice work," Todd offered. Then he handed Max an envelope. Max broke the seal and pulled out his new copy of the *Toad Reports*. Then he groaned.

"What's wrong?" Ernie asked in between bites of a chocolate bar.

Max showed him the report. He was going to have to duel Robert Hernandez. Beating Robert would bring as much satisfaction as kicking a helpless puppy.

"Cheer up," Todd noted. "Hernandez stinks. He was lucky to make it to the second round." He handed the other Griffins their *Toad Reports*.

"You have to be kidding," Ernie said, as he stared at

the name of his next opponent. "Isn't Kenji Sato the kid with the drake?"

"Yep. And if you win, you'd better hope that drake of his doesn't come over and rip your tongue out. He's been known to do that."

Ernie's face turned a pale green, and the chocolate bar fell from his mouth.

ROUND TWO

After the first round, thirty-two duelists remained. A team of workers quickly removed half of the tables from the stage and the curtains rose once again.

Max was about to walk to his table, but he stopped when he saw Ernie and Robert huddled together. They were flipping through a copy of the *Toad Reports* that had the words MAX SUMNER written across the cover.

"No matter what happens, don't fall for that one," Ernie said, pointing to the report. "He gets me with that stupid trap all the time."

"Ernie!" Max shouted.

Ernie blushed and pulled his Kinematic goggles down. Then he rushed past Max and onto the stage. "Sorry," he called back. "Robert had a couple questions, that's all. I would have helped you, too, if you had asked."

"Gee, thanks." Max watched Robert fold the report and stuff it into his back pocket. He avoided eye contact as they walked to the table.

When the duel began, Max and Robert found themselves atop an iceberg in the midst of an endless sea. Using the Kinematic programming function built into the Tesla goggles, Robert made himself look like a knight in heavy armor. With a shout, he sent a wave of creatures crashing against Max's defenses.

For someone so timid, Robert was not only aggressive, but he was unpredictable. That was a dangerous combination. Before Max realized what had happened, his Frost Spider had been squashed under a meteor, and his Snowy Gryphon was knocked out of the game by a chupacabra. Robert had an early lead, and he wasn't letting up.

The battlefield was turned into a smoky ruin, as Robert's archers sent a wave of flaming arrows through the mist. Max rolled his knucklebones to defend his yeti from the attack, but he fumbled. Robert scored again.

Feeling confident before the match, Max hadn't bothered to open the issue of the *Toad Reports* on Robert. There didn't seem to be much of a point. Unfortunately, Max was starting to regret that decision.

A sudden cheer rang out across the hall. Max flipped up his goggles to watch Ernie raise his fists in victory. "Yes!" he shouted, before turning to the crowd and bowing.

Max spotted Xander on the sidelines. He was watching Max's game closely, and Max couldn't help but feel sick from embarrassment. He was losing to a rookie. The Toad brothers were right; Max couldn't be lucky all the time.

Well, at least one of us is going to make it to the next round, Max thought. He turned back to his mounting disaster, sliding the goggles back over his eyes. He was running out of chances, and Max knew he'd have to make a gamble. He took a card from his hand and slipped into his defensive line, holding his breath. It was Robert's turn now.

Robert unleashed a devilish beast from his offensive line. A nine-headed hydra rose above the water, casting a long shadow over Max. Each of the monster's heads was capable of a separate attack. Max only had three cards left — not even enough to slow the monster down.

Robert picked up the dice and rolled, the hydra attacking Max's latest card with a roar.

Max sat back as a thrill crept over him. All at once, the hydra was swallowed up by a sheet of ice, unable to move. Robert jumped up, unsure of what had just happened.

It was Max's turn to go on the offensive. Catapults rolled out, unleashing boulders that slammed into the frozen monster. A moment later, it had shattered like a stained-glass window.

With his prized card defeated, Robert lost his confidence. Max took advantage of the confusion, and before long he took the lead. Moments later, he won the duel.

How to Trump
a War Machine

"Look lively now," Archimedes Thistlebrow announced as he ushered the final sixteen duelists onto the stage. With Harley and Natalia losing in the last round, that meant the only Griffins left were Max and Ernie. The contestants were all greeted with applause, but when Xander Swift walked out, the crowd erupted.

Max scanned the audience, hoping to see Grandma Caliburn, but he couldn't find her. He saw Robert, though. The changeling was wearing an Agent Thunderbolt sweatshirt that Ernie had given him. It even had a lightning bolt stitched across the chest. Then Max spotted Todd and Ross. The Toad brothers were sitting in the back of the balcony. Todd wrote vigorously in his notebook as Ross exchanged slips of paper with a crowd of students that was hovering around them.

"Duelists, please take your seats," Dr. Thistlebrow announced. "Round three will begin in precisely ten seconds."

Catalina Mendez sat down at the table across from Max. It was the first time he had seen her without her Bounder imp, Scuttlebutt, and Max realized then just how attractive she was. Catalina's hair was pulled up with a few loose curls hanging down her neck. She smiled, and suddenly Max felt uncomfortable. He looked away as his neck flushed bright red.

"You may begin," Dr. Thistlebrow instructed after a steam-powered clock whistled.

As his Kinematic goggles flared to life, Max watched Catalina send a snorting minotaur to probe his defenses. According to the *Toad Reports*, Catalina was an aggressive player, but she had barely survived the previous round. She was certain to be more cautious this time around, which made her a dangerous opponent.

Just as Catalina was about to cast her knucklebones, a blinding flash filled the auditorium. The floor rumbled as Aidan Thorne materialized on the stage, flanked by two enormous clockworks.

"What's he doing here?" Max heard Ernie call out.

The audience gasped. War machines were outlawed decades ago, but here two Grimbots stood before them.

Covered in armored plating, the clockworks towered over the duelists, the barrels of their guns sweeping the auditorium.

"I'm baaaaack! Did you miss me?" Smoke challenged, his voice carrying through the hall. He seemed oddly at ease as he paced the silent stage. "Oh, come on now. Are you telling me that nobody here noticed I was missing?"

No one said a word.

"Oh wait, that's right," Smoke continued. "I'm one of those changeling freaks that you pretend doesn't exist!" Then he reached behind his ear and tore out the inhibitor like an unwanted earring. Blood ran down his neck as he tossed the device to the floor and stepped on it. "It's not like it worked anyway," he scoffed, looking directly at Dean Nipkin.

He moved to the center of the stage. "I bring you a message from Otto Von Strife."

A murmur moved like a wave through the audience.

"That's right, he's back, too! He has some unfinished business at Iron Bridge."

"You're in way over your head, Smoke," Xander warned, as he rose from his chair.

In a burst of black smoke, Aidan disappeared from the stage, and then reappeared just as suddenly holding Erica Harkness by the arm. He pushed her toward one of the Grimbots. As Xander moved to help her, Smoke waved a warning finger in the air.

"I wouldn't try to do anything heroic," he said. "These

machines are kind of sensitive, and I'm afraid they might rip Erica's arms out of her sockets if you startle them."

Xander locked eyes with Smoke. Then he sat down.

Max searched the balcony, looking for Logan. But he couldn't see him anywhere.

Smoke casually removed his backpack and pulled out an elegantly crafted brass egg about the size of a football. "This is a little present from Von Strife. Sorry I didn't wrap it, but I figured you wouldn't mind.

"Now if you haven't seen one of these before, you're in for a real treat." With a heave, Smoke smashed the egg against the floor, releasing a swarm of clockworks that filled the air like hornets. Then he disappeared.

The winged machines spread like a pestilence across the auditorium. At first there seemed to be only a hundred or so, but there soon were a thousand. And the swarm continued to grow.

"They are duplicating by scavenging every metal object in their path!" warned a teacher as he swung a chair at a cloud of brass insects.

There was a scream.

"They've got stingers full of poison," a student shouted as everyone rushed for the exits with the swarm on their heels.

"We've got to buy them time to get out of here!" Max shouted. He had ignited his Skyfire, and none of the mechanical insects seemed interested in approaching.

Glancing up, Max could see that Wangai, Ms. Butama's

Bounder spriggan, had transformed into a fiery phoenix and was burning a path through the hornets. Those that didn't melt were eaten.

At the same time, Kenji's drake took flight, mounting an aerial counterattack. Its armored hide was too thick for the hornet stingers, and it tore into them with fury, leaving a rain of scrap metal in its wake.

The hornets quickly rebuilt themselves and took to the air again as the crowd pressed against the exits in a screaming mass. One after another, people collapsed from the poisonous stings. Picking up an axe, Xander rushed to the radiators. With several blows, he cracked open the pipes, releasing great clouds of steam into the air. The mist rolled over the auditorium, providing cover for those trying to escape.

Robert, unsure of which exit to take, had been knocked to the ground by the crush of humanity. He considered resuming his flight, until he heard the buzzing of the clockwork swarm overhead. Rethinking his plan, he dove under a nearby table in hopes that the swarm would move on.

A moment later, a hand reached down to help Robert to his feet. He took it, but he was shocked to find Smoke on the other end.

"Fancy meeting you here, Hernandez," Smoke said with a smile, keeping Robert's hand locked in his grasp.

"You're the one who took Stephen and Becca, aren't you?"

"Guilty." Smoke nodded. "Now, if you don't mind, there's someone who's really looking forward to meeting you."

"Get away from Robert!" Max called as he raced toward Smoke.

Robert lunged for a nearby chair in desperation and started to transmute. His skin turned to metal and his feet became one with the stone floor. Under normal circumstances, he would have been immovable, but Smoke didn't play by the rules. As Max dove at the boys, there was a flash of black smoke. They were gone, taking the chair and part of the floor with them.

The Grimbots suddenly opened fire with their energy cannons. Explosions rumbled through the room and chunks of plaster and chandeliers fell from the ceiling as the roof threatened to fall on everyone.

Angus McCutcheon jumped onto the stage, picked up a table, and smashed it against the back of one of the machines. The wood shattered harmlessly against its metal exoskeleton. The clockwork turned, its red eyes flashing at the boy, before it aimed its cannon at Angus's face.

"No!" Max yelled.

As the Grimbot fired, Xander appeared, plowing into Angus like a locomotive. Both boys hit the stage just as the spot where Angus had been standing was blown into a cloud of debris. In a split second, Xander had rolled to his feet. "Max, your Skyfire!"

Max nodded and opened up on the Grimbot, enshrouding the machine in crackly blue energy. It only managed to slow the Grimbot down, but it gave Xander and Angus enough time to get away safely.

The Grimbot turned on Max, who had no place to go. Luckily, Max had powerful friends. Even as the metal monster approached, Throckmorton appeared, tackling the clockwork. The stone gargoyle battled the machine as the combatants tore into each other with relentless fury, destroying everything around them in their struggle.

Max spotted Natalia and Ernie hiding behind one of the overturned tables. "Go find Grandma and get her out of here!"

Natalia nodded. She ducked away, as one of the stinger drones dove at her from above. She smashed it with Ernie's helmet and then disappeared into the crowd with Ernie close behind.

Max watched the second Grimbot jump off the stage to engage THOR agents that had rushed into the room. The machine raced down the main aisle of the auditorium, barreling through the crowd as one of the agents fired what looked like a harpoon gun. A magnetic projectile raced across the expanse before sticking to the clockwork's chest. Waves of electricity pulsed over the Grimbot's metallic hide, paralyzing it. Then, like a felled tree, it crashed to the ground, where a second agent took a sledgehammer to the Grimbot's head, tearing it from its shoulders.

"One down!" the agent shouted. He was immediately attacked by the swarm of clockwork hornets and lost from view.

"Look out!" Max heard Logan cry.

He spun around in time to see the first Grimbot looming over him.

Then stone hands reached up from behind. With a powerful twist, a battered Throckmorton wrenched the clockwork's head from its shoulders, and the lifeless machine crashed to the floor.

Suddenly the room was filled with a brilliant light. All at once the clockwork hornets froze in midair, sparked like firecrackers, and then fell to the ground in a shower of tiny lifeless bits.

Max raised his eyes to find Baron Lundgren looking at him. He was standing in the midst of the inanimate metal insects. Silver bolts crackled at the end of his cane.

"Where is Robert?" the Baron asked, his voice taut with concern.

"Gone," Max said. "Smoke got him."

"God help us all..."

DECISIONS

When the Griffins entered Cain's office, they found it in a shambles. Books and papers littered the floor. Slashed oil paintings hung askew, chairs were knocked over, and the drawers of the desk stood open. Standing near the Baron were several teachers, along with Logan.

"What happened here?" Max asked, as he walked up to his bodyguard.

"Before he showed up, Smoke teleported here to Cain's office, ransacked it, and let loose a few Grimbots. That's why we were a little late getting to the auditorium." Logan patted Max on the shoulder. "Sorry about that, Grasshopper."

"Is Brooke okay?"

"She's fine," Cain said. "As for Aidan, we have a team hunting for him now."

"Did you send Dr. Thistlebrow?" Ms. Merical asked. Her face was still flushed from the skirmish.

"Of course," Baron Lundgren responded. "Nobody can track a teleporter like Archimedes. He will find Aidan and Robert, I'm certain. I only hope he can intercept them before they reach Von Strife." Cain turned to Logan. "What is the latest on the anti-venom serum?"

"Doc Trimble is making good progress. No deaths so far."

Max shivered at the thought of how close his grandmother had come to being stung. She didn't seem particularly unsettled by the incident, but she also didn't argue when Logan asked if she'd like to be driven home.

"How did Smoke get in here?"

"I made the mistake of bringing Aidan to my office to discuss what happened in the Ward Forest. Unfortunately, it appears that's exactly what he wanted. Afterward, he was able to teleport inside."

"What was he after?" Natalia asked.

"This," the Baron said, pulling out a familiar leather-bound book before setting it on the desk. "Fortunately, I kept it with me today, rather than leaving it in my office."

"Lord Saxon's diary?" Max said, as he looked at the book that Logan had secured from a tomb in Iceland the year before.

"Exactly," Cain answered. "Saxon had a reputation as an eccentric, but he also had a knack for recovering rare antiquities that nobody else in the world could find."

"The man was insane," Dean Nipkin interjected.

"Perhaps, but that is hardly pertinent at the moment," Cain said. "He was, however, one of the most intelligent minds that this world or any other has known."

"Didn't Lord Saxon find the Seal of Solomon?" Natalia asked, referring to a legendary ring that could imprison dark spirits.

"We believe so," Cain replied. "But the Templar relied on Lord Saxon to do more than simply find important artifacts. He hid them so that they would never end up in the wrong hands. This diary contains his coded maps to those artifacts."

"So what was Von Strife after?" Nipkin asked.

"If I'm not mistaken, Otto was looking for a map that would lead him to something called the Brimstone Key."

The Griffins looked at one another.

"Yes," Cain continued. "The same Brimstone Key that you read about in the underground bunker."

"Why would he need a key?" asked Natalia.

"To retrieve his daughter from the Shadowlands," the Baron replied in a matter-of-fact tone.

"As in the home of Oberon? The Shadow King?" exclaimed Ernie. "You have got to be kidding me."

"It was an accident. Von Strife's experiments with

transferring souls into clockworks were very promising. Feeling that time was of the essence, he brought Sophia, his daughter, into the lab for the ultimate test of his brilliance. He succeeded in removing her soul from her body. Unfortunately, the clockwork malfunctioned, leaving the soul no place to go. When that happened, the homeless soul, being part faerie, was pulled into the Shadowlands. She has been there ever since."

"Why not give him the key so he can find his daughter?" Natalia asked.

Dean Nipkin looked horrified. "If you open the gate, you cannot be certain of closing it again...at least not before Oberon breaks through. What is waiting on the other side is, I assure you, far worse than Von Strife or any nightmare you've ever conceived. The gate must remain closed."

Cain nodded. "Von Strife's mania for rescuing his daughter would put the world at risk. Already he has reinitiated his clockwork army—which, like before, he no doubt plans to use when he marches into the Shadowlands to reclaim Sophia's soul. And, judging from the abductions of Stephen and Becca, and now Robert, we have to assume his experiments on changelings have resumed."

Max felt a chill run up his arms.

"Why would he take an army to go get his daughter?" Natalia pressed.

Cain smiled faintly. "You don't think Oberon would just allow someone to walk into his kingdom and take one of his faerie souls, do you?"

"Where is the key, then?" Ms. Merical asked. "Far from here, I hope."

"It was given to Lord Saxon's care, and if we are lucky, it remains hidden," Cain replied. "However, we need to consider the Bishop. His database of knowledge is vast, and I fear he may be the one other person who knows where the Brimstone Key is hidden."

"Then we need to reach the Bishop before Von Strife does," Logan remarked. "I'll put together a team to head to Scotland first thing in the morning."

"Yes," replied Cain, sounding tired. "But if you fail to reach him in time, we must consider alternatives. Lord Saxon's diary has the exact details of where the Brimstone Key can be found. We must use it to locate the key before Von Strife does."

Logan shook his head. "I've seen the page in the journal that you are talking about—the section on the Brimstone Key. It's encrypted. And from what I've heard, Saxon's code can't be broken except by Saxon himself. And he's dead, trust me."

"I concur. However, he never worked alone."

Dean Nipkin shook her head. "Most of Alaric Saxon's students have been hunted down and murdered over the years. What about Percival Pickering? The poor man was over a hundred years old and had dementia. He couldn't read any of those codes if his life depended on it, but only last week he was fished out of the Hudson with a block of cement chained around his neck. Anyone involved with Saxon's diary was cursed. Thankfully, there is no one left."

"That's not entirely true."

"Please tell me you aren't thinking of Obadiah Strange!" The dean was aghast.

"There is no longer an alternative."

PART THREE

BRIMSTONE

A DANGEROUS PATH

Obadiah Strange was an enigma. Having graduated from Stirling with honors, he went on to become a revered member of the natural science and alchemical community. Yet it was his burning ambition that earned the attention of Lord Alaric Saxon. After a chance meeting, the two forged an alliance—or at least as close as two men of their selfish nature could manage. Saxon became the teacher; Strange, his scheming apprentice.

The two never seemed to agree, yet despite their differences, their accomplishments were legendary. There were more articles written about these two daring men than almost anyone in recent history. However, at the height of their prestige and celebrity, Strange resigned his position and retreated to the Himalayas, vowing to never return. That was nearly seventy years ago, and true to his word, Strange had not been seen since.

"It would be best if Throckmorton led the expedition," Cain had explained. "It must be a small group. No soldiers. No one that would alarm Strange. Max and Agent Thunderbolt will go as well."

Ernie had argued against the idea. For one, he and the gargoyle didn't get along. For another thing, he was afraid of heights. The Baron was resolute, however. Apparently he believed that Ernie was actually the most important member of the team, though he refused to elaborate.

"Just be yourselves," the Baron had instructed. "And, with luck, Obadiah may consider our plight."

They traveled most of the way by portal, and soon the three of them stood on a mountainside as strong winds blew swirling clouds of snow into the sky. As a creature of living stone, Throckmorton was immune to the weather. Max and Ernie were a completely different story, though. Despite their identical white parkas, wool underwear, shell pants, and all the other layers that were making it hard for them to walk, the cold seemed to find a way inside. Both boys were also equipped with Rarified Air Respiratory Systems. They wore masks over their faces, with tubes that led to an oxygen chamber. Without these regulators, the lack of oxygen would kill them in a matter of minutes.

Throckmorton cut a path through the deep snow as he trudged ahead. Yet even with the aid of their trekking poles to help lift them out of the snow, Max and Ernie struggled. They traveled for hours before the gargoyle decided to take refuge under a massive overhang littered with icicles. It was time for the boys to eat. Throckmorton broke out a kerosene stove and boiled some snow in a pot. It wasn't long before he had a stew with dried vegetables and meats boiling. Max and Ernie gladly accepted a bowl and sipped the warm broth, though they had to replace their regulators after every bite.

"Eat slowly," the gargoyle warned. "Your body is still adjusting to the altitude, and your digestive tract may struggle."

Ernie didn't bother listening as he downed a second bowl, two chocolate bars, a bag of trail mix, and a stick of beef jerky. A few moments later, he clutched his stomach. "I'm going to vomit into my regulator," he groaned.

The gargoyle melted more snow for drinking water. After the boys had their fill, it was time to ascend the face of the overhang. The climb was well over fifty feet from top to bottom, and Ernie was in no hurry to make it.

"I don't get it," he said. "Me and Max are just kids. We don't even shave yet. So how come Cain sent us up here? If I was in charge, I would have sent a bunch of THOR agents."

"Strange needs to see the faces of those who could

perish if he remains on the sidelines," Throckmorton said evenly.

With that, the gargoyle tethered himself to a rope and sunk his claws into the wall, scaling the icy surface like a spider. Along the way, he pounded metal spikes into the compacted snow so that Max and Ernie had something to grasp as they climbed.

"You go first," Max said after he helped tether the lead rope through carabineers on Ernie's harness. Then he checked Ernie's boot spikes. Losing traction would be dangerous. If the rope failed to hold, it could be deadly.

Ernie grabbed hold of the lead rope before sinking the spikes into the wall. Hand over hand, he pulled himself up, checking frequently to make sure the safety rope never broke free. Though he was relatively safe, the climb was still terrifying. Each step was slow and the wind threatened to tear him from the wall with each gust.

When he was about halfway up, a great rumble shook the mountainside. Ernie looked up to see a wall of ice and snow rolling toward him. With a cry, he flattened himself against the wall and closed his eyes, hoping he wouldn't be torn away. The roar was tremendous, but thankfully it passed.

When Ernie dared to open his eyes, he found Throckmorton standing at the top with snow clinging to his shoulders. Then Ernie looked down and saw that Max had survived the avalanche as well.

"Come," the gargoyle said after Max scaled the wall.

"Daylight is fading, and we don't want to be caught out in the open once the sun goes down. The temperatures will freeze the blood in your veins."

Without another word, he led them through deep snow as daylight gave way to dusk. The terrain was a monotonous blur of white. Max actually thought he was hallucinating when he caught sight of a series of stone pillars that lined the horizon.

"Do you see that?" he asked through the regulator.

"Yeah," Ernie replied. "What are they?"

"Monuments to mark those who have fallen," Throckmorton explained.

"This is a graveyard?" Ernie asked, as he imagined zombies wreathed in ice rising up from the snow.

"Yes," the gargoyle responded. "But you needn't fear, for the dead slumber in peace."

The team continued until they came to the lip of a deep chasm that cut through a river of ice. As Max looked over the edge, he couldn't see the bottom. On they trekked over a vast wasteland of ice and rock, taking few breaks. Then, with his fingers frozen and his nose feeling like a block of ice, Max found himself standing before two tattered flags that snapped in the mountain air.

"Welcome to the lair of Obadiah Strange," Throckmorton called out over the howling wind.

THE BISHOP

"I don't get it," Harley said as Logan drove through the rain-slicked roads of Edinburgh. "If we're in such a hurry to find the Bishop, then why didn't we just take a portal?"

"Too risky," the Scotsman replied. "Your friend Aidan can track our signatures."

"Smoke *isn't* my friend."

"Either way, portals are his territory. The sky is mine, so we flew."

"Wouldn't a phone call have been easier?" asked Natalia.

Logan sighed as he pulled the car into Mason's Close.

"You don't *call* the Bishop. He monitors every airwave, every wire, and just about every thought. He knows what we need already. If he wanted to tell us, he'd have already told us."

"So why bother coming in the first place?" she pressed.

"To give him another chance," Logan replied tersely.

There were stories that the Bishop had once been human. Somewhere along the way, thanks to MERLIN Technology and dark sorcery, he'd managed to stretch his powers and his life across the centuries, at the expense of his humanity. He was now more monster than man, living in a shadowy world. The Bishop was like a spider, consuming when hungry and stealing body parts when his own limbs or organs began to wear out. He smelled bad. He looked even worse. Were it not for the fact that he seemed to know almost everything, even before it happened, he'd probably have been left alone to die. But knowledge is power. As long as the Bishop had it, kings and presidents would give him whatever he demanded in return for a secret or two. And it was no secret that the Bishop made them pay dearly.

"He won't try to eat us, will he?" Natalia remembered Max's warning.

Logan shook his head. "He doesn't eat kids. Usually." Logan smiled when Natalia squirmed. "Anyway, you aren't coming in. Stay in the car and keep the doors locked—this place isn't safe. The vehicle is protected by the best security technology in the world. So unless a troll turns up, you should be able to sit back and watch a movie while I do the talking."

"Where are we?" she asked.

"Mason's Close," Logan replied. The words sounded like a curse as they left his mouth.

"I mean, is it hidden from civilians, like New Victoria? Or is it just a part of Edinburgh?" Natalia asked.

"It's a cesspool filled with thieves and murderers, so mind yourself and keep your window rolled up," Logan said.

"Why can't you just give me a straight answer?"

Logan sighed. "No. The close is not hidden from civilians, but that doesn't mean the degenerates who call it home are all from this world."

"If we're going to be stuck in the car watching television, why did you even bring us?" Harley wanted to know. "I can handle myself."

"There's no doubt about it," Logan replied. "But you're here as my insurance policy, so I expect you to follow orders and stay put."

Harley crossed his arms in frustration as Logan parked the car next to a curb, opened the door, and disappeared into a nearby warehouse.

"What does that mean?" Natalia asked. "Insurance for what?"

Harley shook his head as he flipped on the television. "I don't want to know."

Natalia slid away from the door as a dark figure stumbled up to peer through the mirrored window as if he could see right through. He paused and then reached a shaky hand toward the door handle. There was a blue flash outside the car, and the figure staggered backward in confusion. He scratched his head, looking up and down the street as if he suddenly didn't know where he was. Mumbling to himself, he wandered away.

Logan had been gone more than twenty minutes, and even though Natalia decided to take notes in her *Book of Clues*, Harley was starting to get into the movie. Then the car's engine shut off, and the television died.

"That can't be good," Natalia said, as she looked out the window.

Harley slid over the front seat and tried to turn the backup generator on. It refused to come to life.

"The streetlights are out, too," Natalia noted. "The whole grid must be down."

"The only thing I can think of that could do that is an EMP."

"A what?" Natalia asked.

"An Electromagnetic Pulse," Harley explained. "The military uses it to shut down power prior to an attack. Anything with an electrical circuit is fried."

Natalia glanced down at her digital watch and sighed. "You might be right. My watch stopped."

"But why would anybody use an EMP here?" Harley mused. Yet even as he did, he saw the door to the nearby building explode outward. Logan jumped through, hitting the ground in a roll. His leather jacket was smoking. His face was dark with soot, and his fists were bleeding at the knuckles. With a grunt, Logan leaped over the hood of the car and slid across the hood before jumping inside. He pushed the keys into the ignition and turned.

"It's dead," Natalia warned. "Harley thinks we've been EMPed."

The engine engaged immediately, but it didn't sound right. Then Logan put it in gear and slammed his foot on the gas. The tires squealed as they raced the alley. The dashboard dials had changed. No longer reading miles per hour or how much gas was in the tank, the display was measuring spectral joules. Logan had switched the car from conventional power to MERLIN Tech!

"Seat belts on!" Logan ordered. "We've got company. That EMP was mine, but it won't keep them down for long."

"Keep who down?" Natalia shouted over the roar of the engine.

"The clockworks," Logan responded.

As the words left his mouth, the biggest clockwork they'd ever seen blasted its way through the building Logan had left. The brick structure collapsed in a storm of dust and stone. The machine was even bigger than the Grimbots. It was constructed of brass and iron, and a cloud of steam poured out from its engines. The clockwork had a tiny head that was perched on top of a chest that looked like an oversized potbelly stove. It tore down telephone poles and tossed Dumpsters with its four arms, as it raced after their car.

"What about the Bishop?" Harley asked.

"Gone," Logan replied. "Kidnapped. Or dead. That *thing* and a few of its friends were waiting for us."

"Where are the other machines?"

"Out of commission."

"What is it?" Natalia wanted to know.

"Class Six Nemesis Clockwork," Logan replied, swinging to the side as a Dumpster crashed down to the left of the car.

"How do you know it's a Class Six?"

"If it had been anything less," Logan replied, as he slid around a corner, "the EMP would have finished it off."

The Nemesis rounded the same corner, picking up an abandoned pickup truck along the way and hurling it at their car. Logan hit the brakes and the truck flew harmlessly overhead.

"We won't last in this maze," the Scotsman muttered, as he hit the accelerator and turned down another alley.

The Nemesis smashed through the corner of a building, but the steel and bricks didn't slow it down. Natalia gasped. Logan was barreling toward a dead end. At the last minute he hit the brakes. "Everybody out!" he ordered as a cloud of smoke rose from the tires.

Logan pushed the Griffins into a nearby building before racing back to the car and extracting a suitcase from the trunk. Popping it open, he pulled out what Harley recognized as one of Monti's Plasma Launchers. Logan loaded a glowing-blue canister into its breach and knelt on one knee. Shouldering the Plasma Launcher, he flipped down the targeting reticle and took aim at the approaching Nemesis.

He squeezed the trigger, and the missile shot out of the barrel in a blaze of blue fire, striking the Nemesis in the chest. It reeled backward from the impact, but there was no explosion. As Harley looked on, he could see a slimy gel splattered across the machine, which had frozen mid-stride. There was a creaking sound, like a windmill teetering in the wind, and then it crashed to the ground.

"Back inside!" Logan shouted. "Class Six clockworks have a nasty habit of getting back up."

Sure enough, the three of them watched as the motor inside the Nemesis started to rev up. Then the lights behind its eyes flickered on. It was repairing itself.

"We don't have long. Just stay close, and whatever you do, keep running."

With that, Logan burst into the building, and the Griffins followed close behind. Moments later, the machine was fully operational. It plunged into the building, chasing its targets like a wrecking ball with feet.

OBADIAH STRANGE

Max couldn't believe that such an immense structure could have been built in the middle of nowhere. It looked like a cross between a Tibetan temple and a Victorian mansion. High walls led to even higher gables. There were towering turrets with stained glass, balconies of polished iron, and so many lit windows that it almost seemed like a constellation of stars looking back at them.

The three travelers approached the frosty stairs that led to the front door.

"Strange is the lord of this house, and under his roof, my ability to protect you will be diminished," the gargoyle warned. "Do not speak unless spoken to."

The gargoyle pulled a tasseled cord, and a great gong rang out. A few moments later, the door swung open, revealing a large creature with orange skin who was dressed in servant's attire. It might have been a man, apart from the cloven hooves and horse-like head. The creature's eye sockets were filled with a warm yellow glow that flickered whenever he blinked, and Max thought he could hear a whirring sound.

"I am the servant of his Holiness, the Magnificent and Singular Obadiah Strange. My master is waiting for you in the parlor."

The three travelers were ushered down a long hallway, over thick rugs and parquet flooring, past a gallery of artwork, and finally into the parlor. Leather couches were set to face one another, and a writing desk sat in the corner with an open book and quill at hand. There were several bookshelves that lined the outer walls, and tall windows with honeycombed leaded glass that peeked out from the balcony above. The room had no lights other than the roaring fireplace that consumed nearly a third of the back wall. In front of it stood a dark figure with his back to the newcomers. He was bald and broad-shouldered, and he was wearing green silk robes.

"Throckmorton, a colleague of Baron Lundgren," announced the servant, who then backed out of the parlor, leaving them alone with the master of the house.

"*Baron* Lundgren?" spoke a smooth but commanding voice. "Is that the name he uses these days? Ah, well, times change. Which, of course, brings us to the point of your visit."

Strange turned to his guests and said nothing for several long moments. He had a bronze face and a dark beard peppered with grey, and his eyes were hidden behind large spectacles.

"Von Strife is back," the gargoyle finally announced.

"Is he?" Obadiah responded. "Well, it was bound to happen, wasn't it? The Templar should have killed him when they had a chance. The man is a lunatic."

"Some say the same of you," Throckmorton replied.

"Do they, now?" Obadiah paused thoughtfully with a wry smile. "Curious. I suppose it's a matter of taste. Still, what do these two children have to do with Von Strife? Are you hoping I'll babysit them while you deal with Otto?" Strange paused as his eyes came to rest on Ernie. His expression changed to concern. "This is a changeling!"

Ernie shifted uncomfortably in his seat, feeling rather naked. He hadn't realized his condition had been so obvious.

The gargoyle nodded. "The other is the current Guardian of the *Codex*."

"Now, there's a bit of news I didn't expect," Obadiah said, raising an eyebrow as his gaze shifted to Max. "I don't suppose you've brought the precious *Codex* with you?"

Max turned to Throckmorton for direction, but the gargoyle didn't answer.

"I didn't ask the talking rock; I asked you," Strange

said, his eyes never leaving Max. "So tell me, do you have it?"

"Yes, sir. It's right here," Max replied, raising his hand to show Strange the ring.

Strange started to reach for the *Codex*, but he stopped when Max recoiled. "That certainly is a powerful weapon for someone so young. How is it that you ended up with it?"

"I found it in my grandma's attic."

Obadiah laughed deeply. "Next you'll tell me that you found the Brimstone Key under the cushions of a sofa."

"You know about the Brimstone Key?" Ernie asked.

Throckmorton reached into his jacket and pulled our Lord Saxon's diary before setting it on a table near Strange. "The Brimstone Key is precisely why we've come," the gargoyle said.

Obadiah's spectacles seemed to flicker for a moment as he regarded the book, but he didn't touch it.

Throckmorton continued. "As you know, Obadiah, Lord Saxon knew where the key was placed, and he put the coordinates in this diary."

"And you can't read it," Strange offered curtly.

"But you can?"

"Perhaps," Strange returned enigmatically. "Though I'm curious, what would you do with the key if you found it?"

"Destroy it," the gargoyle said flatly.

Strange seemed amused at the notion. "I'm not sure

you've thought this through. The Brimstone Key can't be destroyed."

"There may be other options," Throckmorton returned. "Yet without your assistance, there are none."

"Lord Saxon was not a simple man," Obadiah replied, as he paced near the fire. "If he wanted something kept a secret, then a secret it would remain. You're free to leave the diary with me, though. If I find time, I may look it over."

"How do we know you'll give it back to us?" asked Max.

Obadiah's face opened in a wide smile, revealing a mouthful of wooden teeth. "My dear boy. You *don't*. But I'm the only hope you have left."

A Dragon Returns

"Get down!" Logan shouted as the railing of a falling staircase shot through the air where Natalia's head had been only a split second before. The three had been moving from shop to shop, and apartment to apartment. The clockwork was relentless.

The Griffins followed Logan over the roofline of a tenement before leaping over a skylight. They took cover behind a nest of chimneys. Logan signaled for them to stay quiet. He scanned the skies for his support team.

"Wait," Harley whispered. "I think it stopped moving…"

Logan signaled for everyone to stay still. He peered over the ledge where the street was choked with debris.

"It doesn't seem like the type of machine that would give up," noted Natalia.

Logan nodded. "Whoever built that thing definitely thought of a few upgrades since the last time I faced a Class Six. It's running on more than simple gears, that's for sure."

"Do you think it was Von Strife?" Harley prompted.

"If it was…" Logan began, and then he heard a familiar pinging sound just beneath his feet. It was followed by a humming roar of an engine whirring to life. Then the roof collapsed under their feet and the whirling of a thousand gears came to life. The clockwork's four hands ripped apart the building as it sliced through the falling debris.

Harley saw a black helicopter hovering overhead. There was a rippling sound, as if the sky were being pushed aside. Then there was a flash from the gun deck. The clockwork shrieked as it was wrenched apart by an unseen force. All that was left was a pile of gears, armor, and twitching fingers. The machine was being eaten away by a strange red liquid.

"Is that a Templar helicopter?" asked Harley.

"No," Logan said gruffly.

The helicopter landed on the roof. Natalia's mouth fell open as a slim female dressed in black stepped through the door. Her black hair was pulled back into a ponytail, with a silver lock hanging in the front.

"I thought you could use some help," Athena yelled over the roar of the blades.

Logan offered a curt nod. Then Athena saw Natalia, and their eyes locked. Natalia was afraid that if she spoke, Athena would disappear.

"I'm sorry about what happened," Athena called out. "Someday, I'll explain."

Natalia was angry, sad, and relieved all at the same time. She had once thought of Athena as an older sister, but sisters didn't betray one another.

"Two more Nemesis Six models are on their way," Athena said. "You have five minutes, tops."

Logan nodded.

"I'll move to intercept, but I can't guarantee that I'll be able to stop them." Then her eyes returned to Natalia. "Will you wish me luck?"

Natalia's voice caught in her throat.

Athena nodded sadly, and then disappeared back into the craft. It rose above the buildings before vanishing over the skyline.

HOPELESS

Back at Iron Bridge, everything was in a state of chaos. The students were terrified—especially the changelings. Each feared he or she might be next to disappear in a flash of black smoke. There had been discussions to suspend school indefinitely, but in the end, Cain decided that it was better to keep the students close so he could better protect them. Besides, Iron Bridge was as safe a place as any given the increased security measures—including the influx of gargoyle sentries standing guard on the rooftops.

Three days after their return, Max and Ernie were summoned to the Baron's office. When he arrived, Cain was sitting at his desk across from Obadiah Strange. No longer in his green robes, Strange was dressed in a charcoal suit, with a top hat resting on his knee.

"I believe the two of you have met," the Baron opened.

Max nodded as Strange reached into his trouser pocket to pull out a pipe and a bag of scented tobacco. Immediately the room smelled of peppermints, and as Strange lit his pipe, Max couldn't help but think of Iver.

"It seems that you impressed Obadiah," Cain said. "So much so, that he has reconsidered our request for his assistance."

Strange pointed his pipe stem toward Max. "You're William Caliburn's grandson."

"You knew my grandpa?"

Strange nodded and chewed thoughtfully on the tip of his pipe. "I did, though he may not have known me. I wasn't really myself at the time we crossed paths, but he saved my life in a manner of speaking. I owe him a debt. No doubt Lundgren knew that when he sent you." His eyes flicked over to the Baron, then back to Max. "Now where is your father, boy?"

Max shrugged. "Dead, I think."

"Missing," Cain corrected. "Lord Sumner, as you no doubt know, was last seen at the battlefield of the World Tree. If it weren't for Max, things would have turned out much differently."

"So I've been told," Strange replied. He took a long

pull from his pipe before turning to Cain. "You know, a gentleman would offer me a sarsaparilla."

"I'll see what I can do," Cain replied as someone knocked on the door. It opened, and Natalia slipped in, with Harley on her heels.

Obadiah walked over to a worktable where several maps were spread out next to Saxon's diary. "Now then, I've made progress, but we have one puzzle left to solve. The true brilliance of Saxon's work is that he never followed a distinct pattern with his ciphers. No two puzzles were ever alike," he said, as he opened the diary. He paused for a few moments over the pages, like a painter examining the works of his master and weighing his own worth.

"As you know, the entire book is written in code," he continued. "Some I understood, most I didn't. In order to appreciate Saxon, you needed to be a master of languages, symbols, mathematics, and even a little backwater sorcery. Unfortunately, every time I solved one of the codes, it unlocked a dozen more. Each of them had a different encryption and new key to work from."

"But?" the Baron prompted.

Strange pulled out a piece of parchment from his breast pocket. He unfolded the paper and spread it across the table to reveal a jumbled mess of codes. "It all comes down to this."

"What is it?" Natalia asked, drawing a frown from Strange before he responded.

"Each puzzle was a part of a larger set of directions," he said, pointing to a tangle of symbols, drawings, and meandering lines. "Much like the pieces of an engine that are linked together, each one is dependent on the other. Discovering how they fit together is the real mystery. This parchment is the key... the final cipher."

"We enlisted Montifer's Babbage Difference Engines yesterday, but he hasn't had any luck," Cain added.

Natalia pulled out her Phantasmoscope and pored over the parchment. "So if we can't solve this last step, is it game over?"

Strange chewed on the tip of his pipe. "Not necessarily. I already know where to find the Brimstone Key. We're missing information to show us how to unlock the impenetrable safe where the key is kept. That's what this parchment is for."

Cain and Obadiah discussed the implications of Von Strife finding the key first. The Bishop might know where to find the key, but opening the safe would be a different game. As they explored these possibilities, Natalia continued to study the parchment, walking from one end of the table to the other, then circling it from time to time.

After a few minutes, Natalia turned to Strange. "Is this the only copy of the parchment?"

Strange shook his head. "The original is in Montifer's lab. Why do you ask?"

"Good, then you won't mind if I try something out."

With that, she began folding the parchment at one

corner, then bending it backward and folding it in another direction. She continued the process, sometimes undoing what she had done before and starting in a new direction. All the while she softly hummed a tune. Then, after folding the last corner and tucking it beneath a slat, she set the parchment back on the desk.

"There," she said triumphantly.

No longer a flat sheet of paper, the parchment looked like two triangles overlapping each other. The first pointed down, the second up, and where they intersected sat a small star. Codes that previously made no sense were suddenly aligned, and as Strange looked it over, his eyes grew wide.

"How did you do that?" Ernie asked her.

"I got the idea from Dr. Thistlebrow. Remember when he made that dove out of paper? You know, the one he set on fire? Well, that was just origami, and so was this."

"Unbelievable," Strange announced, picking up the folded parchment to hold it to the light. "Now all I'll need is a quiet room and a pot of black coffee. If I don't run into any more snags, we'll know how to unlock the Brimstone Key by morning."

After Strange left the room, everyone but Max was dismissed.

"I am afraid that I have some bad news," the Baron began as he leaned on his cane. "Archimedes has returned."

"Did he find Smoke?"

"Yes," Cain replied. "Along with Stephen, Becca, and Robert. There were others that Archimedes could not identify. Apparently Von Strife is keeping them all in an underground laboratory somewhere in Eastern Europe. I'll spare you the details, as they are rather ghastly. However, it would appear that Von Strife has picked up right where he left off."

THE *GRAF ZEPPELIN*

It was agreed that the Baron would remain at Iron Bridge, along with his contingent of gargoyles, to protect the remaining students. At the same time, an expeditionary force would be setting off to secure the Brimstone Key before it fell into the hands of Otto Von Strife.

It was not supposed to be a dangerous mission. Simply a race there and back again. For that reason, Monti and his airship were required. The ship was fast and could land anywhere, and she traveled through portals like a porpoise through the surf. Obadiah would act as navigator and mission leader. Logan was the muscle, and the Griffins were to go along as well. However, Cain maintained that if there was the slightest indication of danger, Logan was to turn the ship around and call in reinforcements.

Never one to miss an opportunity for trying out his inventions, Monti had outfitted everyone with his latest gadgetry. There were sub-zero weather gloves with remote controls for a host of devices that included jump boots, cameras in their goggles, wireless earpieces, holograph projectors, and a special language translator that allowed them to speak in at least thirty different languages, including some faerie dialects and Clockwork Binary v.4. The gadgets were nothing compared to the vehicle that would be taking them on their journey.

"I've never seen anything like this!" Harley exclaimed, as the Griffins approached a colossal airship that hovered above its mooring like a silver cloud. Similar to a blimp, it was streamlined like a bullet and was the length of nearly three football fields from nose to tail. What looked like two pectoral fins extended down from the front third of the airship, upon which were affixed sleek turbines. They rumbled and strained against the mooring ropes, with more wings and additional engines lining the body before giving way to four red tail fins where the Templar symbol was emblazoned.

Diminutive figures were dotted across the vessel, hanging from ropes, polishing walls, wiping the windows, checking the turbines, and measuring the fuel mixture.

"That's the flight crew," Logan explained. "Gnomes."

306

Max headed up the boarding ramp and glanced over-head, feeling like a fly beneath the belly of a whale.

Natalia marveled at the airship, pushing back her amber goggles to restrain her wind-tossed hair. Then she saw the name of the ship painted on its flank: *Graf Zeppelin*.

"I read about this airship in our history book!" Natalia exclaimed. "They said it was destroyed. Where did you find it, Monti?"

The Templar engineer offered a melancholy sigh. "In a rundown off-dimension port where she was left to rot. Can you believe that? I can't even tell you how bad she looked, but I recognized her immediately. And thank-fully I did...they were about to sell her for parts!"

"You restored this whole thing?" asked Harley, amazed.

Monti shrugged. "Restored, modified, enhanced...a few tweaks here and there with the MERLIN engines, and now she's a fine lady. She can even pull three hundred miles an hour with the static discharge engines online."

"What's the deal with all the gnomes?" Ernie asked as one passed by on its way up the gangplank, several life vests in its lanky arms.

"The previous owner converted the *Graf* to handle inter-dimensional flight, and somewhere along the way the airship acquired a crew of gnomes. They're tied to her by a faerie contract and they pretty much do most of the work. Trust me, I'd rather have gnomes than acid-belching basilisks. I got off lucky if you ask me."

The Griffins entered the airship through wide double doors that led into a foyer of cherry wood paneling and tall mirrors.

"So, I've been wanting to ask..." Natalia caught Obadiah Strange's arm as he walked past. "You were Lord Saxon's apprentice, right?"

He stopped and narrowed his eyes. "I *was*."

"I think I might have been a pretty good apprentice for someone like that. I mean, I solved the puzzle last night, didn't I? Admittedly, I am only in sixth grade, but I've got potential, right?"

Obadiah looked at her as one might stare at a two-headed baboon with fleas. He said nothing and then continued on his way, leaving Natalia standing there dumbstruck. She didn't know if she wanted to cry or call him a jerk.

Then there was a lurch, and the ship rose up into the air.

A STRANGE BREW

"Our destination is the city of Durban," Obadiah Strange explained later that evening as the *Graf Zeppelin* passed through a veil of silver-lined clouds. "Like Iron Bridge, Durban resides in the Land of Mist, which separates the human world from the Shadowlands. Several dimensions overlap within its borders, allowing it to act as a trade and commerce center for hundreds of kingdoms. Because of its economic importance, it is considered completely neutral and nobody—not even the Black Wolves—would dare move against Durban."

"Why haven't I ever heard of it?" Natalia asked.

"There are no roads that lead there. No sea charts

describing it. And there are no satellites capable of spying on it," Strange said, sounding slightly agitated. "What was Iverson teaching you?"

"We didn't talk much about geography," Natalia shot back.

Strange shook his head. "Its location is known only by those who need to know, and clearly *you* don't need to know."

Natalia rolled her eyes.

Strange continued. "Once we land, we must be careful. If Saxon's agreement with the Durban dwarves is still binding, they should allow us to conduct our business."

"What was it like to work for Lord Saxon?" Ernie asked.

"Difficult," Strange replied. "He was a towering personality, notoriously impatient and prone to dangerous bouts of rage, particularly when it came to opposing views on his theories. When I first met him in the summer of 1857, I wanted nothing to do with him."

"*1857*? You're that old?" Natalia exclaimed.

Strange smiled as he adjusted his glasses. "I'm much older than that, thanks to my changeling blood."

As if struck by a jolt of electricity, Ernie's eyes grew wide. "Did you just say that you were a *changeling*?"

"We're not as rare as you think, Ernie Tweeny."

"Why didn't you tell us that before?" Natalia pressed.

"You didn't ask."

"So what's *your* changeling power?" asked Ernie. A wide smile was stretched across his cheeks.

"I'm indestructible."

"What?" exclaimed Natalia. "You can't be hurt at all?"

Strange snorted. "Of course I can be *hurt*. I just can't be *destroyed*. There's a difference."

"What if a building fell on your head?" asked Ernie.

"It can happen," Strange replied with indifference. "A piano. A building. It's all the same. I can't die."

"What if something eats you?"

Obadiah shook his head. "Whatever it is will have severe indigestion, I can assure you."

"But..." began Ernie after a moment of reflection. "Don't we change into faeries if we use our power too much? I mean, this kid told me that there aren't any changeling adults."

"It's not about your age," Obadiah replied. "It's about preventing the faerie blood from taking over. If you can do that, then you can be a changeling forever. If that's what you want."

"You've found a way to suppress the change?" Natalia exclaimed, a smile of hope spreading across her face as she placed her hand on Ernie's shoulder.

"Would I be here if I hadn't?"

"Would it work for Ernie?"

Strange placed his hand inside his green robes and pulled out a packet, which he unbound. A wad of dark, loamy substance rolled onto his palm. It might have been dirt, or perhaps coffee grounds. Either way, it smelled like a cross between roadkill and rotten eggs. Natalia, her eyes watering, had to stumble away to avoid gagging.

"This is it," Strange explained, pushing the substance around on his palm. "A pinch of this once every few weeks is all I need. Keep in mind, it's not a cure. It only freezes the changing process."

"What is it?" Ernie asked, standing a few steps away from the pungent substance.

"Dragon dung," the hermit replied offhandedly. "Or more particularly, dung from the nest of the Sabine Cave Drake. Very difficult to acquire, as you might imagine, Sabines being what they are."

"So what do you do with it?"

Strange pulled an elegant cup from the nearby tea service and deposited a wad of dung inside. Next, he placed the cup on a saucer next to him, took the teapot in hand, and filled the cup with steaming water. "You take it as tea."

Strange drank down the liquid, smiling broadly afterward, exposing two grainy black bits on his teeth. "I have studied you, Ernest. Your changeling physiology is very similar to my own. Probably a strain of Holfessen-Streigsin faerie blood, I'd guess. It's a powerful, but relatively stable, form of transformation that responds well to this treatment."

312

Ernie glanced at the teacup skeptically. "If I drink that, I can use my powers all I want?"

"There is only one way to know for sure."

"How does he know it's safe?" Natalia argued. "What if it makes it worse, not better?"

"Your concern is noted, Miss Romanov. However, this conversation is between two changelings. Until you understand what it is like to be one of us, you don't have any right to force your opinion on him." He looked over at Ernie. "Are you ready?" Ernie glanced at a glowering Natalia, then back at the steaming teacup.

"Maybe just one sip."

Strange nodded as he prepared the concoction. Ernie took the cup into his shaking hands and, plugging his nose, swallowed the liquid in a single gulp. Natalia watched in horror as Ernie shuddered. Then he froze, his unblinking eyes locked on the bottom of the cup. He wasn't breathing.

"Ernie, are you okay?" she cried. "Speak to me!"

He blinked suddenly and looked back at Natalia. "I could really use a breath mint."

TRAINING

Ernie and Natalia turned in early, leaving Max on the ship's bridge. Monti was settled into his captain's chair, surveying the stars through the window. Across the room, Harley flipped quietly through a book of shipping charts. He spent most of his free time with Monti, trying to learn everything he could about the wonders of MERLIN Tech.

"I just wish I knew what I was supposed to do," Max confessed.

Monti looked over at him. "That would take all the fun out of life, if you ask me."

"Perhaps," came the voice of Obadiah Strange as he

entered the bridge. He looked over at Max. "If you could ask any question and be assured of an answer, what would it be?"

Max studied Obadiah. "Are you saying that you have the answers?"

"Answers are easy. Forming the right question is the difficult part."

Max looked over at Harley, wondering if this was just a game. Harley shrugged.

"I guess I'd start with the *Codex*. How can I use it if I don't really know what it is? Is it a weapon? Is it a book? Since the Baron showed me how it could change into the gauntlet and channel my Skyfire, I've barely looked at it in book form. But I know there's a whole world inside its pages."

"Fascinating," Obadiah commented. "Keep going."

"Everyone calls me the Guardian of the *Codex*, but I don't know what that means or what I am supposed to do. I know I can release creatures from the pages of the book. Sometimes I can capture things and put them inside. But what's the point? Am I just some sort of zookeeper for monsters?"

"So you've used your Captivity Orbs?" Strange inquired. "I'm impressed. That takes tremendous concentration."

Max shrugged. "I sort of figured it out when a monster climbed in my window one morning. Too bad it doesn't work against clockworks."

"At the moment, that may seem true. But you are young yet. If I recall, Guardians aren't usually given the *Codex* until they are at least sixteen years old. You're barely twelve."

"That's what the Baron keeps telling me. But if I don't learn how to use it soon, I may not live until my sixteenth birthday."

"He's got a good point." Monti laughed nervously.

Obadiah nodded. "Well, let's see if I can help. I'm certainly not an expert, but Lord Saxon was particularly interested in the book. He had me look into it quite extensively.

"The first thing you need to know is that the *Codex* is a part of you. It's not a separate thing, like an umbrella or a sword. Once you touched it, you became fused to it, like two bodies sharing the same soul. The bright side is that the *Codex* can respond to your every thought in an instant. On the other hand, if you are separated from it for any lengthy period of time, you will die. Not in a week. Perhaps not in a month, but you will most certainly wither and die."

"That's a real pick-me-up," Harley noted sarcastically.

Obadiah shrugged. "You take the good with the bad. That's life."

"What is the *Codex*?" Max pressed.

"In scientific terms, it is a Von-Welling Type Seven Singularity...sort of a bridge between two worlds. Only in this case, it bridges the Guardian and several worlds. How many? We don't know. It could easily be dozens. One of which, however, is the Shadowlands. The others act as pocket dimensions for your so-called zoo."

Finally, Max thought, he was getting some answers.

Strange continued. "Originally, the *Codex* was connected to a crystal known as the Jewel of Titania, which increased the book's power a thousandfold. But you already know all about that. So now the Jewel is gone, and it's just you and the *Codex*."

"What can it do?"

Obadiah smirked. "*Do?* Almost anything you can imagine, but it takes time to get the hang of it. Just about the time you think you've got the knack, you'll be too old to use it and will have to hand it down to the next Guardian. That's the way these things usually work. Anyway, why don't we give it a try."

"Right now?"

"Do you have something better to do?"

Max looked down at his ring. He was used to transforming it into the gauntlet. It required a little more effort to change it into a book. As he focused, the ring slowly melted away from his finger and pooled into the palm of his hand, quickly building itself up and out until, in a few moments, he was holding an enormous leather-bound book. He quickly spoke the familiar words of opening. The lock sprung back and the pages unfurled.

"All right," began Obadiah. "The lesson for today is

your empathetic link to the *Codex*. That is, how it can respond to your emotions. You have already sensed it. If I guess correctly, Skyfire works more effectively when you are angry or frightened, correct?"

Max nodded.

"It's the same way with the *Codex*. Now, I want you to open to a page. Not just any page, though. I want you to open to the page you need right at this moment."

"I don't *need* anything."

"Let the *Codex* make that decision. Just let your feelings guide you, and the page you need will appear."

Max paused. "Do I close my eyes and meditate or something?"

Obadiah snorted. "This is science, not some hocus-pocus shenanigans."

Max took in a deep breath and focused on moving the page in front of him. He stared. He glared. He squinted. He even managed to give himself a headache. The book didn't move.

"You're thinking, not feeling! Shut your mind off."

Max focused, trying to feel the page in his mind. He imagined the texture of the paper on his cheek...the smell of the leather...the taste of the ink. Then he tried to imagine *being* the page and falling open. After a few minutes, his mind began to wander, and instead of thinking about his training, all he could think about was being back home, before his parents had divorced, and eating strawberries on the porch with his family. It was one of his favorite memories. Then his mind drifted again, and he feared he might fall asleep on his feet. He opened his eyes.

"Congratulations!" Harley nudged him.

"What?" Max rubbed his eyes and looked down. The pages had indeed turned, without his even knowing it.

"You're a quick study," Obadiah admitted.

Max studied the page. There was a painting of a lush green field of strawberries under a warm sun. He scratched his head, smiled, and looked up at Strange. "Well, I guess I was kind of hungry," he admitted.

Obadiah shook his head. "Those aren't ordinary strawberries. They are a species of *fragaria somnus*, otherwise known as Sleeping Berries. The *Codex* is telling you that you are working too hard. You need to get some sleep."

Max yawned despite himself.

"I think you've learned enough for one night. We have three more days before we reach Durban. Let's try again tomorrow."

"Aren't you going to have Max release the berries from the *Codex*?" asked Harley. "They look pretty good."

Obadiah shook his head. "Unless you want to sleep until next spring, I suggest you try some warm milk instead."

DURBAN

Max trained with Obadiah the next few mornings and was making good progress. Of course, foisting a basket of Sleeping Berries on a horde of clockworks didn't sound particularly heroic, but if he trusted the book, Obadiah assured him that things would turn out all right.

There were other times, moments of quiet as they sailed through the clouds, that Max spent alone. He would walk down the observation decks and stare out the windows, deep in thought. At night, his mind would often return to Sprig, and what she must have gone through. He didn't know what to hope for. Max just knew he wanted her to be happy. If she ever returned to him, he'd promise to take better care of her.

"What the heck is that?" Harley exclaimed as the *Graf Zeppelin* swung over a city that sprawled like a maze on the surface of the Durban Sea. The bridges and white stone towers made it look like it had been constructed from the bones of a dead giant. Every inch of the island was covered by a road or building. There wasn't a single natural rock formation, tree, or even a patch of grass.

"Durban is an island entirely manufactured by dwarves," Strange explained. "With nearly unlimited energy and resources, and a free market economy, there is nothing they can't build or design. The dwarves ensure Durban's neutrality. They have never engaged in war, finding it a waste of time and resources. However, they certainly don't mind benefiting from it by selling weapons of destruction to the highest bidder."

"I just radioed in," Monti announced, as he joined them on the observation deck. "We have clearance to land, but we're supposed to keep our stay short. No more than six hours."

Logan checked his chronometer. "Should be enough."

"How is this place still a secret after so many years?" asked Natalia.

Obadiah smiled and motioned toward his pocket, where Saxon's diary lay. "MERLIN Tech keeps it cloaked under an intricate illusion. It's backed up with a Class

Nine Mesmero Field, which confuses anyone who gets close. Even if someone stumbled on it by chance, they would never understand what they saw. What's more, they would quickly forget."

Max felt a bump. Outside the window, he saw that the *Graf Zeppelin* was being lowered with ropes to the ground, where a team of gnomes hung, swaying like spiders in the wind.

"We have to move quickly," Logan advised, as he stepped onto the ramp. "In and out. No sightseeing."

"Hold on!" Monti exclaimed, as he ran down the ramp with a box under his arm. "You'll want to put these on." He handed each of the Griffins a pair of goggles. "They'll supply a live camera feed so I can monitor your progress while you are away."

Ernie smiled. "Do they work at a hundred miles an hour?"

"Of course," Monti replied. "I can't say the same for the jump boots. I don't recommend activating them at high speed, unless you want to become a permanent part of the ceiling. Anyway, good luck down there."

"Down *where*?" asked Ernie.

"You'll find out soon enough," Logan answered. "Shoulder your packs. We're moving out."

Obadiah, with map in hand, set off with the Griffins trotting behind him. As Max stepped off the ramp, he felt Logan's hand on his shoulder.

"This should be routine, Grasshopper. But just in case, stay close."

Max nodded. The Scotsman was the only continuity in Max's life since his parents' divorce, his father's betrayal, and Iver's death. If it weren't for Logan, Max might not even be alive. He smiled up at the Scotsman, who in turn gave him a wink.

"We'll stick together, mate. You and me."

The entrance to the Brimstone Facility turned out to be just on the other side of the harbor—or so Obadiah assured them. They were standing on the bottom level of a double-decker stone pier, which ran a good way out toward the breakwater. There were seagulls, waddling pelicans, and barking seals everywhere. Nobody could see the Brimstone Facility, though.

"What are we supposed to be looking for?" Ernie asked, as he scanned the waters. "Are we being affected by that Mesmero thing you mentioned?"

"Patience," reprimanded Obadiah, who was busy counting out his footsteps in synchronization with Lord Saxon's instructional map. "Ah, I must have missed it before!" Strange exclaimed suddenly. He retraced his steps, turned left, murmured a few strange words, and proceeded to step right off the side of the pier. Max braced for the splash, but Obadiah didn't fall.

"It's a bridge—invisible, naturally," he explained from his ethereal perch. "Please try to keep up. The bridge will dissipate shortly, so we will have to make this effort count."

The Griffins rushed onto the invisible platform, eyeing the crashing waves just below their feet as they followed after Obadiah Strange.

"Can't everyone see us out here?" Natalia asked, glancing over her shoulder at the town behind them.

Obadiah shook his head as he continued on. "We are now part of the illusion."

A moment later, he came to an abrupt stop, holding up his hand and removing a glove. Obadiah placed his fingers on what Max imagined to be an invisible door. He muttered more unrecognizable words, and the door opened.

Strange stepped through. Max followed.

They were standing in a stone cavern. Two lamps flickered, affording little light. Except for a circular pool in the middle of the floor filled with bright blue water, and an odd-looking brass post with a single ivory button marked *Call*, the room was empty. Obadiah pushed the button and the water bubbled.

"The Bell will arrive in a few minutes," Obadiah assured everyone. "Lord Saxon designed it himself, and even though this place had been dormant for nearly a hundred years, it should be exactly as he left it."

"Checking video feed," came Monti's crackling voice out of an earphone attached to Max's goggles. *"Channel Three. Do you copy, Max?"*

Max nodded.

"Thanks." He heard Monti laugh. *"But if it gets really dark where you are going, I won't be able to see you nodding through the camera, so speak up."*

"Sorry," Max replied. "I copy."

"Good. Let me know if you need anything. I'll check the others," he said. Then his voice disappeared with a crackling noise.

"So what is the Brimstone Key?" asked Ernie, tightening his helmet in preparation for the descent. "What does it look like?"

"It certainly doesn't resemble a house key, if that's what you mean," Strange replied. "It is cylindrical, about arm's length, and very heavy. After all, it is made of meteoric iron. Also, it isn't a single piece, but rather a series of six gears, lined up one beside the other."

The call button on the brass panel lit up, and with a whirring of invisible gears, a round globe blossomed from the water like a shimmering bubble. The vehicle, known as the Bell, was wrought of iron and polished wood. Through the hatch, Max could see a room of padded walls, a circular divan, and a domed roof.

"Looks like our ride is here," Logan said, shouldering his well-stocked weapons rucksack.

Soon, the Griffins had taken their seats and were

looking around in expectation. Strange stood in front of a large, round window with his back to the others. Pressing a similar call button near the window, he closed them in with a hiss of steam.

A chime sounded briefly, and the Bell began its clanking descent.

As the water level rose above the viewing window, Max saw that they were in a glass elevator shaft. The water, light blue at first, gradually grew darker. There were colossal shapes just off in the distance.

"Whales!" Natalia exclaimed as one particularly playful cetacean came close to examine the earthly visitors.

Just when the water became the darkest, Max perceived a soft glow below them. As they approached he saw the rising spires of a city of glass.

"What about Von Strife?" asked Max. "Do you think he beat us here?"

"All that matters is the Brimstone Key," Obadiah replied, as the Bell reached its destination. "But if he *were* here, I think we'd be dead already."

THE BRIMSTONE FACILITY

Logan led them into a cylindrical hallway of glass, framed by thick metal girders and interlocking rings. Its raised floor was plush red carpet, framed on either side by gold. The expeditionary crew stepped out of the elevator and entered the first of many maze-like intersections. Just outside, the sea was dark and menacing.

Obadiah Strange consulted Saxon's diary closely. The wrong path meant death, and there were lethal self-defense systems built into the Brimstone Facility to ensure that any misstep was definitively punished.

"What sort of defenses does this place have?" Harley asked, wondering what they might come up against.

"*Clockworks and other types of security systems,*" Monti replied through the comlink."*Machines don't require oxygen, so if there were ever a breach or some kind of malfunction, there would be no risk of suffocation.*"

At a nod from Obadiah, Logan led the way forward, a flashlight mounted just beneath the barrel of his MERLIN Tech Pulse Rifle.

"*Wow, Saxon was a genius,*" Monti's voice crackled over the line as he watched their progress through the video feed. "*He built this almost a hundred years ago, and it's still state-of-the-art today. I wish I could have met the guy.*"

"You'd be disappointed," Obadiah said flatly. "Saxon wasn't the sociable type and there was only room for one genius in *his* world."

As the Griffins walked through the passageways, it was hard for them to grasp just how immense the Brimstone Facility was. Inside the glass maze, they could only see the next intersection, but outside the window, they could see the faint shimmering of more structures in the distance.

"There it is," Obadiah said, pointing out the window to the right. "The Brimstone Chamber." It was an immense pentagonal structure. Golden light rose like smoke from a ceiling of spider-webbed glass. Only a few more turns and they would be there.

"Hold it." Logan lifted his arm up.

"What?" asked Ernie.

Logan knelt down, swiped his fingers over a dark spot

on the rug, and whispered something into his comlink to Monti. He turned back to Obadiah and the Griffins and held up two fingers. They were covered in grime.

"Grease," he explained. "The same kind used in the Class Six Nemesis we encountered back in Scotland."

"Is it recent?" Max asked.

"It's warm, if that's what you mean."

"They must have used a portal," Strange reasoned. "I have no idea how Von Strife could have done it without alerting the facility's security system, though."

"Smoke…" Max muttered. "He can teleport without using portals."

"Only if he'd been here before, though," Harley noted.

"Maybe all he needs are the coordinates," Harley suggested.

"Should we go back?" asked Natalia.

"We can't be sure they have the key in their possession yet," Obadiah stated. "We must go on, at least a little farther." Strange pointed at the open hatchway in front of them that led into the Brimstone Chamber, where the key rested. It was dark in the room, and there were no sounds of clockwork ticking or energy cannons being charged up. Everything was deathly quiet.

"Do we have to go in there?" Ernie whined.

"There's a remote-control Imager drone in Harley's pack," Monti offered. *"Power it up and I'll take control. You'll be able to see what it sees through your goggles."*

Logan set his rifle down and extracted the clockwork from Harley's backpack.

Similar to the hornets that Smoke had unleashed back at school, this drone was a palm-sized clockwork modeled after a golden dragonfly, with two huge eye-shaped cameras. In a flash, Monti sent it buzzing off through the dark hatchway and into the silence beyond. At the same instant, one of Max's goggle lenses began to feed the drone's video back to him.

The room was circular, dressed in black and white tile and supported by two pillars that rose up to support the massive glass ceiling. Surrounding the room were statues of men whose eyes were trained upon the shattered remains of the resting place that had once held the Brimstone Key: a coffin-sized glass case bound with meteoric iron. Its contents had been ripped out and scattered on the ground. There was no sign of the Brimstone Key.

"*I think we came a little late to the party,*" Monti commented grimly. "*You should probably get back here on the double.*"

Even as he spoke, the sound of clanging metal echoed ominously from the passageway behind them. An instant later, the first of the Grimbots appeared, followed by a stream of blaster fire that lit up the hallways.

"Take cover!" Logan shouted as he pulled everyone behind a steel beam and grabbed his MVX Pulse Rifle. In a blur of professional finesse, he took aim and blew away the arm of the lead Grimbot. Next went the left knee, and finally its head. It took two seconds at most, and Logan had trimmed it like a tree. Several others fell just as quickly, as Logan let loose a deadly barrage of plasma charges.

"Forget about it! Those things are at least Class Five. They have regen sub-programs," Monti warned. *"You don't have enough firepower. Get out of there...now!"*

Already, the Grimbots that had fallen were beginning to repair themselves. Behind those, a dozen more clockworks appeared, blasters firing. At the rate the Grimbots were coming, the Griffins would be overrun no matter how fast Logan could pull the trigger.

"They're blocking our way out," Logan replied as he took another shot, catching a Grimbot in the chest. It crashed into the wall. "Can you find us another exit, Monti?"

"We don't have time!" Obadiah shouted. "Everyone, through the door." He pushed the Griffins through the open hatch and into the Brimstone Chamber. "That goes for you, too," Saxon's apprentice shouted, waving at Logan as the Scotsman protected their escape.

Logan took a final shot that blew the head off the nearest Grimbot, and dove through the door. Obadiah slipped in behind him. Together, they heaved the hatchway shut. Logan spun the lock. The sound of blaster fire faded to a muffled buzz.

"Even if the hatchway holds," Logan began, "we're trapped."

"They've turned off life support," Monti warned. *"Oxygen levels are dropping."*

Logan growled. "I have a feeling that was Von Strife's plan all along."

"We'll have to go on the offensive..." Strange muttered. "It's the only way."

Logan shook his head. "Grimbots are Class Five killing machines. We wouldn't last two minutes. Unless Monti can upgrade my rifle remotely."

"Ha! Not a chance!"

"I have something a little more radical in mind," Strange countered.

VOLT VINES

Max's gauntlet melted away from his arm and reconstituted itself as the *Codex*. With Obadiah's help, Max's mind guided its pages toward a section of green leaves. It came to rest on the image of spiraling vines under the glow of a silvery moon.

Obadiah nodded. "That's the one."

"Are you sure? I mean, I could make this a lot worse."

"I don't think it can get any worse!" Ernie exclaimed.

"Trust yourself, Max," Strange maintained.

Max quickly scanned to the bottom of the page and spoke the words written there. All at once, there was an explosion of light. A tangle of green cords snaked up through the page and spilled onto the floor. The cords began to swell and stretch, turning into twisting vines that slithered across the room.

"An excellent choice." Obadiah nodded, as the *Codex* returned to a ring on Max's finger.

"Vines?" Harley asked, as he jumped over a thick trunk that slithered across the floor.

"Volt Vines," Strange corrected. "Extremely fast growing. They feed on energy."

Soon the vines were as thick as saplings. Natalia sidestepped one of the tendrils as it raced for the door like a dog on the scent of a rabbit. Other vines followed, and then, in unison, they ripped the massive door from its hinges. Like the arms of a sea monster, they seized the closest Grimbot. The machine tried to break free, but the vines only wrapped tighter, crushing the armor plating as they drained the machine of its life. Electric charges crackled through the vegetation as it discarded the lifeless clockwork. Two more Grimbots went down before the others realized what was happening.

"While the Volt Vines keep our friends busy—," Logan began as he sent a volley of blasts through the open hatchway, "we're going through, straight back to the Bell. Everyone stay together and watch your feet," he warned. The Griffins obeyed, following Logan as he leaped over the vines and through the door. More clockworks appeared but were soon engaged with an enemy they hadn't expected. The Griffins raced past them.

Unfortunately, as Obadiah tried to run past, a Grimbot caught him by the leg. Like a cat playing with a mouse, the machine flung Strange wall to wall, ceiling to floor, and it finally slammed him to the ground.

Natalia screamed.

"They're killing him!" she cried.

Already, Obadiah Strange was stumbling to his knees and then to his feet, popping his neck back into place, and then his shoulder and left knee. He replaced his glasses before resuming his race. Natalia's mouth hung open.

"He really *is* indestructible…"

Before the Grimbot could recapture Obadiah, Logan blew its head off with his pulse rifle. At the same time, a Volt Vine caught hold of the rest of the clockwork and began sucking it dry. The machine thrashed until it had no more life to give. The vines moved on, leaving only a dead husk behind.

Out of a nearby tunnel, more Grimbots appeared— ignoring the vines and pursuing the Griffins. They were moving too fast, and Max knew they wouldn't have enough time to make it to the Bell. As he contemplated a final showdown, he heard a strange sound: *Sqwarkkkk!*

Max spun to see several Volt Vines reach around the corner and fall upon two of his pursuers. The vines were growing faster than the Grimbots could run. After each meal, they seemed to become more powerful, swelling to gigantic proportions.

With single-minded focus, the Grimbots continued their pursuit, heedless of their falling brothers. Logan continued his cover fire, but by now the Grimbots were beginning to adapt to his weapon. Soon, his pulse blasts were ricocheting off their armor.

"Seriously, Monti!" Logan shouted into his comlink. "What do I pay you for?"

"How was I to know they were programmed for regen and electrostatic field convergence?" Monti complained. *"I'm an engineer, not a fortune-teller. Besides, you said this mission was a piece of cake!"*

The Grimbots continued to gain, even as they neared their destination. Ernie was the only one who could have out-run the machines. He refused to leave his friends behind.

"We have a problem," Strange called to Logan.

"You think?" Several more energy bolts smashed into the wall above Logan's head.

"I've done the calculations in my head. At the rate the Volt Vines are growing, they'll burst through the walls soon."

"Burying us under a mile of water," Logan growled. "We have to get to the Bell!"

"If I could get one of their transponders, I could repro-gram the Grimbots—like I did at the library," Harley offered, ducking under an incoming plasma blast.

"Wait!" Natalia shouted. "Harley, you're brilliant."

She signaled for the others to go on ahead while she took position at the intersection of three corridors.

"Are you crazy?" Harley shouted, as she said something to Monti through her comlink. "We have to get out of here!"

"Give me a second," she cried, pushing him away. "This will work!"

"She's right!" Logan shouted, grabbing Harley by the arm and pulling him toward the waiting Bell.

Pulling a device from her pack, Natalia flicked a toggle switch and secured it to the wall. She punched in a sequence of codes, as Monti read them off to her. Suddenly she was surrounded by three-dimensional copies of herself and the other three Griffins.

Harley watched in awe as the holograms ran to meet the oncoming Grimbots, screaming and waving their arm. At the last minute, they ducked down a corridor.

Harley held his breath in hope.

The Grimbots took the bait and disappeared down the hall. The Volt Vines followed after them.

The Griffins cheered as they raced aboard the Bell. Even as they did, they could see the glass walls of the underground facility begin to fracture. Pipes started to shake, and an ominous rumble ran through the facility.

"It's gonna implode!" Logan shouted, as he hit the call button. The Bell rumbled to life and began to slowly climb. "Everybody take your seats. This is gonna be a bumpy ride!"

"Wait! Natalia's still outside!" Max cried. She had tripped and fallen, and she was only just getting back to her feet. With a desperate cry, she sprang to her feet, her eyes locked on the rising Bell.

"She's too far away!" Harley exclaimed. "We're rising too fast!"

Logan pushed Harley away from the door and leaned out. "Natalia! Use your jump boots!"

Natalia nodded as she rushed along the fractured passage. Water was beginning to pool at her feet. She pushed a button on her glove and suddenly her jump boots fired up. Silvery fire blasted out from the bottom of her shoes and with a shout, she was launched into the air like a rocket. She hadn't had time to gauge the distance, and Max watched in horror as she shot up the tunnel past the Bell. Then, with a dreadful sputter, the boots cut out and she fell.

At the last minute, Logan grabbed her around the waist and pulled her inside. With a *bang*, Strange sealed the door shut.

"We did it!" Harley laughed in relief. Then the Bell shuddered to a stop.

"The security system was activated," Logan explained grimly. "We have to override it or we'll drown."

Monti's comlink roared with static as his voice came through in pieces. "*...need to...bots...the Bell...be ready!*"

"What?" Max yelled. There was a massive explosion down below, followed by the eerie sound of twisting metal. Then he watched as a wave of icy water rolled up and over the viewing window.

"The Volt Vines have outgrown the facility," Obadiah observed.

The Bell began to shudder against the intense water pressure. Then, just as Max was certain that they were going to be crushed like an egg in a vise, the Bell launched upward like a bullet in a barrel, pinning its occupants to the ground. There was another tremendous explosion and the lights went out. Something heavy smashed into Max's head and he lost consciousness.

When Max opened his eyes, he was lying on the pier in Durban as seagulls flew overhead. At first he thought he could hear Iver's voice, but it was just Obadiah Strange warning Ernie to get away from the water before he fell in.

Max looked up to see Monti's airship hovering nearby. Connected to it by a towrope lay the battered Bell. The heroes had been plucked out of the facility by the *Graf* just in time.

"*Iron Silk,*" Monti explained over the radio. "*I made the towrope myself. My boys here on the Zeppelin were the real heroes, though, spelunking into the shaft and attaching the cable. Gnomes are many things, but timid and slow swimmers they are not.*"

"We can fill the Baron in later," Logan said, before

turning to the rest of the Griffins. "Everyone back on board. We're heading north, engines at full." As he helped Max up the gangplank, they could see the surface of the sea. It was alive with white froth and steaming bubbles: the final, dying breath of the Brimstone Facility.

A Secret Revealed

As evening approached, Monti set the *Graf Zeppelin* on automatic pilot and retired to his bunk, leaving Max and Logan alone on the bridge. Their road lay toward the Inferno Prison, where the Gateway to the Shadowlands had been kept under strict Templar military control in the frozen north. They expected Von Strife to strike there next, using the Brimstone Key to march through the Gateway with his clockwork army, where he would reclaim his daughter.

"Do we really have a chance of beating Von Strife to the Gateway?" asked Max.

"It's hard to say," Logan replied. "Either way, we

shouldn't have to get our hands dirty. The forces at the Inferno Prison have been alerted, and the cavalry is on the way. All we'll do is observe and report.

"We're sending in a team of my best demolitions men to blow the Inferno Prison sky-high," Logan continued. "The Brimstone Key may be indestructible, but the Gateway isn't."

Max thought about Logan's role as a commanding officer of the Templar THOR division. Hardly a day went by when someone from his team didn't risk his or her life. "Do you ever feel guilty when you send people into dangerous situations?"

Logan leaned against the railing, staring into the sky. "Everything is for the greater good."

"Even when someone dies?"

"Everybody dies, Max. Even me. But what we do, the decisions we make, can live forever. And that's the real name of the game."

Max sighed. "I guess."

"I lost my parents when I was about your age," Logan said after several moments of silence. "Did I ever tell you that?"

Max shook his head. Logan had never talked much about his past.

"My father was a diplomat in the Cape Colony, and on a trip to Johannesburg, he stopped to help a man out of a burning car that had rolled into a ditch. There was an explosion, and neither one of them survived." Logan paused, then continued. "A few months later, my mum found out she had cancer. Within the year, she was gone, too."

Max looked up, astonished at how casually Logan spoke about the tragedies.

"Dealing with what happened to my father was hard enough, but when my mum passed away...well, that shook me up something terrible," Logan said.

"I had no idea."

"I guess, after that, I began to understand how brutal this world could be. People can walk into your life, and the next moment, you'll never see them again."

"You aren't going to leave me, are you?" Max whispered slowly.

Logan's eyes were tired and his face lined with concern. He regarded Max for several moments, gauging the boy's thoughts. "No," he offered finally. "At least not if I can help it. One day you won't need me anymore. Until then, you're stuck with me."

THE SECRET TO LIVING FOREVER

Ernie found himself wandering through the luxurious gondola, searching for Obadiah Strange. The dragon dung tea was flowing through his veins, and though he didn't feel any different, he was hoping that it would stunt his metamorphosis into a faerie. Either way, his super speed was still intact. He still had questions, though, and Strange was the only man who might know the answers.

He found Obadiah on the rear observation deck. It was open to the arctic elements, an environment so bitterly cold that only changelings and faeries could even hope to take pleasure in it. Standing there with no walls or windows, a person could almost imagine he or she was flying.

"I can't believe how you survived that clockwork down in the Brimstone Facility," Ernie began as he joined the man.

"Thank you," Strange replied, before sipping at a steaming cup of tea. Then he coughed, his lung rattling. "It wasn't something I'd want to do again."

"But you're indestructible. Doesn't that mean you're going to live forever?"

"In a manner of speaking, I suppose that is correct," Strange said. "What you saw today was only part of my condition. If my body is not entirely destroyed, it can rebuild itself. However, in the event of something more destructive happening—such as the time that I was caught in the Krakatoa lava flow in 1883—my life force is transported backward to a previous point in my life, forcing me to live it all over again so as to regather my strength."

"That's amazing!" Ernie exclaimed. "Think of all the things you could do."

Obadiah raised his hand to cut Ernie off. "One of the conditions is that I must be very selective in what I change. Radical adjustments to the space-time contin-uum can alter history. It's difficult to understand. In fact, after a thousand lifetimes, I am not sure I do. That, my friend, is the secret to my indestructibility. Whatever it takes, my power ensures that I can never die."

"Supersonic," Ernie sighed in awe.

"It's a curse, I assure you," Obadiah returned after a moment of consideration, his eyes following the rising mist from his teacup. "I can only go backward, never forward. If I do go back, I must stay there until time catches up with me. I've watched my friends and loved ones die more times than I care to remember, unable to help."

"You also get to fix your mistakes, right?" Ernie pointed out.

Obadiah Strange sighed in exhaustion. "Each time it is the same colorless world, the same tired house, in the company of the same tedious people. Nothing is novel. Food no longer has taste. Memories move sideways rather than backward. I have no destiny. Nothing to look forward to. I merely exist to continue existing."

Ernie sighed wistfully as he looked out over the sea of ice. "Life isn't easy for heroes, is it, Mr. Strange?"

"No, Agent Thunderbolt, it most certainly is not."

VISIONS

The next night, Max was alone in his sleeping quarters. After checking his DE Tablet for any messages from Brooke, he decided to read a comic book. His eyes scanned the words on the page, but they weren't registering. He was tired and just about to turn off the light when a flash sparked, then faded. Max sat bolt upright.

"Sprig?" he whispered, barely able to contain his excitement. "I know it's you."

There was no answer, but Max heard something shuffling across the floor. He got up to investigate. His eyes were immediately drawn to the dressing mirror, where, staring back at him from the other side, was his Bounder.

Max got down on his hands and knees and knocked at the glass. "Sprig, are you all right? I was so worried about you!"

"Sprig has escaped..." Her voice wavered.

Max sighed in relief, but his smile faded as he noticed that something wasn't quite right. She looked hurt, and Max could sense her pain across the reflection.

"Sprig, what did Von Strife do to you?" Max nearly shouted.

"Sprig will recover..." she breathed. "But the changeling boy. Robert. Sprig couldn't free him or the others.... There were so many."

"I have to get you some help." Max's eyes moved over her, taking in the wounds and the exhaustion in her eyes.

"The Clockwork King will take his soul and put it in a mechanical monster," Sprig told him. "He will make Robert do things he doesn't want to do. Max must remember this. When it happens, there is no going back. Robert will be gone."

The spriggan waved a shaky paw across the reflection, and the image rippled like water. As it calmed, Max could see through the mirror like a magic window. There was a laboratory of steel tables where people were bound and hidden under blue sheets. Max watched with rising fear as the doors to the lab opened. Two men entered in white coats. Their faces were obscured by masks. They worked wordlessly as their gloved hands took hold of one of the tables, wheeling it through the double doors.

Max's eyes followed the men through a series of quiet halls until they entered a semicircular corridor with clear windows on the far wall. Beyond the glass was a cavernous room ringed with a series of balconies stacked one on top of the other. In the center of it all stood a clockwork of colossal proportions.

"The Dreadnaught..." he heard Sprig say.

Towering nearly twenty feet tall, the Dreadnaught was armored like a tank. Its arms were bristling with weapons, and its legs were outfitted with rocket boosters. A small head with a hinged jaw sat on top of broad shoulders, and two figures stood at its feet. One was an older gentleman in a military uniform. Max knew him immediately to be Otto Von Strife. At his side stood a young woman. Her hair was silken red, and tiny flames flickered over the strands. Max had seen her face once before, though it was only a picture. It was Naomi—the girl who had blown up the Iron Bridge Academy long ago. She didn't look a day over eighteen.

After a moment of conversation, she nodded her agreement, and a field of fire ignited around her before she flew up and out of view.

The scientists came back into view as they approached the Dreadnaught. Locking the table's wheels, they drew the sheet away and Max could see Robert lying silently on the table. His skin was pale as a corpse, and tubes filled with blue liquid ran up his nose. The worst part may have been the incision on his shaved head.

Robert's eyes suddenly opened. Instead of brown, they were an unnatural blue. He remained unblinking as the men in white scanned him with a series of strange instruments. Robert's inhibitor was gone, but there was a large device planted in the center of his chest. Von Strife took a thick cable and plugged it into the device before one of his assistants attached the other end to the Dreadnaught.

There was a spark, and Robert screamed.

"No!" Max cried, as he slammed his fist against the mirror. The surface shattered and the image disappeared. Robert was gone. So was Sprig.

"You're going to want to come up here," Harley called over the intercom.

The Inferno
Prison

Max rushed to the bridge. The others were staring out the observation window at a ring of jagged mountains. They could just make out the silhouette of a floating tower that was tethered to the mountaintops by five heavy chains. Smoke was rising from the strange building, and the air was lit up with a barrage of energy pulses and blaster fire.

"We're too late," Strange said. "The Inferno Prison is already under attack."

Just above the floating tower hovered three ships that resembled floating aircraft carriers. Cannons from the ship pummeled the tower, laying waste to the Templar defenses as flying clockworks shot overhead, picking off the heroic soldiers.

The Templar countered. One of the enemy airships had already crashed in the valley below, where a thousand clockworks lay scattered like smoking insects.

"Turn the ship around!" Logan ordered, as he listened to his comlink. "The charges are set. The whole thing is going to blow!"

"We're just going to leave your men to die?" Natalia cried.

Logan ignored her and repeated his order to Monti. The engines roared to life as the airship began its wide turn.

As Max watched out the window, he could see that Von Strife's fleet had realized the danger as well. The carriers were being forced into a desperate retreat. The cannons had been silenced as the crews directed all power to turn the aerial goliaths around.

Max watched as a single ball of flame shot up from one of the towers. It hovered in the air before it turned toward the airship. As it got closer, Max could see that it was actually a girl with flaming hair...Naomi. She crossed the distance between them to hover just outside the window. Her eyes moved over the Griffins as if considering something. Then, with a nod, she blazed off in a trail of fire.

At that moment, the tower erupted in a cataclysmic explosion that sent a ring of destruction in every direction. Before Max could run for cover, the first wave of energy smashed into the side of the airship.

"Get away from the window!" Logan shouted. He grabbed Max by the back of his collar, pulling him to the ground just as the ship's windows blew inward. Shards of glass flew like razors.

The cabin pitched heavily to starboard, and the engines outside the window had caught fire.

"We're going down!" Monti shouted into the comlink. Furniture smashed against the wall and Max barely managed to duck as a heavy table slid like a guillotine over his head.

Natalia screamed.

Stumbling to his feet, Max could see Harley leaning out the window, holding desperately to Natalia's hand. She had fallen through and her feet were dangling a thousand feet above the ice.

"Don't let go of me!" she screamed.

Harley's arm was bleeding, cut by broken glass that was lodged in the window frame. "I think my shoulder is dislocated," he said, wincing.

"Max, get your arms around Harley's knees to steady him!" Logan ordered.

"Eight hundred feet and falling," Monti shouted. *"Firing retro rockets! Dropping ballast!"*

"Harley, I'm going to pick you up like a football lineman hitting a sled," the Scotsman explained as he slid between Harley and the window. "All you need to do is hold on to her."

Harley managed a weak nod, and Logan exploded. Harley's vision went grey as he flew backward, his hand fastened to Natalia's wrist like a vise.

"We're gonna hit!" Monti shouted. *"Brace for impact!"*

STRANDED

Somehow Monti managed to land the airship with minimal damage. The second they hit the ground, an army of gnomes raced to put out fires and repair the engines. Monti was in the middle of it all, trying to bring order to the chaos.

"Looks like Von Strife didn't fare much better than we did," Logan noted, pointing toward two smoking mountains of scrap iron. One of the battleships had managed to get away, but most of Von Strife's clockwork army had been destroyed.

"Where's Obadiah?" Ernie asked, scanning the horizon.

Logan turned to Monti. "Wasn't he with you?"

"He was in the rear observation bridge . . . the one that got blown away."

Natalia gasped in horror, and Logan put his hand on her shoulder. "I'm sure he survived. He's indestructible, remember?"

Logan set his jaw and turned to Harley. "How's the arm?"

"Not good."

"You!" Logan called to a gnome. "First aid. Now." The gnome ran off, returning moments later with a kit of medical supplies. Logan wiped off as much blood as he could before applying gauze and wrapping a linen bandage around Harley's chest and shoulder, pinning his arm so it couldn't move.

"That will have to do," the Scotsman said, surveying his work. "Are you good enough to walk?"

Harley nodded, and Logan handed him a pistol from his belt. "This isn't as strong as my Scatter Blaster, but it'll do in a pinch."

"What does he need that for?" Natalia asked.

"We're going to look for Strange," Logan replied.

With that, he handed each of the Griffins a pack, instructing them to put on the respiratory mask inside. "The air is thin, and it's full of carbonic acid," he explained before slipping one of the masks over his own face.

The sky was filled with ash, and the glow from smoldering fires painted the landscape bloodred. Max could see that the tower holding the gateway had been gutted. He just hoped Robert wasn't among the wreckage.

They wandered silently across the snowy plain, as Logan scanned the surrounding area for any sign of their missing companion.

"Hey, what's that?" Natalia called out.

A large clockwork arm was lying in a snowdrift. It was broken off at the shoulder, still clutching a massive gun.

"Looks like it came from a Nemesis," Logan observed. "Let's hope that there aren't any others hanging around."

"There're more parts over here," Harley said as he crested a hill.

They had stumbled on a graveyard of clockwork parts that littered the valley. Decapitated heads sat at odd angles. Their eye sockets were devoid of life, and their casings were crushed. There were all manner of bolts, gears, and metal rods strewn about.

"Can you see this?" Logan asked into his comlink.

"Crystal clear," Monti replied. *"Wreckage from the blast?"*

"Looks like it," the Scotsman replied.

"Any survivors?"

Logan checked his scanner. "Negative."

Max walked down the hill, searching for anything that looked like the Dreadnaught he had seen. It was hard differentiating one component from another. Most of the metal was just scrap.

"What are you looking for?" Harley asked.

Max stopped for a moment, debating whether or not he should say anything. "Robert."

THE DREADNAUGHT

"What do you mean, you're looking for Robert?" Ernie wanted to know.

Max took a deep breath. "I didn't want to say anything, but before we crashed, Sprig showed me an image of Robert through a portal inside the mirror in my room. He was hooked up to some kind of a machine."

"Don't joke around about stuff like that."

"I'm not," Max replied solemnly. "Von Strife was using a machine that was sucking out his soul and placing it into a Dreadnaught."

"Hold on," Logan said, looking down at his tracking device. "I picked up something big moving this way."

"Do you think it's Robert?" Ernie asked hopefully.

"Look, Ernie," Logan started to explain, "even if it is Robert inside one of these machines, the longer he stays there, the less likely he'll be able to recognize any of us. He's gone, and he's not coming back."

"You're lying!" Ernie exclaimed as tears started to well in his eyes. "I bet Monti could help him."

The device on Logan's wrist started to beep rapidly. "It's almost on us," Logan said, raising his pulse rifle.

"I can't see anything," Max said.

"Me, either," agreed Harley. "Do you think it has some kind of cloaking device?"

"It might," Logan admitted. "According to this, it should be right on top of us."

"Then why isn't it firing?" asked Natalia.

Without warning, Ernie took off. Snow kicked up as he raced to find the Dreadnaught.

"He's going to get himself killed," Logan growled.

"Robert!" Ernie called. "Robert, are you out there?"

There was no response.

"Look, if you can hear me, it's Ernie! You know, Agent Thunderbolt!" Ernie called out, hoping that if Robert was nearby, he would show himself.

The air in front of Ernie began to ripple like the surface of water in the wind. A moment later, Ernie found himself standing in the shadow of a menacing clockwork. The war machine was wrapped in thick armor and bristled with weapons.

Natalia gasped as she stepped behind Harley, looking around his shoulder.

"Robert, you have to listen to me," Ernie continued. "I know you're in there. I promise, if you let us help, we'll find a way to get you out."

The Dreadnaught's head rotated like a turret as it took focus on Ernie.

Agent Thunderbolt smiled weakly through his respirator. "That's right. It's me!"

The monstrous machine seemed to consider Ernie before it scanned the metal bones of destroyed clockworks. Then it turned back to Ernie and raised a hand toward him.

The air exploded with electrical fire as a missile smashed into the Dreadnaught, sending it reeling backward. At the same time, a black shadow raced overhead. It was a Templar hover-copter, and it was coming back for another shot.

"No!" Ernie cried out.

Logan activated his comlink and tried to call the pilot off, but it was too late. As the copter flew by, the clockwork launched into the air. Boosters embedded in the bottom of its feet kicked in. With a metal-crunching thud, it punched a hole through the side of the hover-copter. There was a terrible explosion and the wreckage of the ship smashed into the earth in a cloud of fire and smoke.

The Dreadnaught landed on top of the smoking ruin

360

and began hammering at it like an enraged animal. Pieces of metal flew everywhere, but Ernie still moved closer.

"It was a mistake, Robert."

The Dreadnaught turned toward Agent Thunderbolt. One of its shoulder plates flipped up, and a large Gatling gun appeared. Suddenly twenty barrels were leveled at Ernie.

"Please, Robert." Ernie held his ground. "If you come with us, we can help."

There was no hesitation this time. The Dreadnaught opened fire, its barrels spinning fast. The explosions sent a shower of ice into the air. When the war machine's barrels died down, Ernie was nowhere to be found.

With Ernie out of the way, the Dreadnaught unloaded on the other Griffins. Cannons fired wildly as its fists crushed the earth.

Max felt a rush of wind over his shoulder. Logan had sent a plasma rocket smashing into the chest of a massive clockwork. The explosion was blinding, but the metal beast wasn't even stunned. It swung a giant fist at the Scotsman's head, narrowly missing as Logan threw himself between the machine's legs. He rolled back to his feet on the other side and fired another round directly into its face. The clockwork was barely fazed.

"The Mark Six Plasma Charges aren't working!" Logan shouted into his comlink.

"*I know,*" Monti called back. "*It looks like it's time for Plan B.*"

Logan signaled Max and Natalia. "You heard the man."

Max was the first to drop his pack into the snow. He tore open the top and fished out a strange device that was about the size of a hockey puck. He ignited his gauntlet and slapped it onto the circular THOR emblem on the top. Instantly, a spark of red energy crackled across the surface.

Natalia was next. She removed her backpack and pulled the ripcord as it hit the ground. The bag opened up, and thirty brass spheres rolled out into the snow. Each was covered with etched lines connecting a series of flashing lights that pulsed like tiny heartbeats.

Just as Logan was about to get smashed into oblivion, two more Templar hover-copters appeared, engaging the Dreadnaught from a safe distance. They didn't have the firepower to take the brute down, but they would buy the Griffins some time.

"Hit the activator!" Logan ordered.

Natalia complied and the spheres began to twist and rotate, unlocking themselves to transform into small Assembler clockworks.

"Your turn, Max," Monti called across the comlink. *"This is our only chance!"*

Max prepped his jump boots and raced toward the Dreadnaught. It was distracted by the hover-copters. As he sailed toward the Dreadnaught, he raised his gauntlet and swung with all his might. Max could feel the machine's head crumple as he hit it. The impact sent Max flying off into a snowdrift, as the Dreadnaught fell to the ground.

The machine struggled to regain its feet as a plume of smoke rose from the gash in its head. Sparks flew out of its joints, and the light behind its eyes flickered erratically.

"Quick!" Logan ordered Natalia. "Before it starts to repair itself!"

Natalia flicked the control panel, and the Assemblers went to work. They swarmed over the fallen giant like a metallic pestilence. With hands made from wrenches, drills, grinders, cutters, hammers, and torches, they were efficient and fast.

One of the Assemblers deactivated the Dreadnaught's regen system, and from there it was just a matter of time before the war machine was scrap. The Gatling gun was removed, and then its right arm. Two Assemblers pulled a knee apart, and a third stripped its fingers.

"No!" Ernie cried as he raced to the Dreadnaught.

Natalia ran to hug him. "We thought you were dead!"

Ernie pushed her away. "Max, you have to stop them. They're killing Robert!"

"I'm sorry, Ernie, but you heard Logan. That isn't Robert anymore."

"What happened to you?" Ernie shouted. "If Iver had been here, he never would have let this happen!"

Ernie jumped on the colossal machine and kicked

at the Assemblers. Several fell, but it was too late. The machines had done their job with mechanical efficiency, splitting open the Dreadnaught's chest before unscrewing the head. Ernie watched in horror as the light of the Dreadnaught's eyes extinguished.

"No!" Ernie screamed. "You guys are monsters! You killed him!"

A wisp of vapor swirled up out of the metal shell. It gathered there for a moment, taking the shape of a young boy who regarded Ernie with tired eyes. Then, out of the north, a cold wind blew. The figure dissolved into nothing.

Logan walked solemnly to Ernie and placed a gentle hand on Agent Thunderbolt's shoulder. Ernie tried to pull away, but Logan held firm. Then Ernie's chest heaved, and his shoulders shook. He couldn't hold back the sobs, and he didn't care.

GOOD-BYE

A grey December sky hung over Iron Bridge Academy. Classes had been canceled so the students and faculty could gather in the courtyard to honor Robert. A stone memorial had been erected, surrounded by colorful flowers that were warmed by faerie magic.

Robert's parents were dressed in black, their eyes hidden behind dark glasses. Ernie stood beside them in silence as tears ran down his face. Natalia slipped her arm around his shoulder. He smiled weakly, only half listening as Baron Lundgren continued the eulogy.

"...and this garden will stand in constant bloom to symbolize Robert's indelible spirit. Yet despite our sorrow, we must push forward. The weak must be defended. The helpless, protected. Robert may have died, but his spirit remains. He will be with us in our fight, never far from our thoughts."

Cain's voice was melancholy as he leaned on his walking stick. Brooke was standing next to him. It was her first time back on campus since the Reaper attack. "The Templar have a long history, and we know well the pain of losing loved ones. We have been victims of hatred. We have been outcasts. We have known the pains of torture, but we have never been defeated. Our anguish will only serve to strengthen our resolve. Long live the Templar."

"Long live the Templar!" the crowd answered.

Max looked up at Obadiah Strange, who had returned to Iron Bridge a few days before. The indestructible man looked grim. He also knew that Von Strife still had the Brimstone Key and that the mad genius was more than capable of rebuilding his clockwork army. A man with his determination and wherewithal would never give up.

"I have asked Ms. Burrows to make her office available should any students wish to talk with someone today," Cain added. "The rest of you are free to return to your homes."

As Ernie turned to leave, Robert's mother placed her hand on his shoulder. Then she reached into her purse and pulled out a package. "This was Robert's journal," she explained with a raw voice. "He spoke so highly of you, Ernie. I know he would have wanted you to have it."

Ernie shook his head and stared at the ground.

"We insist," Mrs. Hernandez said firmly, handing Ernie the journal before she kissed him on the forehead.

Ernie removed the brown paper wrapping and opened the book slowly. As he thumbed through the journal, he stopped at a passage that Robert had written the day before he was abducted:

We were given powers for a reason....

Max walked over and threw his arm around Ernie's shoulder. Natalia took Ernie's hand as Harley stood silently. There was nothing more to say.

TIRED OF BEING A VICTIM

An hour after the memorial service, more than a dozen changelings were crammed into a storage room on the top floor of Sendak Hall.

Word had come down that another changeling had gone missing. This time it was a geokinetic from Nova Scotia who could move the earth with his thoughts. He was supposed to have transferred to Iron Bridge for the second semester, but now it didn't look as though that would happen.

"I know you're upset," Tejan Chandra said. "We all are. But what can we do? Von Strife is one of the leading military minds of the last century. Most of the changelings in this room haven't even graduated from grammar school."

"Are you kidding?" Ernie argued. "You can wipe people's memories with a touch of your hand. Annie can interface with anything that can be plugged in to an outlet or run on a battery, and I bet Denton can lift a Grimbot over his head. If we work together, we can do anything."

"This isn't some scenario in the SIM Chamber," Denton pointed out. "If we go after Von Strife, people could die."

"People are already dying," Ernie reminded him.

"What about the THOR agents?" Tejan asked.

"They couldn't find Robert until it was too late," Ernie replied. "What makes you think they'll find the others before Von Strife rips out their souls and stuffs them into a bunch of clockworks?"

"I don't know.... Maybe Ernie is right," Denton said. "I mean, going after Von Strife beats waiting around here for Smoke to pop in and pick us off one by one. I'm in."

As Ernie looked around the room, he saw anxiety slowly give way to determination.

"Count me in," Laini said, her pink hair bouncing as she joined the boys in the center of the room. "If we don't look out for each other, nobody will."

One at a time the others came forward, ready to join the fight for their survival. The changelings of Iron Bridge had been awakened.

WILL THE CLOCKWORK KING
RETURN TO FINISH HIS
UNSPEAKABLE PLAN?

CAN THE CHANGELINGS LEARN
TO UNITE AND FIGHT BACK?

WILL THE GREY GRIFFINS
SURVIVE THEIR FIRST SEMESTER
AT IRON BRIDGE ACADEMY?

THE THRILLING ADVENTURE
CONTINUES IN BOOK 2 OF

COMING SPRING 2011.